SPACEMAN

A Post-Apocalyptic Thriller

Part One of The SpaceMan Chronicles

Tom Abrahams

**FT
Pbk**

tomabrahamsbooks.com

Join Tom's Preferred Readers Club. You'll be the first to
know about new releases, promotions, and special opportunities
reserved only for members. It's free to join.

PITON PRESS

WORKS BY TOM ABRAHAMS

For the ones who keep me grounded while lifting me skyward:
Courtney, Samantha, and Luke

Extinction is the rule. Survival is the exception.

— Carl Sagan, Astronomer

A diagram of the International Space Station is available for reference at the end of the book.

CHAPTER 1

MISSION ELAPSED TIME:
72 DAYS, 3 HOURS, 5 MINUTES, 31 SECONDS
249 MILES ABOVE EARTH

The alarm sounded.

It was shrill, echoing through the station until Clayton Shepard typed a series of commands into the computer to disarm it.

He ran his finger across the screen, not believing what he was reading, what the alarm was warning. It was outside the bounds of what was reasonable or even possible. It appeared out of nowhere, and yet, it didn't. They should have seen it coming. They *did* see it coming. They chose to ignore it.

WARNING: GEOMAGNETIC K-INDEX 9 OR GREATER EXPECTED
SPACE WEATHER MESSAGE CODE: WARK9<
SERIAL NUMBER: 476
ISSUE TIME: 2020 JAN 25 0225 UTC
VALID TO 2020 JAN 25 2359 UTC

He pressed a button that keyed the microphone nearest his mouth. "Houston," he said, "station on space-to-ground one. Are you seeing the alarm?"

"Station, this is Houston on space-to-ground one. We see it. We have a team looking at data. Stand by."

Clayton rolled his eyes. "Are you kidding me?" He keyed the mic. "Houston, this is station on space-to-ground one. I don't think we have time for that. I'm asking we abort the spacewalk now."

He looked through the window to his left. Astronaut Ben Greenwood stopped his work, turned around to face Clayton through the mask on his helmet, and joined the conversation.

"Clayton," said Ben, "what alarm?" Greenwood's helmet reflected a fish-eye view of the Cupola, in which Shepard was monitoring the first emergency spacewalk of their expedition, what NASA called extravehicular activity or EVA.

Clayton read the alert again. A severe magnetic storm was coming. The earlier anomalies were indicators they should have paid closer attention to. He swallowed and cleared his throat before keying the mic again. "The onboard coronagraph is giving indications of large, transient disturbances on the Earth-facing side of the Sun."

"You mean solar flares?" Ben asked. "I knew it. I knew we shouldn't be out here."

"We've checked with Boulder," the radio call from mission control interrupted. *"They confirm the alarm, as does Huntsville. Loops are growing in intensity. There is a coronal mass ejection within striking distance. Our original assessment about the CME may have been incorrect."*

"Incorrect? That's an understatement," muttered Clayton, cursing the antiseptic language ground controllers were apt to use.

The third member of the expedition, Cosmonaut Boris Voin, was ten yards from Greenwood, tethered to the exterior of the station. "Clayton," he said through his mic, his English barbed with his native Russian accent, "are we killing spacewalk?"

Shepard took a deep breath before answering. Days earlier, they'd seen evidence of a coronal mass ejection, what they'd believed was a part of the corona tearing away from the Sun.

First there was a ridiculous X-ray burst registered by the Geostationary Operational Environmental Satellite.

"It's nothing critical," was the original assessment, even after that initial blast was soon followed by a strong detection of solar energetic particles in the Earth's atmosphere. That kind of detection was rare. However, the South Pole station, which was responsible for measuring the intensity of solar eruptions, had been malfunctioning for months. Instruments were in the midst of recalibration.

That was one excuse for ignoring the signs. The urgency of the spacewalk was the other.

The ISS relied on its large photovoltaic solar panels to track the sun and provide power. That rotation was enabled by large bearings called solar array alpha joints. Sixty days into the mission, the joints were hard to turn, and the crew had to shut them down. If they weren't fixed quickly, the solar panels' ability to track the sun and provide power was diminished. The ISS would lose much of its power. The crew's life would be in danger.

After looking at the data and considering the needed repairs, mission control determined the reading was an anomaly. Coronal mass injections, or CMEs, as they were called, happened nearly every day. This one, they concluded, was no real threat.

The numbers seemed so far beyond anything they'd ever seen, they concluded there was a system malfunction and the sensor was wrong. If it was even close to being correct, they concluded the CME was unlikely to hit Earth.

"We'll need an EVA," ground controllers had told the crew. "Greenwood and Voin will attack the problem."

"What about the CME?" Greenwood had asked. "If we're out there when it hits, that's a bad thing. We're also at half crew. The previous expedition is back on Earth and the replacement team is delayed from launch for another four days. Wouldn't it be better to wait for our full complement of six?"

"Negative."

"Have to admit," Greenwood ha said, "I'm not thrilled."

"We're confident our assessment is correct," ground had insisted. "The risk is minimal; the reward is great. At worst, the storm would temporarily interrupt our communication. Nothing more."

Now they knew they'd been wrong.

Clayton keyed the mic. "Houston," he said, aware the spacewalking astronauts could hear him, "it's my recommendation that we immediately kill the EVA."

Mission Control replied immediately. "*We agree that out of an abundance of caution the best course of action is terminating the EVA. Move immediately to the Soy —* "

The line went dead. The station went dark.

Clayton pressed the mic. "Houston," he said, a hint of panic in his voice, "do you copy?"

No answer. He looked out the window.

"Ben," he said, "do you copy?"

No response.

Clayton tried Boris, then Ben again. No response. He wasn't even sure his radio was working. Shepard switched channels.

The station talked to the ground through one of two methods. One was the Tracking and Data Relay Satellite System, TDRS, and it had multiple options. The ISS could use antennas that pointed away from Earth and toward satellites in geostationary orbit. They were government owned and operated. If one satellite didn't work, perhaps the next would.

"Houston," he said, "station on space-to-ground two for comm check."

Static.

He repeated it three more times and then switched to channels three and four. Neither produced more than a hiss and a crackle.

His other option was trying to communicate with the Russians from their side of the station. Their antennas aimed directly at Earth, but were only operational when the station was flying over that part of the world. Not an option at the moment.

"This cannot be happening."

It was.

Astronaut Clayton Shepard was ten weeks into his first mission in low Earth orbit when the impossible happened. The coronal mass ejection experts thought couldn't exist carried with it sixteen billion tons of hot plasma and charged particles. It outraced the solar wind at an astonishing two million kilometers an hour, creating a blast wave ahead of its impact with Earth and its orbiting satellites. The cloud, larger than any ever recorded, collided with Earth's magnetic field and created an enormous surge.

High-energy protons peaked at over two hundred and fifty times the norm and slammed into Earth, where the effect was instantaneous. Electrical currents in the atmosphere and on the ground surged repeatedly at varying degrees.

Within ninety seconds of impact, chain reactions began to shut down power grids and damage oil and gas pipelines across the entirety of the planet. Satellites orbiting the Earth absorbed the electrical surge, and those that had not shut down the high voltage on their transceivers were either destroyed or significantly damaged.

Unlike solar flares, the CME had left the Sun gradually, gathering speed as it accelerated outward and away from the star's surface. It traveled nearly twice the speed of any previously recorded CME and carried with it sixty percent more material than the typical value of a CME cloud.

By the time it hit the ISS, the station was in the worst spot possible, racing above the Atlantic Ocean in a highly magnetic region of the planet called the South Atlantic Anomaly. It only worsened the impact on the station, which was radiation hardened to withstand minor event upsets. It couldn't handle anything like the invisible tsunami that had just surged and crashed over it.

Without knowing exactly what had happened, Shepard knew what had happened. He steadied himself in the darkness of the Cupola, a dome-shaped module with seven panoramic windows, and pressed his hands against the glass. It was almost five feet tall and a little more than nine feet across, but it felt like a coffin.

He looked to his right, out window three, and saw the Canadarm2, the station's large robotic arm used to build parts of the station and to grab incoming cargo vehicles. Beyond the arm was his home planet.

From the underside of the station, the Cupola was the perfect spot from which to watch Earth as the ISS moved at five miles per second around the globe. He was speeding past North America.

It was dark. The familiar spider webs of lights that marked large metropolitan areas across the continent were missing. Like the ISS, the planet was virtually powerless.

"Jackie," he breathed, looking toward the area he thought was Texas. A thick knot grew in his throat as he suppressed his emotion. "The kids." His lips quivered, his eyes welled, but Clayton Shepard, the mechanical engineer and astronaut, steadied himself. He'd have to worry about them later. Right now, his own survival and that of his crew was paramount.

Shepard gripped the sides of the laptop display directly in front of him. The screen was black. He thumped the spacebar with his thumb. He hit the power button as if he were trying to score points on a video game.

Nothing worked.

To his right, facing the Canadarm2 underneath window three, was a joystick. It controlled the arm. He jockeyed it back and forth and then slapped at it with his hand. Nothing happened, not that he expected it.

Shepard spun one hundred and eighty degrees. Cosmonaut Boris Voin was still there. He was tangled in the tether that connected him to the ISS. Feet away was veteran Astronaut Ben Greenwood. Ben had his hands up in surrender. Shepard didn't know if they were dead or barely clinging to life.

He took a deep breath and closed his eyes. "Tell me this is a dream," he said to the empty room. "This has got to be a dream."

He opened his eyes and reaffirmed what he already knew to be true. If he couldn't restore power, they were screwed.

MISSION ELAPSED TIME:
72 DAYS, 3 HOURS, 19 MINUTES, 28 SECONDS
249 MILES ABOVE EARTH

Clayton Shepard didn't usually take shortcuts; however, if he was going to save Ben and Boris, he'd need to cheat physics and biology.

He was in the Russian side of the ISS, inside the airlock, lowering the pressure to a little more than ten pounds per square inch. It was a process that normally took nearly twice as long as he planned to give it.

As tempting as it was to slip into one of the two do-it-yourself Russian Orlan space suits and rescue his friends immediately, he couldn't risk nitrogen poisoning. Still, he could not take the usual four hours to prep his body.

Ben and Boris were both in US suits since they'd exited on the American side of the station, and they were working on the port photovoltaic arrays. Assuming they were alive, which was a giant leap, their suits wouldn't last more than eight hours before their life-support systems would begin to fail.

They'd been outside for four. Clayton had less than three hours to acclimate as best he could.

In the seconds after the CME hit, Clayton had understood the gravity of the damage. His best option had been to reteach himself the manual Soyuz procedures and evacuate.

He couldn't do it.

He couldn't leave his expedition teammates floating in space. If they were alive, he could save them. If they were dead, he could bring home their bodies to their families.

He knew his wife wouldn't be thrilled with his decision, but she'd understand. Jackie was a smart, strong woman who'd always understood his pull toward the risky, the dangerous, and the unknown.

Clayton checked his analog, battery-operated watch. It wasn't working. It was stuck at 9:23 CST. He'd done a lot in what he calculated couldn't have been more than fifteen minutes since the CME cloud shut them down.

"I should have packed my Breitling," he lamented. The self-perpetuating watch, with no digital parts or battery, would have survived the electromagnetic blast. "Idiot."

From the Cupola, he'd quickly maneuvered his way into Node 1, the central part of the station, the oldest piece upon which the rest of it was built. Inside Node 1 were a series of computers that controlled basic life functions on board the entirety of the ISS.

Clayton had known instinctively all of the computers were shut down from the magnetic blast. Rather than check the Command & Control computers one by one and hope he could restart them individually, he pushed himself the shortest distance necessary to keep himself, and hopefully his compatriots, alive.

He had checked the systems on the Node 1 computer and gone through the restart sequence. It hadn't worked.

He'd tried it again and held his breath for three seconds. Five seconds. Fifteen seconds.

Bingo.

The Node 1 computer had clicked and buzzed to life. Its indicators had flashed and blinked. Simple systems were on.

Next, he'd entered a series of commands to reboot the Command & Control computers. There were three of them on either side of the ISS. Although he couldn't know from his position if the Russian side was operational, it didn't matter yet. He'd needed at least one on the American side to reboot and function, and that was what he got.

Step one was complete. He had basic power inside the American half of the ISS, and external systems had rebooted as well. Clayton had hoped those systems returned quickly enough for the men stuck outside. He'd checked life-support monitors on their EMUs that indicated heart rate and breathing. There was no biofeedback available. He still had hope though. Those monitors frequently malfunctioned because of sweat or poor skin contact. The lack of data wasn't good news, but it hadn't deterred him from what he had to do.

It could be they were unconscious but alive. It was a small chance, but it was there. At every chance, Clayton had peeked through the small windows that gave him narrow glimpses into the space around the station. The men weren't moving. Clayton was nauseous with each panicked look through the glass. His pulse thumped. Sweat clung to his face.

From Node 1, Clayton had quickly maneuvered to the Destiny module, a twenty-eight-foot-long cylinder that housed the ECLSS— the Environmental and Life Support System—on the American side of the station. Before he could do anything else, he'd needed to ensure the main control computers and the ECLSS were functional, most critically the carbon dioxide scrubber. If that wasn't working, he'd suffocate.

Clayton had hovered in the module for a moment, holding the rack supporting the system with one hand, and with the other he'd held a crude sketch he'd drawn to remind himself of the electrical systems on board the station. He'd kept it in his pocket, folded inside a small red journal, since the launch from Baikonur in the Kazakhstan Desert more than two months earlier.

He'd essentially created a simplified flowchart. At the top was the Command & Control computer. Remarkably, it was working.

To the left was Guidance; to the right were Payloads and other internal functions that were mostly redundant. He didn't care about those.

The two center boxes were labeled Internal Systems and External Systems. Connected to the Internal Systems was a trio of boxes labeled Thermal, Audio, and ECLSS; the External Systems connected to Communications and Electrical.

It had appeared to him the ECLSS was functioning properly, at least as far as the most critical systems were concerned. The atmosphere was preserved, and the scrubber was working. The water recovery system, however, which recycled water from the toilets and humidity in the air, was fried.

That would only be a problem if they planned on staying aboard the ISS for a long period of time. Clayton didn't.

The Russian side also had a similar system in the Zvezda service module. Also considered the "central post," the Zvezda contained Russian and American computers and was the gathering place for the crew whenever an emergency arose.

Pushing himself past the camera equipment lining the walls and into the service module, he made a cursory check of the Russian systems, which appeared okay, though he didn't have time for a thorough evaluation. He'd needed to start the EVA procedure as quickly as he could. When he hit the airlock and the mechanical process had clicked, he'd known, at the very least, the critical electrical components on the Russian side of the station were functional for now. The radios were down. Even the HAM radio they used to communicate with schoolkids and interested radio operators wasn't functioning. He was alone.

His heart was pounding. The thoughts of his family coping with…whatever had happened…was untenable. It was exacerbated by the idea of waiting for hours inside the ISS while his friends were helpless in space, just beyond his reach. He chewed on the inside of his cheek and tapped out syncopated beats with his fingers. He was like a child in the middle seat on a long road trip.

To comfort himself, to erase the fires of Armageddon from his mind's eye, he imagined Jackie might not even know what had happened. It was nighttime. She could be asleep. She could be reading a book. She loved to read. Steinbeck and Hemingway were her favorites. Jane Austen wasn't far behind, although she considered Austen summertime beach reading.

Clayton forced a chuckle, thinking about his wife with a stack of books beside their bed, all of them dog eared and coffee stained. He could feel her feet under the covers, rubbing up against his calf. He longed for the gravity of Earth, the weight of her arms around him.

He sucked in a breath of filtered air and sighed.

If she was awake and she'd lost power, she'd probably chalk it up to a surge of some kind. Jackie wouldn't know how dire the situation truly was until the next day.

He hoped that was the case. He prayed she'd have one more good night of sleep before her world turned upside down, and he was stuck in orbit, passing by every ninety minutes, unable to help.

She'll be okay, he silently assured himself. *She's got neighbors. She's got a Concealed Handgun License.. There's plenty of food in the freezer she can cook on the charcoal grill. And we've got gallons of water and gasoline left over from hurricane season.*

He kept repeating the mantra, trying to convince himself it was so.

CHAPTER 2

FRIDAY, JANUARY 24, 2020, 9:25 PM CST
CLEAR LAKE, TEXAS

Jackie Shepard was two pages from finishing *The Grapes of Wrath* for the fourth time when the lights went out. "Seriously? You have got to be kidding me."

She pulled the covers back and planted her feet on the cold Spanish tile floor. She'd made it from her master bedroom into the kitchen when her daughter called from upstairs.

"Mmmommmm!" yelled the aggrieved sixteen-year-old. "The Internet died. I can't get YouTube."

Jackie stopped at the large granite island and leaned on it. "The power's out, Marie," she called back. "It's not just the Internet."

"So unfair!" Marie yelled.

Jackie chuckled. "Snap your displeasure. Or Tweet it. Whatever it is you're using these days."

Marie appeared at the top of the stairs and bounded down the steps. "I can't," she whined, walking into the kitchen. "I've got no service."

Jackie looked at the glowing white screen and took the iPhone from her daughter's hand. "Huh," she said, noticing the lack of cellular signal. "That's weird."

"What do we do?" Marie had headphones around her neck, her shoulder-length hair pulled into a ponytail.

"Good question," said Jackie. "I guess you could hang down here with me. You could fill me in on the last dance team drama."

Marie shrugged. "I guess," she said. "I've got nothing better to do."

Jackie popped Marie on the bottom as her daughter led her back to the bedroom. "Gee, thanks."

Marie giggled. "Anytime, Mom. I guess it's just us girls tonight."

The two climbed into Jackie's bed and pulled the covers up to their necks. Jackie lay on one side to face her daughter.

"Yeah," she said. "Tomorrow night too. Chris isn't back from his camping trip until Sunday."

Marie fluffed the pillow on her side of the bed. "I don't know why he likes that stuff. Camping is so totally unsanitary."

"He's a thirteen-year-old boy," Jackie replied. "Everything about him is totally unsanitary."

"True."

Jackie rolled over to check her phone. It was plugged into a charging dock on the bedside table. Its display was off. She punched the home button; it didn't respond.

She pulled the phone from its base. "Huh. It's not working at all."

"Try a hard reset," Marie said. She grabbed her mom's phone. "I'll do it."

Jackie chuckled. "Okay."

Marie tried the reset sequence. It didn't work. She tried it again. Nothing.

"Power surge," Marie suggested.

"Maybe," said Jackie. "No big deal. I've got insurance. So, about the dance team…"

Marie wasn't looking at her. Instead, her attention had shifted from the phone to beyond Jackie's shoulder and the window that faced the backyard.

Her eyes widened. "Um…Mom?"

Jackie frowned, sensing something was wrong. "What?"

Marie pointed out the window. "That! What is that?"

Jackie looked out the bay window at the red light bathing the sky through the slats of the white wooden shutters. She slid out of bed and moved to the glass, pulling open the shutter casement to get a better look.

The sky was undulating with a multihued red wave. It pulsed, seemingly breathing in the atmosphere above southeast Texas before exhaling.

"C'mon," Jackie said to Marie. "Let's go check it out."

The two scurried back to the kitchen and through the door leading onto the covered rear porch. The brick was colder than the tile on Jackie's feet. They walked from under the porch onto the stained concrete pool deck.

"Except for the color, that looks like the northern lights," said Jackie, her breath visible in the cool winter air. "You know, the aurora borealis?"

Marie stepped close to her mom, looping her arm around her for warmth. "I know what it is. It does kinda look like it, right? The color though…"

"That's really weird," Jackie said. "They're magnetic. They typically only appear at the poles. And they're green."

"So what does it mean?"

"I don't know." Jackie curled her toes underneath her feet. "But all the power is out. Look around the neighborhood. There isn't a single light. Even the light pollution off near the shopping center isn't there. Everything is dark."

Marie let go of her mother's arms and stepped out onto the grass. She folded her arms across her chest and looked up at the sky. "You think Dad's okay?"

Jackie took a deep breath. "I don't know."

"And Chris?"

"I don't—" Jackie stopped mid-sentence.

In the sky behind their house was a dark shadow growing exponentially by the second, blocking out the red aurora. At first, Jackie thought it was a bird. But as it grew in size, the shape of its wings and its tail told her it wasn't a bird. It was a plane.

It was falling; the only sound was the air rushing through its engines, whistling fiercely as it dove toward them. Jackie stood mesmerized for a moment by the surreality of what was happening in front of her.

She grabbed Marie's arm and pulled her into the swimming pool. Jackie sank to the bottom of the pool, the cold water sucking the air from her lungs. From beneath the water, she felt the ground rumble and shake.

Still holding Marie's hand, she pulled her daughter to the surface, both coughing up water as they swam to the edge of the pool.

Marie's teeth were chattering, her lips trembling. "What was that? What happened, Mom?"

Jackie pushed herself from the water and spun to sit on the edge. "I think a plane just crashed," she said, helping Marie from the water.

"Our house looks okay," Marie said.

"We need to go see," said Jackie. "It felt like the plane crashed on top of us."

Shivering, both of them ran around the side of the house past the silent pool pump. The crushed granite path poked and jabbed at Jackie's bare feet. Before she'd cleared the side of the house, she could see the bright orange glow strobing across the cul-de-sac. There were people yelling and screaming. Jackie thought it was raining until she realized the specks of whatever was hitting her shoulders and pinging off her head were tiny pieces of debris.

Jackie led Marie to the front yard. Across the wide circle that marked the end of their street was an enormous fire. Twenty-foot flames lit the thick black smoke pouring from the wreckage of the plane and the remains of the home that had stood there moments earlier.

Jackie stopped in her driveway. The heat emanating from the fire warmed her cold, wet body.

"Oh my God," she said. She drew her daughter to her chest, wrapping her arms around her. "My God. There are people alive in there."

The screams and cries for help that pierced the air when Jackie and Marie reached the front yard died within seconds as those trapped in the burning wreckage succumbed to their injuries, the flames, and the smoke.

Jackie's eyes adjusted the glow of the fire and she saw the houses on either side were also burning. It wasn't just one house, it was three. She kissed her daughter's head.

"I'll be right back," she said.

"Mom, no!" Marie cried, holding on to her mother. "Don't."

Jackie pulled away and jogged toward the heat. "I'll be right back."

She made a wide berth around the fire to the left. It was too hot to get any closer. When she neared the burning house on the end of the three, she saw neighbors dragging garden hoses into the narrow area between the home that was burning and the adjacent that wasn't.

"Jackie," said an older, retired neighbor named Reggie Buck, "that you?"

"Yes," Jackie said, smoke burning her eyes. "What can I do, Reggie?"

"Help my wife here with the hoses," he said. "I'm gonna crank on the water. Just keep the house wet. Get any flames that start to creep."

Jackie reached the hose and helped detangle its end. Reggie's wife, Lana, was grappling with another hose attached to a spigot at the front of their house.

"Got it!" she called. "You can turn on the water."

Reggie spun the spigot at the side of the house and water sprang from the high-pressure nozzle attached to the end of the hose. He ran to his wife and helped her with the second hose.

Jackie aimed the spray at the flames licking the side of the burning home. It wasn't doing much. She shifted the nozzle to the side of Reggie and Lana's house, painting the HardiePlank siding with water.

"Help! Please help! We're stuck." The frightened woman's call came from the burning house next door. There was a window above the two-car garage. From her spot between the homes Jackie couldn't see who it was, but assumed it was Betty Brown. She lived in the house with her son, who had special needs. Her husband had died of metastatic melanoma two years earlier.

Reggie bolted past Jackie, limping on his bum knee to the garage of the burning house next door. He'd taken off his white undershirt and wrapped it around his face like a mask.

Flames dripped from the house onto the yard, sparking the dry ground. Lana joined Jackie at the hose, trying to beat back the fire.

Lana yanked on her hose to move closer to the neighbor's driveway. "Be careful," she called after her husband.

Reggie waved at her before ducking into the house through the open front door. A moment later he was manually lifting the garage door.

"Drop the hose, Jackie!" he said, his voice muffled by the shirt. He coughed and waved her over. "I need help with the ladder!"

Lana reached out with her free hand. "Go, Jackie," she said. "I've got the hoses."

Jackie handed Lana the hose and sprinted to join Reggie on the driveway. She grabbed one end of the long aluminum extension ladder when Reggie emerged from the garage. Together they raised the ladder against the brick face of the house.

"I'll climb it," Reggie said and began climbing the metal rungs. "You keep it stable."

"Got it."

Jackie glanced back and saw Marie sitting in their driveway. Her knees were pulled up to her chest and she was rocking in the orange flicker of the fire. Jackie's heart sank.

"Marie!" she yelled above the crackle of the inferno. "I need you! Come here!"

Marie snapped from her daze and pushed herself to her feet. She raced across the street and joined her mother at the base of the ladder. Her eyes were swollen with tears, her nose was running, and her lower lip quivered.

Jackie locked eyes with her daughter. "Worry about us later, okay? Right now others need us."

Marie sniffled and nodded. She grabbed the rail on her side of the ladder.

Jackie tightened her grip on her rail. "We'll be okay."

They both looked up toward the window in time to see Reggie's foot disappear inside the house. His head reemerged and he looked down at Jackie.

"I'm sending down Betty first," he said. "Help her if she needs it."

Jackie nodded. The fire was thickening along the roofline and had consumed much of the right side of the home closest to the crash. They had mere minutes until the entire home was engulfed.

"Hurry up!" she called up to Reggie. "I don't think you have long!"

Betty appeared feet first. She descended the ladder slowly, skidding her hands gingerly along the aluminum rails. She was barefoot and in a nightgown, her hair in curlers.

Reggie poked his head through the window. "Okay, Betty," he encouraged. "You're good. You're almost there."

Betty made the final few steps down the ladder. Marie helped her to the last rung and she planted her feet squarely on the driveway.

"Thank you," Betty sobbed. "Thank you." She cupped her shaking hands over her mouth and looked back at the window.

Her son, Brian, was standing at the top of the ladder, shaking his head. The smoke was intensifying and he coughed.

"My eyes," he said, letting go of the ladder with one hand to pinch his eyes shut. "They hurt. My eyes hurt."

The smoke grew denser, moving in thick puffs that began to obscure Brian atop the ladder. The heat was intensifying, the dry radiation of it forcing Jackie to close her eyes and look away. The aluminum ladder was getting hot to the touch.

"My eyes," Brian said. He wasn't moving. The fire was.

Jackie swung herself onto the ladder. "Hold it," she told Marie. "Don't let go."

She pulled herself up the ladder, skipping rungs where she could, to meet Brian at his feet. She gently grabbed the boy's calf.

He shook her off, kicking his leg. Jackie nearly lost her footing. She recovered and grabbed at it again and held on.

"Brian, keep your eyes closed. I'll help you down."

"Don't touch," he said. "Don't touch."

Betty called from the ground below, "Let her help you, Brian."

"Let me," Brian said. "I'll do it. I'll do it!"

Jackie lowered herself a rung at a time as Brian did so above her until they reached the ground. Betty threw herself at Brian, trapping his arms with her hug.

"Go to Lana, Marie," said Jackie. "Go help her." She coughed against the thickening, acrid smoke.

Marie reluctantly let go of the ladder and joined the others in the Bucks' yard next door. Jackie gripped the ladder, ignoring the burn of the aluminum rails, to steady it for Reggie.

"Reggie! I've got it. C'mon!"

Reggie didn't respond.

The fire was eating its way across the house, the flames lapping at the roof and walls. Jackie couldn't hold on much longer. She let go of one rail and pulled her shirt over her nose and mouth, her eyes watering.

She tried looking up, but she couldn't see anything. She tucked her chin against her chest and squeezed her eyes shut. The heat was searing on the right side of her body. Another couple of seconds was all Jackie could take.

She was about to let go when the ladder shifted and she felt the vibration in her hands of someone moving down the rungs.

Clunk. Clunk. Clunk.

Reggie's feet appeared two rungs above her hands. Jackie moved out of the way and let her neighbor jump to the ground.

"C'mon," he coughed, and took Jackie's arm. "We need to move. The house is about to collapse."

They stumbled away from the house, collapsing onto the grass, coughing and rubbing the sting from their eyes as the fire engulfed the garage.

"The hoses aren't working!" Lana shouted, her voice warbling with emotion. "The flames are about to jump. Our house is going to burn too."

Reggie pushed himself to his feet. "Let's forget about saving it, then," he said. "Let's run inside and grab critical things we'll need."

Lana dropped the hose. The glow of the fire reflected the glisten in her eyes. "Just give up on our house?"

Brian started jumping up and down next to the hose as if he were avoiding an ant pile. "Water. Water. It's wet! Too wet!"

Marie bent down and pulled the hose away from Brian, letting the water run toward the street.

"We've got suitcases in the foyer coat closet," Reggie said to the group. "Let's get those and fill them up. I'll handle the kitchen and garage with Betty and Brian."

Betty nodded. "Okay."

"Lana, you get clothes from the bedrooms. Whatever you think we might need. Shoes too."

"What about us?" asked Jackie. "What can Marie and I do?"

Reggie puffed his cheeks and exhaled. "The garage. Batteries, tools, tape, glue, whatever. I've got some fishing poles. There's a box with some odds and ends. A shovel."

"Got it. We'll hurry."

"We've got no choice," said Reggie, motioning toward the fire. It had fully consumed the Browns' home. In minutes it would be burning his.

Lana put her hand on Jackie's arm. "Is it too much to ask if we could stay with you for now?" she asked nervously. "I know Clay isn't home."

"Of course, Lana." Jackie smiled. "Clay wouldn't want it any other way if he were here. In fact, Betty and Brian are welcome too."

"Thank you. You're too kind."

"We're going to need each other for a while," said Jackie.

A remarkably loud, inhuman shriek pierced the air. It was coming from beyond the smoke and flames.

"Did you hear that?" Reggie asked.

"I did," said Jackie. "I was hoping it was my imagination."

The shriek morphed into a wail, carrying with it the deep sound of irreversible despair. It lingered, drowning out the pop and crackle of the flames licking at Reggie's house.

"We should go," said Reggie. "The heck with our stuff. There could be survivors over there."

"You deal with salvaging what you can from your house," she said. "Keep an eye on Marie. I'm running over there."

"I don't know about –"

"Reggie," said Jackie. "You take care of everybody here. You're the strongest."

Before he could protest again, Jackie was off. She sprinted up her street onto the main loop that encircled the neighborhood and bolted right, cutting across a lawn. She trod through the thin St. Augustine grass, the blades crunching under her feet as she darted from one yard to the next, her wet clothes sticking to her. She cut another corner and bounded onto the street running parallel to hers. Ahead she could see the orange strobe of the flames consuming houses at the end of the cul-de-sac. Another wail cut through the air and made the hairs on Jackie's neck stand up. She was back on the asphalt, pounding toward the cries. People were hurt. They needed help. She passed a pair of For Sale signs in the yards of empty houses. Then it hit her.

The carnage was worse than on her street. Six of the homes were ablaze. The tail of the aircraft was smoldering in the middle of the circle at the end of the street. She slowed to a fast walk, trying to absorb what lay in front of her.

Another wail drew her attention toward the houses. The smoke was too thick.

To her right, on their sides, were a pair of seats. They were connected to each other, as were the crisp of passengers melted into the fabric. One of them still wore a high heel on one foot. The other's blackened features were drawn with agony. The mouth was agape and white teeth seemed to glow in contrast.

A torrent of nausea coursed through Jackie's body. With every step, another horror greeted her, each new vignette more grotesque than the one before. She sidestepped a pink child's backpack. She saw a doll next to it, its plastic limbs twisted into unnatural positions. Then she saw…

"Dear God," she whispered, tears flooding her eyes. It wasn't a doll.

Jackie heaved and bent over at her waist, vomiting into the grass. Her stomach churned, her muscles contracting in spasms until the burn of hot bile was all that remained.

Another wail. This one was weaker, peppered with resignation.

Jackie spat onto the grass and wiped her mouth with the back of her forearm. She resumed her march toward the smoke and flames, her eyes stinging from the particulates in the air.

She pulled her shirt collar over her nose and mouth and moved deeper into the haze. She dodged bodies, parts of bodies, and debris as she hopscotched to a spot where she thought the wail was emanating from.

There was nothing now. Only the sound of the flames consuming the homes and lives of her neighbors remained.

Then from behind her came a soft voice dripping with pain. "Help me."

Jackie spun and saw a man lying on the ground near the engine. He was on his back, his arms reaching over his head toward her. Jackie coughed through the smoke and knelt next to the man. She didn't immediately recognize him. His face was black with soot. He was shirtless and wore only boxers. She surveyed his body, looking for the source of his immobility. It was too dark and smoky, even with the ambient orange flicker from the fire, to see much. Then she spotted a Woody Woodpecker tattoo on his bicep. She knew the man, Walter Fleming, who lived alone.

"Jackie?" he said, his voice garbled. "Jackie? Oh, thank you."

"Walter?" she asked, another lump blooming in her throat. The man in front of her looked nothing like her neighbor Walter Fleming, the realtor. He sounded nothing like Walter Fleming. But it had to be him.

"Yes," he coughed. "I can't feel my legs," he said. "I'm…I can't…please."

Jackie leaned in and took his hand. It was cold. Blood trickled from his ears and nose. She felt for a pulse in his wrist but couldn't find one.

"I was in bed," he said. With each breath, his lungs rattled. "I got up to go to the bathroom and then I'm here. Outside. I can't feel anything, Jackie."

"Okay, Walter," she said. "It's okay."

"I don't..." His voice trailed off and his eyes looked past Jackie, fixing on something far beyond the smoke.

She squeezed his hand. "Walter?"

He stiffened and then relaxed, air escaping with a gurgle from his open mouth. Walter Fleming was dead.

Jackie looked over her shoulder. There had to be survivors. Somebody. Somewhere.

She pushed herself to her feet and, keeping her profile low, wandered the cul-de-sac, looking for signs of life. The dry heat of the fire burned like an open oven, the choking smoke was thickening. She couldn't stay much longer.

Coughing, Jackie stumbled over another body. She struggled to maintain her balance but did and found herself in front of a woman on her knees, giving mouth-to-mouth resuscitation to someone.

Jackie knelt down and crawled the remaining few feet. "Can I help?"

The woman jerked away from the victim, a man, and fell back onto her bottom. Her eyes were wide with fear, the whites exaggerated by her soot-dirtied face. She stared at Jackie without saying anything.

"Can I help?"

The woman blinked. "Yes," she said breathlessly. "Can you try? I'll start chest compressions."

Jackie nodded and moved to the man's head. His eyes were closed. She scanned down his body. His shoulder looked dislocated, and one of his legs was broken. He was wearing long-sleeved pajamas.

Jackie inched into position and cradled the back of the man's neck to open his airway. She pinched his nose with one hand and drew his chin downward with the other to open his lips.

She'd taken a CPR class years earlier when the children were younger, so she vaguely remembered what to do. She bent down, tugged her shirt from her face, and puffed air into the man's mouth. She counted and then repeated. Counted and repeated.

She felt for a pulse and found none. She laid her head on his chest. He wasn't breathing. His heart was stopped.

The woman moved to the man's side and leaned over him. She locked her elbows and flattened her palms. Coughing, the woman pumped up and down. Up and down, crying as she worked.

"I don't think it's helping," she whimpered. "I think he's gone." She stopped the compressions.

Jackie didn't know the couple. She didn't recognize them at all. Still, she bent over again and lowered her mouth onto his, puffing large volumes of air into his lungs.

For minutes the two women alternated tasks. Neither worked. The woman sank back onto her heels and buried her hands in her face, coughing through her sobs.

"I can keep going," Jackie offered, pulling the shirt back above her nose. She was drenched in sweat. Her face felt as it did after a day at the beach without sunscreen. Her lungs burned from the waves of smoke.

The woman shook her head. "He's dead," she said. "He's dead."

"Are there any other survivors here?" Jackie asked. "Have you seen anyone?"

"There was screaming," the woman said. "It stopped. I don't think anyone is alive."

Jackie reached out and put a hand on the woman's shoulder. "Come with me," she said. "I'm a street over. My house is okay. I've got others staying with me."

The woman looked at Jackie and cocked her head as if she didn't understand the offer. She coughed again and gagged against the smoke.

Jackie stood, staying as low as possible, and wrapped her fingers around the woman's thick upper arm. "C'mon," she said. "Let's go."

The woman vacantly complied and followed Jackie down the street, away from the flames and heat. They ran like helicopter blades swirled just above their heads until they'd turned left twice and found themselves on Jackie's street.

Jackie blinked away the sting of the remnant smoke and lowered her shirt. She stood tall and walked. Her back ached. Her head throbbed. Her lips felt swollen and cracked.

"My name is Jackie," she said. "I live over here." She motioned toward her house with her chin.

"I'm Candace," the woman said. "I just moved in last—" She hesitated. "We just moved in last week. My boyfriend Chad." Her face contorted and she stopped walking. Tears pooled in her eyes and streaked clean wet lines down her face. "That was Chad," she sobbed.

Jackie stopped and pulled Candace into an embrace. She gathered the young woman in her arms and held her in the street. The snap of flames crackled in the distance.

CHAPTER 3

FRIDAY, JANUARY 24, 2020, 10:40 PM CST
DINOSAUR VALLEY STATE PARK, TEXAS

Rick Walsh stood overlooking Opossum Creek on the western edge of the park. "We should start heading back to the tent, boys. It's late."

His son, Kenny, and Kenny's friend Chris Shepard were twenty feet below him, perched halfway down the steep limestone ledge that led to the water below. For much of the late afternoon, they'd spent their day looking down at their feet, trying to identify the sauropod and theropod tracks preserved in the creek bed. For the last hour, they'd gazed skyward at the red aurora that undulated and floated in the northern sky to their right.

"Five more minutes?" Kenny called to his dad.

"Please?" Chris chimed in.

"Five minutes," Rick agreed. He stared at what he was sure was an aurora. He'd seen the northern lights on a business trip to Canada years before and they were unmistakable. He didn't understand, however, why they'd be so far south or why they were red.

The only explanation was a magnetic storm of some kind. They'd had no warning, however, and he hadn't received any news alerts on his iPhone, which was odd.

They'd finished dinner at their campsite and walked over to the communal restrooms to clean up for the night when the boys had insisted on a nighttime hike back to Track Site Area One. Even though he'd been exhausted from the five-hour drive and setting up camp, Rick had relented.

It wasn't often he got time with his son. Every other weekend, alternating holidays, and two weeks during the summer didn't cut it. So when he had the chance, he tried to make the most of it. His ex complained he spoiled Kenny. He didn't disagree with her. The whole mess was his fault. There was no point in arguing with her anymore. She deserved that much.

Rick pulled a sports bottle from the pack he'd slung over one shoulder and squeezed a shot of warm Gatorade into his mouth. "Remember to drink, boys," he called out. "Even if it's cold out, you can get dehydrated.

The boys were pointing at the sky, their hands waving excitedly as they talked. He smiled. Kenny was a good kid. He surrounded himself with good kids. Rick had worried the divorce would ruin his boy and send him down a bad path. So far, so good. Although it had only been six months, still, it was a small victory.

"Excuse me, sir."

The voice from behind Rick startled him. He tensed, spun quickly, and backed up a step. "Yes?"

It was a park ranger straddling a mountain bike and holding a flashlight aimed at Rick's feet. "I'm sorry," he said. "I didn't mean to scare you, but I need to ask you to return to your campsite."

Rick studied the young ranger. His uniform was neatly pressed, creases along the sleeves and down the front of his pants.

"Okay," Rick replied hesitantly. "Why is that?"

The ranger pointed his light toward the aurora. "We're asking all campers to return to their sites."

Rick followed the bluish white LED beam with his eyes. "Because of that?"

"Yes, sir. Well, not exactly. But yes. We've experienced a park-wide power failure. For everyone's safety, we're asking you return to your campsite."

"Power is out park wide?"

"Yes," he said. "My truck isn't working either. None of them are."

"Sounds like an electromagnetic pulse," Rick said. "I read a book about it by that news guy Ted Koppel."

The ranger shrugged. He took his flashlight with both hands and used one to wind a crank on the top of it. "This still works at least," he said. "So, you'll head back to your site, please?"

"Sure thing." Rick turned his attention to the boys. "Kenny, Chris, c'mon. We need to go."

The ranger nodded his thanks and hopped back onto his bike. He affixed the flashlight to a clip on the handlebars and sped off into the darkness.

Rick watched him disappear. "He had no idea what I was talking about," he mumbled, shaking his head. Despite warnings, he knew a lot of people were ignorant to the threat of an electromagnetic pulse, an EMP. That didn't explain the aurora, necessarily. And he didn't understand why it was red and not green.

Rick was a pencil pusher in the energy industry. He wasn't a scientist, so he couldn't connect the two definitively. But something bad had happened, that much he knew for sure.

The boys finished their climb up the limestone steps and joined Rick in the parking lot. Both of them stopped and downed long swigs of their Gatorade.

"You guys ready? We should head back."

"Dad," said Kenny, "this is so cool. Seriously."

"Mr. Walsh," Chris said, "you should have come down there. It was awesome."

Rick smiled and tousled Kenny's hair, then patted Chris on the shoulder. "I got a good look from here, but I'm glad you enjoyed it. It is pretty cool."

He led them across the wide parking lot toward their campsite a quarter mile away on the edge of the meandering creek. As the three of them trudged in the relative red-hued darkness, Rick looked to his left.

The air was still. The night was sinking from chilly to cold. Rick adjusted the pack on his back, tightening his grip on the strap. As beautiful as it was, he was sure that aurora was a harbinger of doom.

SATURDAY, JANUARY 25, 2020, 11:03 PM CST
DINOSAUR VALLEY STATE PARK, TEXAS

Rick leaned against the hood of his 1978 Jeep Cherokee Chief. His boot heel was resting against the bottom well of the large wheel on the driver's side. He was chewing on his thumbnail, watching the aurora with less enthusiasm every passing minute.

The boys were in the tent a few feet away. They'd fallen asleep after some resistance and negotiations for an early wake-up call.

Rick only relented to their demands because none of their watches or phones were working. There was no way they'd wake up early. At least he hoped that was the case.

"Hey," a timid voice whispered through the trees behind Rick. "Sorry to bother you. You got a second?"

Rick squinted to see an older man standing at the clump of pines separating his campsite from the one next to it. His hands were stuffed into his pockets. His eyes were peering over the tops of reading glasses, and he was bald. The red aura reflected off the smooth dome of his head.

Rick pushed his boot onto the tire and forced himself straight onto both feet. He moved toward the visitor.

"What's up?" Rick asked. "You need something?"

The man pulled up his loose-fitting pants with his hands still in the pockets. His long-sleeved shirt was buttoned to the collar. "I don't reckon I need anything," he said in a slow, deliberate drawl. "I just wanted to take a survey."

"Yeah?"

The man pulled his hand out and offered it to Rick. "I'm Mumphrey," he said. "I'm here all the time. Grandkids love the place. I come on my own sometimes."

Rick shook the man's bony, frail grip. "I'm Rick."

The man let go of Rick's hand and fingered his glasses higher onto his thin nose. He stretched his face, making a perfect oval with his lips as he adjusted the frames. His movement, like his speech, reminded Rick of a wise old turtle working as fast as it could.

Rick folded his arms across his chest. "A survey, you said?"

Mumphrey's forehead wrinkles deepened. "I've got some concerns, that's all. I already checked with my neighbor on the other side and figured I might pick your brain too."

Rick shrugged. "Go ahead."

"I've got a camper," said Mumphrey, nodding toward his site. "It's a little pop-up. Ain't much. But it's enough space for me and the grandkids. Like I said, they come with me most times."

"I saw it earlier," said Rick. "Looks nice."

A sheepish smile stretched across the old man's face. "Thanks," he said. "I try to keep it up. You know, clean and all. It's easy to let something like a pop-up go to pot."

"I'm sure."

"It's got an icebox, a little microwave too. The grandkids like popcorn. So it's good for that."

"I'll bet."

Mumphrey leaned toward Rick, his eyes big behind the slipping black frames of his glasses. "Well," he said, "none of it's working. Plum broke. Icebox, microwave, everything. Nothing's working. I checked fuses; I tried shore power on them little posts they got at the sites. Nothing."

"You have a generator?"

Mumphrey nodded. "It's a nice little Honda EU 2000. Got a computer inverter on it for laptops and whatnot. It won't start."

Rick glanced back to the aurora. "Huh."

Mumphrey crossed his arms and scratched his pointy elbow. He looked like he was playing an instrument. "I'm asking if you got any problems like that. I asked the other neighbor too."

"What did he say?"

"She."

"What did she say?"

"She's by herself," he said. "I think she's an athlete or something. She was sitting at the picnic table, looking at the sky. I think I might have startled her. But I asked her."

Rick took a deep breath through his nose and bit the inside of his lip. Mumphrey seemed like a nice enough guy. "What did she say?"

"Her car wouldn't start. Her phone was dead. She was a tick nervous, I think. That's why I think I startled her. She does have a flashlight that works, though."

"Our flashlights are working too. You said she was an athlete?"

"Yeah. She's real fit looking. She has one of them stickers on the back of her car. It's got numbers on it, like a marathon or something."

"What about your phone, Mr. Mumphrey? Is it working?"

The old man smiled and raised a finger into the air. "Come to think of it," he said, "I ain't checked it yet." He reached into his back pocket and pulled out a phone. He flipped it open and stared at it.

"Doesn't work?"

Mumphrey looked over the tops of his glasses. "I'll be," he said, shaking his head. "It's deader than a doornail."

"My phone doesn't work either," said Rick. "None of ours do."

The old man cocked his head to the side. "Ours? You got somebody with you? Sorry if I'm intruding and all. Just wanted to take a survey."

"My boy and his friend."

"I bet they like it here."

"They do."

"All right then," said Mumphrey. "Just wondering what's going on. That's all."

Rick smiled. "No problem. If you need anything, you let me know."

"Nothing yet," said Mumphrey. "I might need help starting that woman's car in the morning. You got jumper cables?"

"I do," said Rick. "Happy to help."

Mumphrey nodded and waved goodbye. He trudged back to his pop-up. Rick rubbed his chin with his hand, the idea of an EMP sparking again in his mind.

The lines in his forehead deepened as he considered the implications of an EMP, of a prolonged loss of power. There were various causes, a nuclear attack being one of them.

He couldn't, didn't want to, wrap his head around the idea of war. It couldn't be that. They'd already know if the Russians, the Chinese, North Koreans, or Iranians had bombed them.

Wouldn't we?

He pushed the thought from his mind and looked back at the aurora. Maybe this wasn't a foreign power exerting its will, but rather Mother Nature. It was some sort of geomagnetic storm. That would explain the aurora.

Wouldn't it?

Rick felt the sting of fatigue in his eyes. He yawned. There was nothing he could do. He might as well try to sleep.

He walked over to the tent and unzipped the entry flap. Inside, hanging from the center of the pitch on a vinyl tab was a circular LED light. It was attached with a carabiner and swung a bit when Rick spread the flap open and squeezed into the space.

The swinging light gave Rick a good look at both boys. They were neck deep in their sleeping bags. His son wore a beanie to cover his head.

Rick lowered himself onto all fours and rolled over to sit on the edge of his sleeping bag. He slipped off his hiking boots one at a time and pushed them to the corner of the tent before reaching up to turn off the light.

He slid into his own bag and pulled it up to his chest and closed his eyes, feeling the bubble of air seep from the quilted polyester. Regardless of the cause of the power outage, his gut told him it wouldn't be short-lived. He'd need his rest.

Saturday would be a long day.

CHAPTER 4

MISSION ELAPSED TIME:
72 DAYS, 4 HOURS, 23 MINUTES, 43 SECONDS
249 MILES ABOVE EARTH

Clayton was sick of waiting. He couldn't do it. He couldn't give physics and biology the time they needed. His friends were in danger of dying, if not dead already, and his family was grappling with an apocalypse. The faster he got outside, the faster he could get back and go home.

He stared at the Russian Orlan suit, an MKS model. It was semirigid, which made it easier to don. He could suit up by himself. If he'd had to use an American suit, he'd be stuck. Those took two people to outfit. With the Orlan, he could prep alone in a half hour.

Clayton considered the task ahead and cursed. He could die by trying to rescue to men who might already be dead. An image of Jackie flashed in his mind. He could hear her voice pleading with him to forego the rescue mission and climb into the Soyuz.

The astronaut always buried the black rot in his gut that told him he was selfish. He was an adventurer, an adrenaline-seeker, an avid outdoorsman. Those were all code words for someone who cared only about himself, without thinking about the consequences his needs had on those around him.

His mind drifted to a conversation he'd had with Jackie a couple of weeks before leaving for Moscow. He could remember every word, the glisten in her eyes, the tight grip of her fists as she spoke through a clenched jaw.

"I didn't ask for this," she'd said. "I didn't marry an astronaut. I fell in love with an engineer. A safe, boring, brilliant engineer. This wasn't part of the deal. You blowing up in a rocket wasn't written in our vows."

He'd been sitting on the foot of the bed, listening without interruption. He knew better than to argue. He'd been married long enough and she'd been making salient points.

She was standing as far away from him as she could and still be in the room. "I knew you liked parasailing and hiking and crap like that, but that's not space travel."

Against his better judgment, he'd put a finger to his lips. "The kids will hear you."

Her eyes widened with rage. "I don't care if the whole neighborhood hears me!" she'd blasted. "The children are more frightened than I am. Chris keeps talking about *Apollo One* and *Challenger* and *Columbia*. Marie has asked what we do if you die in space and there's nothing to bury."

Clayton had slumped where he sat, each word stinging more than the last.

"It doesn't help that they watch these stupid movies with astronauts dying on asteroids or on Mars," she'd said. "And with YouTube…"

Her face had gone from anger to worry. Tears had streaked down her face. Without saying anything, Clayton stood from the bed and moved quietly to her, his arms outstretched.

She'd backed away, then relented, the tight balls of her fists relaxing and then gripping his shoulders when he embraced her. They'd cried together. Clayton could still feel the syncopated rise and fall of their chests and backs as they'd wept.

Seconds had turned to minutes before they'd let go of one another. Jackie had searched his eyes, he remembered. He'd wondered then, and now, what she'd hoped to find.

He'd swallowed hard and fought the warble of his voice before he spoke. He'd measured his words, not wanting to make promises he couldn't keep.

"You are as selfless as you are strong," he'd said. "You are what grounds our family. You ground *me*."

She had chuckled through her tears. "Not well enough."

"You have every right to be afraid. The kids do too. I get your anger. You're right, you didn't sign up for this."

"That wasn't entirely fair," she'd admitted. "You did ask if you could apply for the corps and I did say yes. I just never thought they'd take you."

Clayton had started to laugh, but saw she wasn't joking.

"We've been training for a long time. We wouldn't be going up there if I thought for a second I wouldn't be coming back," he'd said. "I plan on living a ridiculously long life with you and our children and our grandchildren."

"You need to talk to the children," she'd said. "They need to hear the same thing. They won't tell you how they're feeling."

Clayton had agreed. He'd talked with Marie and Chris. He'd told them to stay off of YouTube. He'd told them no American had ever died in space. He'd told them there were a zillion safety measures designed so he'd get home safe and in one piece.

He'd never promised them he'd be back though. He'd never promised them he'd survive the mission. Their frightened faces were the ones seared into his mind as he glanced over at the Orlan helmet and refocused his attention as best he could on the task ahead.

Its gold reflective visor reflected his image as if he were looking into a funhouse mirror. The patch on the suit was triangular. It was the Expedition patch the Russians had designed. In its center was the ISS encircled by yellow sun rays. The names Voin, Greenwood, and Shepard were stitched across the top of the station. Expedition 58, written in English and in Russian, was embossed along the bottom of the patch in a semicircle.

"*Ek-spe-dit-see-ya*," Clayton said in his best central Russian dialect. "*Pee-aht-des-yat vosem*." He laughed at himself. "More like, *Ek-spe-dit-see-ya pos-led-niy*," he said, recalling one of the few Russian words in his vocabulary. *Posledniy*. In English it meant last.

Clayton chastised himself for not having studied enough Russian before his trip. Jackie had bought him Rosetta Stone as a Christmas gift a year earlier. He'd listened to the first couple of hours before procrastinating on the rest. Then time ran out and he was on his way to Moscow. He could read the language better than he could speak it, although that wasn't saying much. And really, the words he could read were bastardized English forced into Cyrillic lettering.

He was able to pick out some of the sounds because the letters were similar enough to the Greek alphabet. Still, all in all, he had the vocabulary of a two-year-old.

Fortunately for him, donning an Orlan MKS EVA suit was relatively self-explanatory in any language. The suit had a fully automated thermal control system and a built-in computer. Incredibly, the suit was undamaged by the magnetic blast.

The MKS was a brilliant piece of engineering. Its pressurization layer was much more durable than the American suits. It was a Belgian polyurethane that was so strong, it enabled the Russian designers to lose a backup layer, making the suit lighter and more flexible. It was also height adjustable. Most importantly for Clayton, a crew member could suit up without any help.

He slipped into his LCG, the periwinkle blue liquid cooling garment that was laced with tubing along his arms and thighs. With a pneumohydraulic control panel on the outside of the Orlan, he could adjust the level and temperature of water circulating through the LCG. It would help prevent him from freezing or overheating during the EVA.

Unlike the American extravehicular mobility unit, the EMU spacesuit, the Orlan was one size fits all. The EMU was built like clothing and was customized for each user. The Orlan had custom gloves. That was it.

Clayton looked at the timer; he had twenty minutes left before he could open the airlock to the outside. It might take him that long to finish outfitting himself.

To put on the suit, he opened a door on the back of it. With a little help from the microgravity environment in the airlock, he floated into the suit feet first and sat on the lower ledge of the doorframe. He slid his arms into the sleeves and then ducked into the suit, his head fitting into the affixed helmet.

He took a deep breath and reached down to his right side. He pulled a lever to close the back of the suit, and with his right hand reached across to his left side to connect a metal hook that sealed the door. The arms were too big, his fingers barely reaching into the cuffs at the end of the suit. At each bicep there was a crank lever he could spin to shorten or lengthen the arms. One turn at a time, he shrank the arms until his wrists were free of the suit and his fingers slid into the attached, custom gloves.

At his waist dangled a pair of tethers, one white and one orange. He'd use them to attach to handrails once he exited the airlock. They'd allow him to slide along the edge of the station with some modicum of safety should he lose his footing.

The specialists on the ground, who'd trained him in the use of the Orlan and the EMU, called the movements along the outside of the ISS "translating." He shook his head. NASA and its vocabulary.

Clayton held the orange tether in his hand and rubbed it with his gloved thumb. He chuckled thinking about it.

"Just call it floating," he mumbled. "*Translate*? Seriously?"

He looked down at his chest. On the right was the ECP, the electronic control panel that regulated the fans and pumps inside the suit. There was also a small computer there with a digital display for error messages.

At his ribcage, on the left side, was the pneumohydraulic control panel, which controlled the oxygen that kept him alive, and the lever that regulated the liquid inside the LCG.

The suit was lightweight. Clayton thought it less clunky than the EMU. The Russians were always a step or two ahead technologically. They weren't as afraid to take risks.

Maybe it was because they'd never had a *Challenger* or a *Columbia*. Maybe it was because they didn't lose *Apollo* astronauts to a devastating fire on the ground.

Whatever it was, the Russians were better at space. They were the cowboys Americans once were and that Clayton wished they still were.

It wasn't NASA's fault, Clayton reasoned. It was bureaucrats in Washington who turned over every four to eight years and couldn't think beyond their own reelections.

They hamstrung the ingenuity and genius of the people at NASA and her contractors. They bombed JSC and KSC with eggs and then forced the brilliant, hardworking dreamers who put men and women into space to walk on the broken shells for fear of losing everything related to exploration.

It was as simple as an iPod or a Nikon. NASA would take months or years to test the off-gassing of some new work-enhancing product they could employ in the Shuttle, when it existed, or on the ISS.

Russia would fill the *Progress* supply vehicle with the latest and greatest techno-toys and tell their people to have at it. They didn't worry about the minutia of if the big picture made sense.

The Orlan was the perfect example. The Russian brass listened to their people, the operators in space who knew what it was like to live in orbit, and they adjusted.

The Americans didn't. They tested and retested and retested on Earth. While the Russians were using the rear-door entry suits for decades, the Americans were still working on one for future missions to the moon and Mars.

The moon. A place they'd gone a half-century earlier and hadn't returned to.

Mars might as well be outside the Milky Way. If they couldn't cope with a burst of radiation in low Earth orbit, how would they function two hundred and twenty-five million kilometers away?

Clayton was venting as he tried to distract himself from the fear that washed over him when he stepped to the airlock. Fear didn't fit him. He wasn't sure what to do with it.

He unhooked the suit from an umbilical and flipped on the Orlan's internal battery before checking the computer at his chest and adjusting the flow of oxygen into the helmet. His body was warm, but he didn't adapt the temperature of the LCG. He knew once he stepped out into space, "translating" along the handrail outside the airlock, he'd get cold.

"This is what I call a major pucker factor," he said. "No doubt."

It was time.

Clayton's pulse quickened, thumping against his neck as he lowered the airlock pressure to near zero. He depressed the airlock, maneuvered the lever as he'd been taught in training, and exited the hatch.

He found himself on the verge of hyperventilating, like the first time he'd scuba dived in Pennekamp Coral Reef State Park in Key Largo. Gliding through the lock, he reminded himself to breathe in and out slowly and evenly. The breathing kept him calm and conserved air.

He floated from the lock to the station's exterior without taking in the remarkable view in front of him, then turned to close the hatch and affix his dual straps to the handrails along the outside of the Russian module.

Once connected, Clayton took one final deep breath and exhaled. His eyes widened and sweat bloomed on his brow. The seriousness of his task mixed with the excitement and anxiety of his first spacewalk created a tingling sensation that caught him off-guard.

All of the hours of training in the Neutral Buoyancy Laboratory in Houston hadn't fully prepared him for a real EVA. The NBL pool was two hundred feet long, one hundred feet wide, and forty feet deep. It held more than six million gallons of water designed to mimic weightlessness by providing the neutrality between floating and sinking in water. In the NBL Clayton had felt the weight of his suit, felt the drag as he moved. In space, he felt the weight of the mission.

It pressed on him like gravity.

Clayton shuddered, a tingle running along his spine. He'd taken the DRINK ME potion without realizing it, but he could taste it on his lips.

"What a curious feeling! I must be shutting up like a telescope." Louis Carroll's famous, prescient words from *Adventures in Wonderland* hung in his mind.

The vastness of space washed over him and he instantly felt infinitesimal. The station, the moon, and the Earth were tiny. Their place in the universe shrank as he scanned the overwhelming depth of blackness surrounding him. The sun was on the other side of the planet. It was darker than he'd imagined darkness could be.

He was at once hot and cold. In space there was no up or down. Everything was relative. He felt twisted inside. He looked down at his feet and saw the Earth below him. Or was it above him? Regardless, it hung there away from him, speeding and spinning through space. A true spaceship on an endless voyage.

Clayton looked away from Earth and outward toward the stars. They were brighter than he imagined, more crystalline even than they appeared from the Cupola, sparkling and strobing light years away. He thought about that light, the energy released from those stars. It was the same energy that tore away from the Sun and churned through the ISS and Earth.

He recalled Astronaut Rick Mastracchio's words. He finally understood them. Mastracchio, a veteran of three shuttle missions and one ISS expedition, once said, "Seeing Earth from inside the spacecraft is great, but it is nothing compared to seeing it through the large visor of the helmet. Imagine looking at the ocean from the deck of a boat versus jumping in the ocean and splashing around. Everyone wants to splash around, even in space."

Clayton was in the ocean, all right. He was in the deep end without a life vest.

He listened to the sound of his own breathing and refocused on the task at hand. He moved carefully along the rails and then gently pushed away from the relative security of the station's exterior hull. It didn't take much until he was floating free.

As he drifted from the ISS, he held on to the twin tethers at his waist, not ready to let go. They extended to their full length, stretching the fabric when Clayton's body jerked, his pelvis pulled forward as he swam helplessly back toward the station.

He quickly let go of the tethers and held his hands out, preparing for the impact against the Russian module. It was coming at him faster than he expected. He managed to raise his hands at the right moment and stop himself. He grabbed onto the railing with one hand and gripped his glove tight around the bar as his momentum carried him away from the station again. He strained and pulled in with his arm, steadying himself at the side of the station.

Clayton evened his breathing and found the dial on the left side of his chest. He spun it to lower the temperature of the cooling liquid. He blinked away the sweat in his eyes and licked it from his upper lip.

Enjoying the cool rush across his arms and legs, he regrouped. He had to get to his crewmates.

"Get it together, Shepard," he told himself. Then he whispered the secret astronaut prayer frequently muttered by the few men and women in the history of the planet who'd ventured beyond the bounds of Earth's atmosphere.

"Lord," he prayed, "please don't let me F this up."

Clayton looked down at his feet again and saw the familiar outline of the Baltic Sea. It was morning there.

The ISS was over Russia.

He spoke, activating the hot mic in his suit. "Korolyov, this is station on space-to-ground one. Comm check." He spoke so quickly his words slurred together.

He tried in butchered Russian. *"Korolyov, eto stant-siya- na zem-ly-u o-din,"* he said. *"Test sv-yazi."*

No response. Frustrated, he manually keyed the mic. Nothing.

He switched channels and tried again in both languages. Nothing. He reached out to Roscosmos Headquarters in Moscow, Russian Launch Control in Baikonur, and GCTC in Star City. Either nobody could hear him, or his radio wasn't transmitting. His breath and the pulse thumping blood through his head were the only sounds he could hear.

Clayton clenched his jaw. *"Der'mo,"* he muttered. It was one of three curse words Boris Voin had successfully taught him during their meals together on board the station. The ISS had hosted more than two hundred spacewalks in its twenty-year life. None of them, Clayton was sure, were like his.

He gripped both gloves around the railing on the edge of the Russian module and worked his way toward the port photovoltaic arrays. The station generated power with the help of eight solar arrays, four on either side. Together, they produced eighty-four kilowatts of power to what was effectively the size of a six-bedroom house. The arrays spanned wider than the wings of a Boeing 777. If laid side by side, they'd cover an acre of land.

Voin and Greenwood had quickly maneuvered their way, more skillfully than Clayton, to the port one truss segment. It was effectively the joint that connected the central components of the ISS with the interior port array.

In addition to the debris, or space dirt, they'd found underneath the cover of the malfunctioning joint, they'd discovered cell damage. They'd concluded that much in the first ninety minutes of the EVA. That damage had further reduced the array's output, compounding the potential danger. Once they'd cleaned the debris from under the joint cover, they were painstakingly trying to repair the damaged cells.

The irony wasn't lost on Clayton. The very power they harnessed to operate their modest orbiting outpost was the same that was killing it.

Greenwood's tethers were affixed to port trusses three and four. Voin was connected on the opposite side of the array at port truss five.

The station fit together like Legos from different kits. Over the course of nearly two decades, the station grew exponentially from the single forty-two-foot-long Russian Zarya control module launched in 1998.

That same year, the United States added another eighteen feet with Unity. Gradually, the ISS expanded piece by piece. The trusses held the variety of nodes and modules in place and were the mounts for unpressurized components. There were eleven of them and they were what engineers called the "bus structure" for the ISS. They were named for their planned positions on the station. Z for Zenith, P for port, S for starboard.

The S0 truss was none of the above. It was essentially at the effective center of the station. Officially designated the Center Integrated Truss Assembly Starboard 0 Truss, S0 was the backbone of the station. All of the external utilities for the habitable ISS modules and nodes ran through S0. Power, data, video, and ammonia for the automatic thermal control system connected from the S0 across the station. It also housed four GPS antennas. Running along its length was a track that provided a path for a robotic arm to move along the truss. That arm was also known as the Canadarm2.

Clayton floated smoothly across the forty-foot-long truss on the side opposite the arm. Methodically he crept along the rails, focusing on each movement. He felt the urgency boiling up within him the closer he got to the array and fought the urge to speed up. His attention was focused fully on the truss in front of him. He worked it as if he were walking the thin ledge of a skyscraper. He looked straight ahead at the truss. Not down. Not up. Not to either side.

As he inched closer to the port edge of the large gray structure, he swung around to look directly ahead at where he was going. His heart sank.

"I'm an idiot." The words bounced around inside his helmet. "A total freaking idiot." He clenched his jaw and bit the inside of his lip.

Straight ahead, blocking his movement to the arrays and his crewmates, was the P1 truss segment. He was on the wrong side of it, the side from which a long radiator extended, blocking his path. There was no way around it.

Not all astronauts were created equal. They came from different backgrounds and had different mentalities. Together they made complete mission teams. Separately they each had their strengths and weaknesses.

If instructed to flip a light switch, an astronaut who was militarily trained would do it without pause. A scientist serving as a payload or mission specialist would ask why. He or she would question the order, the reasoning behind it. They would ask not only about the switch but the need for light. What color light? Did the task even need light?

An engineer, though, would play with the switch, remove its housing, understand how it functioned, and then after making sure a switch was the best way to engage the mechanism and initiate said task, he or she would flip it. Or, alternatively, the engineer would replace it with a dial, a knob, or a lever.

At that moment, Clayton was glad he was an engineer. He was a problem solver who could think quickly and remove obstacles blocking the completion of any task.

That was why NASA had chosen him from among the thousands of astronaut applicants in his class. He saw a problem; he mentally and physically parsed it into its essential pieces; he fixed it.

Clayton stared at the radiator. It was a problem. He'd solve it.

First, though, he lowered the temperature of the liquid snaking through his suit. A chill spreading over him forced an involuntary shiver.

Clayton turned as would a man with a stiff neck to look back at where he'd already translated. It would take too long to move all the way back to where he started and then maneuver to the opposite side of the truss. His friends' lives might depend on his speed.

He spun back to the radiator and then faced the truss. He looked down.

"All right," he said. "That's the answer."

Clayton accessed the rough blueprint of the station's exterior in his mind. Why he had ignored it when first exiting the ISS was a question he couldn't answer. He hoped it hadn't ruined the mission.

He closed his eyes and mentally traversed the underside of the truss. He would clip and unclip the tethers as he moved, like a rock climber would edge up the sheer face of a peak. He'd then maneuver to the opposite side of the truss, beyond the Candaarm2 and at the beginning of the P1 truss. That would allow him to find the rails on that side of the ISS and move outward toward the array, Voin, and Greenwood.

"You can do this," he assured himself. He took a deep breath and unhooked the first tether.

From a distance, the S0 truss looked vaguely like the underside of an Imperial Class Star Destroyer. Up close it was a series of beams and connectors that provided plenty of spots to attach the tethers.

Clayton worked along the truss with ease. Like a child on monkey bars, he unhooked one tether, pulled himself in the right direction, hooked the tether, and unhooked the other before repeating the process.

A confident smile spread across his face as he moved. He felt it in his cheeks as the plan he envisioned propelled him to the underside of the truss.

Once underneath the large structure, he pulled his legs even with his torso. Lying on his back, parallel to the underside of the truss, he slowed his momentum. Unhook. Pull. Hook. Unhook. Pull. Hook. Unhook.

He neared the edge of the underside and stopped, using his arms and hips to lower his legs beneath him. He was close to the Canadarm2 and was on the correct side of it. He unhooked the longer tether and hung there for a moment before turning back to look at how far he'd moved. As he did, he lost his grip. Worse, he'd gotten out of his rhythm when he stopped and didn't retether the smaller cord.

Clayton was suddenly floating free.

It happened slowly and yet impossibly fast. It didn't take much of a movement to create tremendous momentum given his mass.

He reached with both arms, stretching as far as he could. He grabbed nothing. In space it was more difficult to judge distance. The relativity of things was off. How could it not be when he floated above a planet with a four-thousand-mile radius?

To make his predicament more dire, he was in an Orlan and not an EMU.

Despite all of the advantages of the Orlan suit Clayton wore, there was one major disadvantage. It was not equipped with SAFER.

SAFER—Simplified Aid For EVA Rescue—was an emergency jet-propulsion pack on the back of NASA's EMU. It was specifically designed for a moment like this.

In an emergency, astronauts who became untethered from the ISS could use the system to guide themselves to safety. It was a smaller version of the MMU used regularly on EVAs. He was wearing an emergency Orlan. This eagle, the English translation of the Russian suit's namesake, had no wings. Clayton floated free of the structure. He was moving, untethered, away from S0 truss.

The suit suddenly felt hot. He reached out with both hands, sweat dripping into his eyes. He flailed as the vacuum of low Earth orbit carried him away in its unending current. He twisted, trying to turn around and grab something. Anything.

Flashes of his family flickered in his mind; Jackie's trembling hand as he slipped the ring onto her finger, the bright blue of Marie's eyes staring into his the first time he held her in the minutes after she was born, Chris splashing in the water at Dinosaur Valley State Park, convinced he could attract a *T. rex* if he made enough noise. The bright flashes turned dark.

He saw his father's cancer-ravaged body holding his mother's hand as they walked along the Seawall in Galveston. His steps were fragile as he looked out at the waves crashing against the jetties. Her weight held up his; her balance was his.

He saw his twin's open casket and the white makeup that caked her young face. The injuries that killed her were hidden beneath the new satin dress their mother had purchased for a middle school dance. She'd been the smart one. She'd been the achiever. She'd been the one not wearing a seatbelt even though he'd reminded her when they'd climbed into the backseat of their family sedan.

There was Jackie again, closed off and distant. He'd chosen his own needs and wants over that of the family. He was a selfish prick, she'd told him more than once. He'd gone for the glory and the fame and the adulation instead of what really mattered. He'd placed love of self above love of family. Jackie had warned him the children were drifting from him. Now he was the one drifting.

Clayton's stomach lurched. His pulse pounded against his temples and neck. He fought against the panic spreading through his core like a virus.

"Think," he said aloud in his helmet. "Damn it. Think, Shepard. Do something."

It was too late. He was free of the truss. He was floating away from it. There was no jetpack to help him. There was nobody to save him. Clayton Shepard was drifting to a certain silent death.

He didn't feel it through the panic coursing through him like a numbing agent. But when the Canadarm2 elbow hit the back of his own, he instinctively reached behind his back and grabbed.

His gloved hand slid along the robotic arm for several feet, his fingers unable to grasp anything. Clayton tried spinning to face the arm but couldn't. He blindly grabbed and prodded at the arm, watching the truss and the body of the ISS drift farther away. He was easily thirty or forty feet from the structure. Momentum shifted his body as he floated, the action of his hand grappling at the arm rotating him enough that as he inched toward the end of the arm he caught one of three wrist joints with a clawed glove.

He grabbed it, hanging on against the invisible force tugging at him, urging him deeper into space. Clayton's muscles tensed and he gnashed his teeth.

His fingers slipped but held on as the momentum slowed and dissipated. His feet floated back toward the ISS. He was upright, or what felt like it, and he pulled himself toward the arm. With his right hand he found one of the tethers and connected it to the other. He took the elongated tether and looped it around the arm like a lumberjack might attach himself to a tree. He latched the large loop at his waist and exhaled deeply.

He turned to face away from the ISS. He was at the very end of the fifty-seven-foot-long arm. Had he missed the wrist joint…

No. He didn't want to think about it.

He pushed himself back to face the ISS. From the end of the Canadarm2, he could see much of the station. He scanned the structure, and to the right of it, for the first time since exiting the airlock, he saw his crewmates.

Both of them floated lifelessly near the interior port array. Their long tethers snaked from their waists to the trusses. Both men looked like they were awaiting hugs with their arms floating wide.

Clayton hoped they were unconscious and not dead. Regardless, it didn't change his mission. He shifted back to put the arm at his left hip. The arm was bent at a slight angle, but it was close enough to straight that Clayton could navigate a clean shot back to the ISS structure.

The SSRMS arm—the Space Station Remote Manipulator System—was based on the much smaller version housed inside the now decommissioned Space Shuttle. Unlike that shuttle version, the one permanently affixed to the station wasn't limited by its length. The tracks along the trusses allowed the arm to move and reach virtually every part of the station. Clayton admired its engineering, its simple complexity. The Canadarm2 had much of the flexibility of a human arm. It had seven degrees of freedom. There were three shoulder joints, one at the elbow, and three more at the wrist. One of the joints stayed locked. The other six of them could rotate an astonishing five hundred and forty degrees, which was greater flexibility than the most advanced yogi.

Clayton slid the tether and carefully moved along the SSRMS, using one hand to gently propel himself toward his goal. More cautious than he was before his near-death experience, he deliberately navigated the fifty-seven feet back to the main structure with his gloved hands. When he reached the elbow, he noticed two of the arm's four cameras. He looked into the one closest to him and started talking to it.

"I've never thought much of Canada," he said. "It's not that I have anything against Canadians. I've known a few. Nice people, grounded, good hearts. I've just never thought about their country."

He glided past the camera but kept talking to himself as he worked. "When I do think of Canada, I think of Dudley Do-Right from the old *Rocky and Bullwinkle* cartoons. I think of John Candy. Ryan Reynolds."

He moved robotically, an inch at a time, and kept his mind focused on the absurd. "Candy was hilarious. Everything he touched was gold. And Reynolds. I didn't really like *Green Lantern*, but the dude killed it in *Deadpool*."

"Aside from that," he said, his voice hollow in his helmet, "there's syrup and Canadian bacon, which is, like, ham. There's ice hockey. The oil sands. Not much else. Canada is the kid from high school you forget about until you crack open your yearbook years later, right?"

Clayton was three-quarters of the way back to the station. He moved with an unconsciously confident rhythm.

"That has all changed now," he said. "For the rest of my life I am praising Canada first thing in the morning and the last thing at night. I am rooting for the Canucks or Canadiens. Hell, I'll even pull for the Raptors as long as they're not playing the Rockets. I'll fill my iPad with movies only starring Canadians. I'll stop ordering the Sausage McMuffin and stick with the original, the one with the Canadian bacon. I'll even listen to Nickelback."

He chuckled as he reached the base of the arm, which was connected to the Mobile Servicing System. The MSS was the mechanism that rolled back and forth along the tracks. He unhooked the elongated safety tethers and drew the loop around the SSRMS. He disconnected them and hooked one tether to the MSS, then pushed himself back to the S0 truss and grabbed with both hands.

"Yeah," he said. "On second thought, no Nickelback. I won't go that far."

Clayton turned to face the port side of the ISS. He'd wasted a lot of time with his miscalculations. He checked the display on the computer at his chest. There were no error messages, but he knew the Orlan could only process his breathable air for seven hours. The mechanism that removed, or scrubbed, carbon dioxide from his air would slowly fill, and he'd suffocate.

"All right," he said. "Shallow breaths. In and out. No more mistakes."

Clayton translated along the truss toward the array, drawing closer to his crewmates. Both were friends. Both were good men. Both had families awaiting them back home.

He used his tether method to move outward along the side of the ISS, making compact movements rather than larger, risky ones. The farther out he moved, the farther away he was from the life-saving Canadarm2.

His thoughts shifted from Boris's and Ben's families to his own. He knew from the missing yellow spider webs of light that North America was without power. The density of those lights represented large cities, big populations. He loved looking at them from the Cupola. He and the others would try to identify the cities by those lights. It was an impossible task now.

The dark Earth was as frightening to Clayton as what he was facing, translating the edge of the ISS without communication or backup. He knew Jackie was strong. She'd always been the foundation of their family. She was smarter, funnier, and a better parent than him. He loved that about her. He loved her toughness, her grit, her blunt no-holds-barred approach to life.

While she'd not liked the idea of his applying to the astronaut corps, once he was a part of it she'd pushed him to play the political game it took to get a good mission.

"If this is what you want, then you need to sing your praises," she'd repeatedly told him. "Nobody else will."

However, strength and chutzpah were one thing. Surviving the apocalypse was something else altogether. Clayton clipped a hook and looked down at the planet below. For the first time he noticed the red aurora dancing in the atmosphere. How had he not seen it before?

Tunnel vision was both a blessing and a curse, as Jackie often reminded him.

He tried to recall everything he'd learned about the sun during his college astronomy and physics classes. It wasn't much, at least not as far as what the experts at NASA knew.

Then again, they'd known so much they'd discounted the abnormal readings as an anomaly, as faulty data. What he knew could fit into a thimble by comparison. That was a good thing. Clayton picked his mind, the obvious facts surfacing first.

The sun was at the center of the solar system. It was the largest object and contained more than ninety-nine percent of the solar system's mass. A million Earths could fit inside the sun. The outer part of the star reached temperatures of ten thousand degrees Fahrenheit. The core could be as hot as twenty-seven million degrees. Clayton couldn't fathom either number.

He recalled the nuclear energy the sun generated was like a hundred billion tons of dynamite. It was a young star, one of one hundred billion or so in the galaxy.

It was positioned perfectly for life on Earth, or vice versa. Clayton's home planet traveled in what scientists called the Goldilocks Zone, a small area at just the right distance from the star to enable liquid water. Water was the foundation of all life.

Without the sun, the Earth would be a lifeless, frozen orb. With it, life teemed. But the sun was also close enough to cause problems.

Coronal mass ejections were among those issues. Balloon-shaped bursts of solar wind that expanded out from the sun's corona. The plasma trapped inside was heated, broke free of the sun, and could travel mind-numbingly fast. Most of them didn't affect Earth. Sometimes they did.

As man became increasingly reliant on technology, the damage from a CME aimed at Earth became increasingly acute. Nothing had ever approached what hit them hours earlier. This was an end-of-days type magnetic storm; the kind of event Clayton feared could knock mankind back into the Dark Ages.

From satellites traveling in orbit to energy pipelines, power grids and anything plugged into them, the CME could force a surge of magnetic energy into those systems and kill them.

Cars, phones, computers, GPS systems, gasoline pumps, even water filtration and treatment were at risk. Clayton shuddered, thinking about how bad it could be at home.

Worst of all, he couldn't communicate with Jackie. He couldn't tell her he was okay, that he was working on a plan to get back home. He hated worrying her. Then again, as he drew within a few feet of the first crewmate, he thought it better she didn't know he was risking his life to save two men who might already be dead.

He hooked the orange tether as far to the right as he could reach. He unhooked the white tether and floated free of the structure, pushing himself to Boris Voin.

Voin's name was on his helmet and on his suit. He floated at the end of his tether like a helium balloon leaking air.

Clayton eyed the name patch and sighed. It was nothing against Voin. Boris was a fine man who'd become a good friend. But Ben Greenwood was a mentor and a hero of sorts for Clayton. He'd hoped to reach Ben first.

A wave of guilt washed over him. "You shouldn't think that way," he mumbled.

He drifted to him and reached out to grab Voin's tether, slowing his speed. He reached the cosmonaut and tackled him in what felt like slow motion. Immediately, he knew Boris was dead.

The systems on his chest were flashing with errors. The flashes were weak and intermittent, not as they should be. The EMU was a death suit.

He inched his hands up Voin's suit and placed his gloves on either side of his friend's helmet. Voin's sun visor reflected Clayton's own warped image with a fish-eye effect until he pulled a lever on the helmet's left side, which lifted the visor like an eyelid.

Clayton flinched at the face staring back at him. He gasped and momentarily lost his grip. Boris's eyes were open, the fear frozen in his tiny pupils. He was slack jawed, his tongue hanging over his lower lip. He looked as if something had scared the life out of him.

Regaining his composure, Clayton said a silent prayer on behalf of his Russian crewmate, apologized for having wished he were Ben, and raised the reflective visor to hide Boris's death stare. He reached down to Boris's waist and found the connector for his tether, took his own free tether, and connected it to Boris.

Clayton then used Boris's tether to pull himself backward to the ISS structure. Once there, he disconnected Boris, hooked it to himself, and disconnected the one he'd originally attached at Boris's waist.

"There's gotta be a better way to do this," he muttered.

His stomach ached, his chest felt tight, and a wave of nausea washed over him. It was the kind of feeling he'd not experienced since pulling all-nighters during his final months of graduate school at the University of Florida. It was the overwhelming exhaustion that accompanied stress, a lack of sleep, and the knowledge there was so much left to do.

The display at his chest told him he was running short on time. He'd need to speed up the process. With Boris floating behind him, Clayton maneuvered his way to Ben Greenwood. Hand over hand he traversed the underside of the array structure until he'd reached the astronaut. Before he reached for Greenwood, he turned around and used one hand to grab the tether connecting Boris to his waist. The cosmonaut's momentum carried him forward after Clayton had stopped. Clayton worked the tether like a whip and tried to guide Boris's body around his own to avoid a direct hit. It didn't work. Boris's body moved closer and closer. Clayton tried to shift himself away from the impact, but he miscalculated Boris's speed and distance.

Boris's body tackled him, knocking him from his position underneath the array. Both men floated past Greenwood until Clayton's tether snapped taut and reversed his direction. He had only seconds to grab onto something to hold himself in place; otherwise, Boris's tether would pull tight and yank him backward again. He was low on air. He couldn't continue the zero-gravity seesaw he'd created.

He felt the frustration of a golfer who kept missing a short putt from one side of the hole to the other. He clenched his jaw. He was nearing the end of the breathable oxygen. He knew the CO_2 scrubber had to be getting full.

Clayton drifted to the edge of the truss and extended his fingers as far as they would stretch. With the tips of the gloves he managed to cling to one of the triangular pieces that, together, formed the structure. No sooner had his fingertips curled around the piece than he felt the strong tug of Boris's body. Thankfully the pull was a few degrees to the side of his free hand. That enabled him to bring that hand closer to the truss and grab it.

He held his position for a moment and then used one of his hands to shorten the length of Boris's tether. He wrapped it around his elbow, drawing in the increasing slack. It was the only way he knew to stop the endless swing.

To his right, Ben Greenwood pirouetted slowly, like a music box ballerina in need of a key wind. With most of the tether now wrapped around one arm, Clayton pulled himself free of the truss and aimed for the spot where Ben's tether connected with the ISS.

"Should have done this with Boris," he said. It would lessen the momentum shifts if he drew Ben to himself and rolled up the tether slack as he floated to him.

Clayton was learning as he went. He was a quick study. Always had been. Space, though, was unrelenting. Even without gravity, the curve was steep and arduous. Mistakes, as he'd learned already, were unforgiving in a vacuum.

He looked at his chest. Time was short. He resisted the urge to suck in a deep breath of exasperation and focused on reaching the hooked tether in his sights.

If only I could cut a hole in my glove like Matt Damon, he thought. *Then I'd be able to speed this up.*

Clayton wondered for a moment if Damon was Canadian. No, he remembered. He was from New England. Coping with the stress, his mind played a game of free association as he inched closer to the hook.

Damon. The Departure. Boston. Harvard. JFK. The speech at Rice that sparked the race to the moon.

That speech was burned into Clayton's mind. He'd memorized it as a kid for a school project. It was always on the tip of his tongue.

There is no strife, no prejudice, no national conflict in outer space as yet. Its hazards are hostile to us all. Its conquest deserves the best of all mankind, and its opportunity for peaceful cooperation may never come again.

But why, some say, the moon? Why choose this as our goal? And they may well ask why climb the highest mountain? Why, thirty-five years ago, fly the Atlantic? Why does Rice play Texas?

We choose to go to the moon. We choose to go to the moon in this decade and do the other things, not because they are easy, but because they are hard, because that goal will serve to organize and measure the best of our energies and skills, because that challenge is one that we are willing to accept, one we are unwilling to postpone, and one which we intend to win, and the others, too…

Many years ago the great British explorer George Mallory, who was to die on Mount Everest, was asked why did he want to climb it. He said, "Because it is there."

Well, space is there, and we're going to climb it, and the moon and the planets are there, and new hopes for knowledge and peace are there. And, therefore, as we set sail we ask God's blessing on the most hazardous and dangerous and greatest adventure on which man has ever embarked.

Hazardous. Dangerous. Adventure.

That speech had never meant more, its words never clearer in their meanings, than they were as Clayton reached the clip connected to the first American astronaut to die in space.

Ben Greenwood had suffocated in his suit. Clayton suspected as much when he'd seen the pain painted onto Boris's face. He confirmed it when he reeled in his friend and turned the lever on the visor. He flipped the lever back immediately. He couldn't bear to look at Ben. Not like that.

Clayton clipped Ben's tether to Boris's waist and prepped himself to lead a convoy back to the Russian airlock. The first error message appeared on his chest.

The trip back to the airlock was faster than the journey away from it. Well, at first it was faster. The closer he got to the airlock, the less room he had to maneuver, the more he worried about the remaining oxygen in his suit, and the slower he moved.

Counterintuitively he became more deliberate and less sure of himself as he reached the lock. He slowed significantly when he reached the Russian module, fearful of the momentum gathered by the two men trailing him.

A second error message flashed on his chest when he opened the hatch and climbed inside. Once in the airlock, with the hatch still open, he loosened Boris's tether to allow for as much slack as it could take. Then he started gathering it, hand over hand, pulling the men closer to the hatch.

It was a fisherman's job, and Clayton's back and neck and legs strained as he worked to brace himself inside the hatch while reeling in Boris and Ben.

It worked. Clayton closed the hatch and began the depressurizing process with just enough breathable air remaining. He would be okay. The two crewmates floating in the hatch next to him would not be.

Clayton floated silently in the cramped airlock, unable to free himself completely of the heavy bodies of his friends. He closed his eyes and ran through a checklist of what needed to happen next.

He had a lot to do and not a lot of time to do it.

CHAPTER 5

FRIDAY, JANUARY 24, 2020, 11:38 PM CST
CLEAR LAKE, TEXAS

Marie and Jackie stood holding hands, watching the flames burn the remnants of Reggie and Lana's house.

"When do you think the fire department will get here?" Marie asked.

Jackie shook her head. "I don't think they're coming," she said softly. "There's no power, there are no working phones, our cars won't start. There's no way the fire department knows there's a fire here. And if they did, I don't know how they'd get here."

"It was like that plane just fell out of the sky, Mom. I mean, it was silent, like its engines just died."

"Yeah, it did seem that way." She let go of Marie's hand and draped her arm over her daughter's shoulder. She pulled her closer and scanned the smoldering houses across the street that had long run out of sufficient kindling. The outlines of the char were backlit with the orange glow of the fires still burning one street over.

"Whole families are gone," Marie said quietly. "Parents, little kids…and that's not counting the people on the plane." She shuddered and hugged her mother tightly, pressed her face into her mother's neck and softly sobbed.

"I babysat for the Wickards," she said between heaving cries. "The babies, Mom. The babies."

Jackie stroked her daughter's head. "I know," she whispered. "I know."

Jackie felt a hand on her back, and Reggie spoke. "You two okay?"

Jackie nodded.

"When you get a minute," he said, "you might want to come inside. We're taking inventory of everything we've got. Lana's been in your garage, checking what you've got. I hope that's okay."

"It's fine," she said. "How are Betty and Brian?"

"In shock, I think."

"And Candace? Is she okay?"

"I don't think she's processing what's happened," said Reggie. "She knows her boyfriend is dead, but the scope of this event isn't registering."

Jackie laughed nervously. "Is it with any of us?"

"I'll see you inside," said Reggie. "Take your time."

Jackie took a deep breath of the sharply scented air. She'd been standing in and around the smoke for so long, she'd almost become immune to it.

Marie pulled away and wiped the corners of her eyes with the backs of her fingers. She looked up at her mom. "What about Dad? And Chris?"

Jackie bit the inside of her lip, suppressing the bruising knot in her throat. She swallowed against it and forced as reassuring a look as she could muster. She held her frightened daughter's stare.

"You know your father," Jackie said evenly. "Above all else, he is a survivor. For all we know, he's in better shape than we are. Whatever happened may not be happening in orbit."

Marie nodded and blinked back tears.

"As for your brother," she said with a chuckle, "that little boy isn't so little anymore. He's with Kenny's dad. They're camping in the middle of nowhere. Chances are they don't even know what's happened. His face is probably sticky with marshmallow and chocolate residue."

Marie laughed. "Gross."

"It is, right?"

"Why is he so gross?"

"All boys are," said Jackie, content to shift the conversation. "Your father was as disgusting as they come when I got ahold of him."

"Really?"

"I've told you this, haven't I? About his socks?"

"No."

Jackie looked skyward, wishing she could see the ISS silently arcing across the sky. Instead there was blackness from the tendrils of smoke spiraling upward from the half dozen burning homes across from their driveway. Snapshots of the Wickards' children toddling in the yard popped into her mind.

Babies. Just babies.

They quickly dissolved to a different image of a baby she didn't know. An infant she'd thought was a large doll. She tasted the remnant bile in her mouth.

"Mom?"

"Sorry." Jackie swallowed hard and refocused on the distraction. "Your father would wear his socks until they were ink black on the bottoms. I mean black. Like 'absence of color and light' black."

It was such an oddly timed discussion, so out of place and yet so needed. Jackie sensed Marie needed a distraction.

Marie sniffled. "I get it. Black."

"He would flip them inside out," Jackie continued. "He would, I don't know, wear them until they could stand on their own."

"That would gross me out."

"Oh" — Jackie's eyes widened — "it grossed me out. You know me. I'm a bit of a clean freak."

"A bit."

Jackie laughed. "It was almost over between us before it began. I mean, who does that?"

"What did you do?"

"I bought him new socks. A lot of new socks. Maybe twenty pairs. I also threw out the old ones."

Marie looked over her mother's shoulder beyond the roofline of their house at the aurora still dancing in the sky. "I bet his socks up there are disgusting."

Jackie turned and put her hand on her daughter's neck, massaging it gently, then stroking Marie's ponytail. "You know they are. They only have so many pairs up there. He probably feels right at home."

The two giggled until the laughter dissolved into the reality of the moment. Jackie sighed. Her eyes drifted from the sky to the front of their home. Through the large paneled windows, she could see the flicker of candles illuminating the large family room that ran the length of the first floor. Some of the windows were cracked, spidery veins distorting the candlelight. The concussion of the plane's impact must have done that.

Jackie's faint smile evaporated. "We have work to do. We should get inside."

SATURDAY, JANUARY 25, 2020, 1:40 AM CST
CLEAR LAKE, TEXAS

Jackie Shepard sat in a leather easy chair adjacent to the fireplace, holding court in her family room. Marie sat cross-legged at her feet on the ottoman.

Across from her on the long matching sofa were Reggie, Lana, and Betty. Betty's son, Brian, was sitting by himself in a parson's chair on the other side of the fireplace.

"We know the Wickards are dead," Jackie said. "All four of them. There's no way they survived the impact or the fire. And Marie knows they were home."

"The Robinson family," said Reggie. "They were home too. No way they're still with us."

Candace was sitting apart from the group. She was at the kitchen island, sitting on a barstool. "My whole street is dead."

Betty's shoulders slumped and her body shuddered. She pulled her hands to her face and choked back tears. Lana reached out and put an arm around her, patting her shoulder.

"It's okay," Lana said. "Let it out."

Betty dropped her hands into her lap, tears glistening in the flickering candlelight that colored her face.

"I can't," she said, inhaling deeply through her nostrils. "It's not right for me to feel sorry for myself, Lana. She lost her boyfriend. You lost your home too." She leaned into her neighbor and reciprocated Lana's kindness with a hug.

Jackie didn't say anything. The women needed their moment. Jackie, though, didn't want to spend time on what had happened. She couldn't do anything about that. If she paused to think about her husband and her son, she'd cease to be of any use to anyone. Like Reggie, she wanted to press forward.

After a minute, she exhaled. "Okay," she said, smiling faintly against Lana's and Betty's focused glares. "Let's talk about what we do now. It's critical we focus on what comes next. It will keep us sane amidst this insanity. Reggie, I know you've taken inventory."

Reggie cleared his throat and looked down at a pad of paper on which he'd made a list. It was obvious he was avoiding eye contact with his wife.

"I've already taken the ice we salvaged from our freezer and yours," he said. "I nearly filled the Yeti cooler you have in your garage and then I put some of the frozen foods in it. That'll give them a little longer life."

"Good," said Jackie. "What else?"

"I've filled all of the tubs with cold water," Reggie said. "We don't know how the power outage will affect the water treatment plants. Better to use what we've got now. The tubs are a last resort but are better than nothing."

"Okay," said Jackie. "We can all use the shower in my bathroom until the hot water runs out. We have two large hot water heaters in the attic. It'll last a few days."

"We've got a good supply of nonperishables," he said. "We also have bread, milk, eggs, some ground beef, and some frozen steaks. We'll probably want to eat that stuff first."

Betty's wide eyes darted between Reggie and Jackie. "Wait," she said, waving her hands in front of her face. "How long are we planning on being without power? I need to call my insurance company. I have to talk to the adjuster."

"We don't know," Jackie said in a calm, even voice. "It could be a couple of days. It could be a lot longer. Maybe weeks. That's why—"

Betty stood up from the sofa. "No." She shook her finger. "That's not possible. We can't be without power for weeks. We need clothing. We need to start rebuilding. We—"

Lana gently took Betty's hand in hers. She led Betty's eyes to the parson's chair across from her where Brian was rocking in the chair. His arms were folded tight across his chest, his fists hidden in the pits of his arms. He was mumbling and rocking back and forth.

Betty sat down. "Brian, it's okay. I'm sorry for raising my voice."

Brian looked up from the floor. "The dark isn't good. It's not good. Not good."

Betty stood and glided to her son, kneeling in front of him. "It's okay," she repeated softly. "It will be sunny and bright again in a couple of hours."

Marie looked up at her mother with worry and mouthed, "Mom?" Her young face was aged with wrinkles across her forehead, frown lines leaving deep crevices along her cheeks.

Jackie didn't remember seeing them before. She leaned into Marie and whispered, "I know. It's tough. We'll get through this together."

Reggie stood from the sofa and held up the notepad. "We should do this in the morning once the sun comes up. Brian is probably right. The dark isn't good."

"The dark isn't good," Brian echoed.

Jackie didn't want to go to sleep. She wanted to formulate a plan.

Reggie implored her for support with arched brows. "What do you say, Jackie? We could all use a couple of hours of rest. If this does last—"

Jackie held up a hand. "You're right, Reggie. We're all struggling with a mix of shock and exhaustion. We can talk over breakfast in the morning."

"Where did you want us?"

"Marie will sleep with me," she said. "That will free up her room. We also have a guest room. Take your pick."

The group stood and said their goodnights to each other. Betty led Brian up the stairs and stopped at the landing. "Thank you, Jackie," she said. "I mean that."

Jackie smiled. "I know," she said and then blew out the candles before heading to her room.

Marie was already in bed, lying atop the covers, curled on her side, her hands between her knees. Her face was half buried in a down pillow, the glow of the lone candle in the room illuminating her sad features.

Jackie closed the bedroom door behind her and sat on her side of the bed. "The whole house smells like smoke," she said. "My clothes, my hair, everything. I'd change before bed, but I don't think it would do any good. These sheets will need changing anyhow."

She swung her legs up onto the covers, not bothering to tuck herself underneath them. She felt confined enough given the bizarre turn of events. Jackie propped up two pillows against the cherrywood headboard and leaned back, resting her head for the first time in what felt like days.

Marie reached out and touched her mother's leg. "This is going to get worse before it gets better, isn't it?" she asked in a tone that told Jackie it was more rhetorical than not.

"The smell?"

Marie huffed. "No, Mom, the—"

"I know what you meant," Jackie said, reaching out to caress her daughter's arm.

They were in a house with five neighbors, one of whom had special needs, and one woman they'd never met. They had finite supplies. There were dead, burned families buried in the charred hulks of homes across yards from their home. Chris was incommunicado in North Texas. Clayton was in orbit, hundreds of miles above Earth.

She picked up the candle on the bedside table to her right, pulled it close, and blew out the flame. Its pomegranate scent wafted across her face as the room went nearly dark, taking on the faint red hue of the aurora sneaking through the gaps in the shutters.

CHAPTER 6

SATURDAY, JANUARY 25, 2020, 7:13 AM CST
DINOSAUR VALLEY STATE PARK, TEXAS

Rick Walsh awoke to the sound of two boys laughing. His eyes popped open and he immediately felt the sharp stiffness in his back that came with a night on the ground in a tent. He winced as he sat up and then twisted at his waist to loosen the tight muscles. He dragged his phone into his palm and pressed the home button, having forgotten the device was dead.

He cursed the technology and tossed it into the corner before leaning forward to unzip the tent flap. Crawling from the tent, he pushed himself to his bare feet and stood up. His lower back protested, as did his neck, but he ignored it and walked over to Kenny and Chris. They were playing cards at a picnic table.

"Hey, boys," he said. "You might want to keep it down a bit. It's still early and people are sleeping."

Kenny slapped a card on the table without looking up at his dad. "Nobody's asleep, Dad," he said. "Everybody's up. They're all talking about the apocalypse."

Rick stepped to the table and leaned in. "The what?"

Kenny slapped another card. "The a-poc-a-lypse, he said. "You know, the end of the world."

Rick shook his head in disbelief. "I know what the apocalypse is, Kenny. Where did you hear people talking about it?" He looked over his shoulder, scanning the looped road that connected the campsites. "What people?"

"People at the bathrooms," Chris said. "They were saying all of the electricity is out, their phones don't work, their cars won't start."

Rick was dumfounded. "Why didn't you wake me up?" he asked with incredulity.

Kenny shrugged. He held a card above the table and looked at Rick. "We're camping," he said as if it were the most obvious answer in the history of questions. "What do we care if nothing works? It's cool."

Rick tilted his head. He was raising an idiot. Better yet, his ex was raising an idiot. He was only responsible for the stupidity every other weekend and on select holidays.

"It's *not* cool," Rick replied.

"War," said Kenny.

"We don't know that," said Rick. "It could be —"

"No, Mr. Walsh." Chris laughed. "We're playing war. The card game?"

Kenny chuckled. "Sheesh, Dad. You're so uptight."

"Why so serious?" Chris laughed, aping Heath Ledger's Joker, much to Kenny's amusement.

Rick planted his hands on the table, ready to let the boys know just how serious a situation this might be, then thought better of it and bit off his retort.

If the boys were oblivious, so be it. That wasn't a bad thing. The longer they could go without comprehending the potential severity of whatever it was that had happened the night before, the easier it would be for him to cope with it.

"You're right," he said. "It's cool. You guys want breakfast? I can do eggs and bacon or oatmeal."

Kenny wrinkled his nose as if he'd smelled something rotten. "Not oatmeal, please."

"Anything's fine," said Chris.

"Bacon and eggs it is."

Rick walked over to his Jeep and opened the rear tailgate. Inside was a large Igloo cooler filled with ice. He unclipped the lid and cracked open the cooler. Fishing through melting ice, pushing aside bottles of Gatorade and cans of Shiner, he reached a carton of egg whites and a package of precooked bacon.

He spun to walk back to the charcoal grill when he caught the glimpse of someone in his peripheral vision and almost dropped his breakfast.

It was Mumphrey. "Sorry to frighten you," he said. "Got a bad habit of it, I guess."

Rick exhaled a shaky breath. "No problem. What's up?" He walked over to the grill, aware Mumphrey was following him.

The man greeted the boys and then stuffed his hands into his pockets to pull up his pants. "I need your help." Mumphrey peered over the top of his glasses expectantly.

"No luck with the camper?"

"No," Mumphrey replied. "It ain't that though. Like I said before, there's that woman. You know, the athlete? She's got that sticker on her car. Got numbers on it that says she runs forever."

Rick placed the egg whites and bacon package on a camping stool. "Right," he said, picking up a bag of charcoal and unloading a pile of it into the grill. "I remember."

"So" — Mumphrey scratched his elbow through his long-sleeved shirt — "she needs that jump I mentioned to you. You said you've got some cables."

Rick was piling the briquettes into a pyramid. "Sure," he said. "Let me get the charcoal going and I'll be right over."

"That's mighty kind of you. I'd help her by myself, but I ain't got my cables. Guess I left 'em at the shop or something. So you helping out is good. Mighty kind."

Rick doused the pyramid with lighter fluid and then lit it with a match. "That'll do it, don't you think?" he asked rhetorically.

Mumphrey nodded. "Oh sure. I like the charcoal myself. I like to sprinkle some mesquite chips in there too. Gives everything a mighty nice smoky flavor. I also like smokers. I got one back at home. It's a nice one. I could do up a fine turkey in it."

Rick smiled. "I'll bet," he said and patted Mumphrey on the shoulder. "Let's go help that lady."

He reached back into his Jeep and pulled out a set of jumper cables. He told the boys he'd be a couple of sites over and to yell if they needed anything. They were oblivious and totally preoccupied with their card game.

Rick followed Mumphrey along the circular drive, passing the much-discussed pop-up camper. Mumphrey pulled his shoulders back and puffed his chest as he pointed to it. Rick acknowledged how nice it looked.

They passed another thicket of tall oaks and pines before the next cleared site came into view. Leaning against the back of a Honda Accord was a young woman with short dark hair and bright green eyes.

She was wearing a tank top and running shorts. Her toned arms were folded across her chest, her legs crossed at the ankles. Her full lips were pouting. She was a living, breathing example of Rick's weakness. He caught himself staring a little too long at her when her eyes met his, and he quickly looked away.

Rick cleared his throat. "Car won't start?"

The woman shook her head. "Nope. Doesn't even turn over."

Rick stepped to the woman, drawn into her eyes. "My name's Rick," he said, offering his hand. "And you are?"

"Stranded," she said with a smile and took his hand. "Mr. Mumphrey here was kind enough to offer your help."

Rick chuckled. "Okay, Mrs. Stranded. Let's see if we can get you started."

"It's miss," she said. "And you forgot something."

"What is that, *Miss* Stranded?"

"Your car," she said. "It would be kinda hard to start mine without yours."

Rick felt the warmth grow in his cheeks. He looked at his feet and nodded. "Yeah." He sighed. "You have a point. I'll be right back."

Rick handed the cables to Mumphrey. "Go ahead and get these hooked up, please."

Rick started jogging back to his site with an insecure confidence, making certain his shoulders were pulled back as he pounded the dirt away from the woman. He tried to ignore her disinterested vibe.

She was his type. Young. Pretty. Athletic. She was a triathlete too. He'd noticed the 140.6 sticker on the rear window of the Honda and the expensive Thule bike rack atop its roof. She'd finished an Ironman.

Then again, most women were his type. That was the problem. He was a good dad to Kenny. He was never late to pick him up. He texted and "snapped" him every day.

But when he'd cheated on Kenny's mom, over and over again, he'd been cheating on Kenny too. His infidelity, his narcissism, had ended Kenny's comfortable two-parent life and thrust the young teenager into a never-ending game of ping-pong in which he was the ball.

In his darkest private moments, alone in his sparsely furnished apartment with a beer in his hand, Rick could admit his failings. He knew he was selfish, and no matter how hard he tried to make it up to Kenny, nothing could equal the damage he'd inflicted on his son and his ex-wife.

Rick climbed into his Jeep and glanced over at Kenny and Chris. He considered the ramifications of that red glow in the sky the night before and the loss of power. If the world were ending, would he float skyward or take a nosedive into the depths of that other place?

He sat there for a moment with the key in the ignition, lost in thought. This wasn't the time or place for his usual barstool antics. He needed to focus. If he was going to be the kind of dad he aspired to be, this was the time to step up. His gut told him as much.

He cranked the ignition without even considering it might not start. The Jeep whined a protest then rumbled awake. Its idling rev startled Kenny, who looked sideways at his dad. He held up a finger to Chris and trotted over to Rick's window.

"Where are you going?"

"Just two campsites over. A woman needs a jump."

Kenny's eyes narrowed with suspicion. "What does that mean, Dad?"

Rick knew what his kid was thinking. "It means her car won't start. I'm going to try to help her."

The boy's eyes softened with relief. "Good," he said. "Just hurry up, please. We're hungry and the charcoal smells ready."

Rick looked over at the grill, where waves of heat stretched upward in ambling streams, distorting the trunks of the trees in the distance. "Got it."

He gave his son a thumbs-up and then shifted into gear, pulling right into the circular drive and rolling to the stranded Ironwoman and her Honda. She and Mumphrey were talking. Really, Mumphrey was talking, gesticulating wildly with his hands. She was listening, an interested smile glued to her cheeks. Even her cheeks looked toned.

Rick shook the thought from his mind. "All business," he mumbled, averting his eyes from her physique.

He slipped the Jeep into park and left the engine running. He popped the hood and hopped out. Mumphrey already had the cables connected to the Honda's battery terminals.

"All right," Rick said, heaving the heavy hood into an open and locked position. "Let's do this."

The athlete was standing close behind him. She was smiling at him, and Rick assumed some of her ice must have melted. Instead of returning the flirt, he looked at his feet.

He resisted the strong reflexive urge to compliment her or use one of his ridiculously douchey pickup lines that worked despite their lack of charm.

"Why don't you give her a shot," he said without any hint of his earlier flirtation. "Mumphrey here has the cables hooked up."

"Oh," she said, batting her eyes with surprise. "Okay then." She raised her arms with balled fists and flexed her biceps. "Let's do this," she mocked with a deepened voice and walked to the Honda.

Rick sat behind the wheel and waited for her to give the thumbs-up. When she did, he pressed on the accelerator, revving the three hundred and sixty horsepower V-8 two-barrel engine.

The athlete cranked the ignition. The Honda wasn't responding. Rick revved the engine again.

Nothing.

He got out of the Jeep and walked over to the Honda, leaned on the open driver's door, and looked down at the athlete. She was cursing her car and slapping the top of the steering wheel with her palm with one hand while uselessly pushing the start button with the other.

"You want me to try?" Rick asked.

She glared at him. "Seriously? You think you can do a better job of pushing the button?"

Rick grinned. "Seems like I just did a pretty good job of pushing one."

She rolled her eyes. "Good one."

"I try."

"Thing is" — she gestured toward the dash with her hands — "it's not just the engine or the battery. The display isn't working either. It's like someone fried the computer."

Mumphrey peeked around the Honda's hood and blinked over the top of his glasses. "Just like my pop-up," he said. "Deader than dead."

"Why is *your* car working?" the athlete asked. "It looks like something Henry Ford built by hand."

It was Rick's turn to roll his eyes. "It's not that old. It's—"

Then it hit him. The magnetic blast, whatever it was from, had fried electronics and anything plugged into an outlet.

His old Jeep was computer-free. There was nothing to fry.

"Looks like you're ruminating on something," Mumphrey remarked. "You got an idea there?"

Rick nodded. "My car doesn't have a computer. Yours does."

"So?"

"Didn't you see that magnetic storm last night?"

The athlete shrugged. "The aurora?"

"Yeah," Rick said. "The aurora is an electrical phenomenon. It's like a visible magnetic disturbance."

She looked at him sideways and planted both hands on the top of the steering wheel. "Are you a scientist or something? You don't look like a scientist."

Rick stepped back from the open door. "I'm not sure how to take that," he said. "But, no, I'm not a scientist. I can't really explain why we saw that aurora last night. It shouldn't happen this far south unless there's a magnetic cause. That's about all I know. That and they're usually green."

"The green ones are borealis and australis," said Mumphrey, slinking around the side with his hands in his pockets. "Those are the two auroras. One's North Pole, the other is South Pole. I watch a lot of the Discovery Channel. I'm an outdoors kind of fella. The red one means there's a big sun storm, I think. There was one back in the 1850s. It was red."

"So what do we do?" she asked. "I need to get back to Galveston."

"Galveston?" said Mumphrey. "That's where I'm headed. Well, not exactly Galveston. But Spring. You know, a bit north of Houston?"

"I know Spring," she said. "Right off I-45. You're on the way."

Mumphrey's eyes lit up. "Exactly right."

Rick knew neither the athlete nor Mumphrey were going anywhere. Their vehicles were as good as scrap metal. He drew in a deep breath and exhaled.

"I'm headed that way," Rick said reluctantly. He didn't need the temptation or the bother. He felt obligated, though. Mumphrey was a nice guy, and it wouldn't be right to leave a woman stranded in the woods. Especially a woman who looked like her.

"I hadn't planned on leaving today," he said. "But the boys are from Clear Lake. I'm on the west side near Memorial."

The athlete's eyes widened. "The boys?"

"My son and his friend," Rick explained. "I've got to take them back to Clear Lake. I've got room in the Jeep for both of you."

Mumphrey hiked up his pants. "When were you hitting the road if not today?"

"Tomorrow," Rick said. "Given we've got no cell service, though, and I can't get in touch with the boys' moms, we probably should head back after breakfast."

"I'll take you up on the offer," Mumphrey said. "Mighty kind of you. I'm in Spring right off the highway."

Rick nodded at Mumphrey and then shifted his eyes to the athlete. Part of him wanted her to decline the offer. Admittedly, it wasn't as big as the part that wanted her to say yes.

Her eyes narrowed on Rick then relaxed. She shrugged. "All right," she said, exhaling loudly. "Might as well. I've got no other choice."

"Don't sound so enthused," Rick said and walked back to the front of the Honda. He disconnected the cables from her car and then from his Jeep. When he slammed shut the hood, she was standing next to him.

"I'm sorry," she said, extending her hand. "I didn't mean to sound ungrateful. I'm just frustrated. I'm usually pretty self-reliant. I can handle my business, you know? Plus..."

"Plus what?"

Her cheeks flushed. "Plus you make me uncomfortable."

There was an undeniable electricity. Rick felt it, and he believed she did as well. It was his sudden disinterest that attracted her. Maybe not. It didn't matter. He immediately regretted inviting her.

"Huh," Rick said flatly. "That's funny. You make me uncomfortable too." He shook her hand and pulled away before he might have usually done so.

"What time you wanna leave?" Mumphrey asked.

"Give me a an hour," said Rick. "Meet me over at my site. Bring what you want and we'll make room for it."

He put the Jeep into reverse and started backing out of the campsite. He'd stopped and shifted into drive when she jogged up to his window.

"What?" he asked, pressing the brake while trying to keep his eyes above her neck.

"Nikki," she said. "My name is Nikki."

"Okay, Nikki," Rick said. "See you in an hour."

SATURDAY, JANUARY 25, 2020, 8:01 AM CST
DINOSAUR VALLEY STATE PARK, TEXAS

Rick hosed off the camping pan from the site spigot and used a grease-stained towel to dry it as best he could. He folded the handle into the pan and looked up to see Nikki walking toward him. She had a large pack on her shoulders, her thumbs tucked inside the straps.

"Ready to go?" she asked. "Mumphrey said he'll be here in a second."

"Just about," Rick replied, motioning toward the boys. "They're taking down the tent and we'll be on our way."

"How was breakfast?"

"Good enough," Rick said. He tucked the pan into a bag that held other camping utensils. "Bacon is always undercooked and greasy when you do it out here. Even the precooked stuff. Eggs were fine. It's hard to screw up a carton of egg whites."

Nikki chuckled. "So you're a chef, then?"

"Iron," he said. "I'm a regular Mario Batali." He zipped up the bag and reached for Nikki's pack. "Let me get that for you."

"Oh," she said, appearing surprised at Rick's chivalry. She shrugged the pack from her shoulders and slung it toward him. "Thank you."

"A chef and a gentleman," Rick said.

"Stop being a player, Dad," said a cracking pubescent voice. "Seriously."

Kenny stood there, his nose crinkled with disgust. Rick's cheeks grew hot. Leave it to a teenager.

Nikki belly laughed and stepped over to Kenny, offering her hand. "I'm Nikki. You guys are giving me a ride."

Kenny's eyes flashed with disappointment, darting between the woman and his father. "Are we?" He didn't take her hand.

Rick glared at his son. "Be polite," he said through clenched teeth.

Kenny shook Nikki's hand but didn't look her in the eyes. "Nice to meet you," he mumbled. "I'm Kenny."

Nikki bent over, trying to draw Kenny's attention. "So your dad's a player?"

Kenny rolled his eyes. He nodded and then looked at her. "You look familiar. I've seen you before."

"I just have one of those faces." She winked. "Seems to me you're the cute one."

Kenny's cheeks flushed. He nodded toward Chris. "This is Chris. His dad's not a player."

Nikki waved. "Hi, Chris."

Chris waved back. He was sticking the last of the fiberglass poles into the large tent case.

"Am I late?" Mumphrey appeared from nowhere. "I had a few things to lock up, seeing as how I gotta leave my car behind."

"You're good," Rick said. "Nikki, your car locked up?"

"Yes. I hate leaving it here, but I can't call Triple-A or Honda, so I've got no choice, really."

"Guess not," Rick said. "Hopefully, this is a temporary thing, and as soon as we get you home, you can take care of it."

"Hopefully," she said.

Rick adjusted her pack in the back of the Jeep and made room for Mumphrey's US Army standard-issue duffle bag. "You sure you don't want me to tow the pop-up?"

"Nah," Mumphrey said. "I appreciate it, but you don't have a tow package on the back of the Jeep. Might do more harm than good. She'll be okay for a couple days until I can get back up here."

Rick heaved the duffle into the back of the Jeep. He'd feel uneasy leaving anything behind. There was no telling who or what would be hanging around once they left. The cars and pop-up were as good as abandoned.

He walked over to Chris and helped the boy finish zipping up the tent case. It was always tough getting all of the pieces in the bag just right. When they finished the job, Rick thanked Chris for his help and tossed the case into the back of the Jeep and closed the tailgate.

"Okay," he said with a sigh, "we can hit the road. Everybody hop in."

"I'll get in the back with the boys," offered Nikki. "Mr. Mumphrey can have the front seat."

Mumphrey faked a bow with a wide, toothy grin. "Mighty kind of you. Are you sure you don't want to be up front?"

Nikki slung open the heavy passenger side door and climbed into the back. "I'm good," she replied, sitting in the middle.

Rick put his hand on Kenny's shoulder and whispered into his son's ear, "Don't be a player."

Kenny rolled his eyes. "Funny, Dad."

Rick climbed into the driver's seat and cranked the engine. He checked the fuel gauge. It was nearly full. Thankfully, he had filled up on Highway 67 outside of the park entrance.

He adjusted his rearview mirror and caught Nikki's eyes. She held his gaze for a moment before she turned away to talk to the boys. Rick pulled out onto the circular loop that connected the campsites to Park Road 59.

He drove west, passing the same scene over and again. People were trying to jump the cars or their SUVs. They had their hoods up. Men and women were flailing their arms at each other or pointing with frustration at their children.

"Seems everybody's stuck," said Mumphrey. "So thankful to have you help us."

"Not a problem," Rick said. He turned on Park Road 59 and drove south toward the exit. He felt the stranded campers watching when they rolled past. He tried to keep his eyes straight ahead, as if trying to avoid a beggar shaking a can at a stop light.

They navigated the Park Road in silence until they reached the fork where the road merged with FM 205. Just south of the merge and before they connected with Highway 67, they saw a crowd of people off to the left of the road. A few of them stood in the northbound lanes, threatening to block Rick from passing.

Kenny pressed his nose to the glass. "Dad, what are they doing?"

Chris leaned forward, almost sitting in Nikki's lap. "They look angry, Mr. Walsh."

As they approached, they could hear the chanting. Dozens of people were dressed in all white. Some of them had their eyes closed, heads tilted back toward the sky. They held their arms in the air, palms pressed open flat.

"That's the Creation Evidence Museum," said Rick. "The people who don't believe in dinosaurs."

"What are they doing?" Kenny asked.

Mumphrey pointed at the people spilling into the road. "Looks to me like they're praying."

The chanting grew louder. It was another language, perhaps Latin or Aramaic.

Rick pressed the accelerator, hoping to skirt past the crowd flowing onto the road. He wasn't fast enough. By the time he'd shifted the wheel to go around the group, they'd blocked him.

They were men and women, even some children, all of them with the same wild look in their eyes. They had something to say and they were going to make sure Rick listened to them.

Rick looked in the side-view mirror and shifted into reverse. He started to back up, but when he turned around, some of the white-clad chanters had blocked him. He cursed under his breath and slipped the Jeep into park.

Kenny reached across the seat and gripped Rick's shoulder. "Dad?"

Rick took one of his son's hands. "It's okay, they won't hurt us," he said, although he wasn't so sure. He glanced in the rearview mirror and caught Nikki's eyes again. She wasn't sure either.

A tall, thin man standing on the shoulder moved, almost floated, to the center of the road. His white shirt was buttoned up to the collar, his hair short and trimmed neatly along his temples. He had a long, birdlike nose that flared as he spoke.

"And there appeared another wonder in Heaven; and behold a great red dragon, having seven heads and ten horns, and seven crowns upon his heads," he recited.

His voice was loud but controlled. The others kept chanting. It was like a scene straight out of a horror movie.

Rick reached down to crank open his window.

"Dad," Kenny said, his voice trembling, "don't."

"It's okay," he assured his son and opened the window. He leaned his head out. "Could you please let us pass? We need to get home."

"Where did they come from?" asked Nikki. "I don't see any cars. Did they all walk here? Are they with the museum?"

The tall man with the bird nose glared at Rick but didn't respond. He blinked and took a step forward. He held up his hands to silence the throng. The chanting stopped and all of their eyes focused on the Jeep.

Rick muttered under his breath, "What the hell?"

"We might want to get a move on," said Mumphrey. "These folks look like they got bad intentions. They ain't got nothin' to do with that museum."

Through clenched lips, Rick said, "I can't go anywhere. Ichabod Crane and his minions are blocking me."

A broad smile wormed its way across the tall man's thin lips, drawing his nose downward. His eyes narrowed, crow's-feet deepening on either side.

The man pointed past the Jeep with a long, bony finger. "You came from the dinosaur park?" he asked through the creepy smile.

Rick nodded.

"So you know the lies of that place," the man said. "You saw them in the sky. You saw what the true creator has wrought."

Nobody in the Jeep responded.

"We have said for so long that He would show Himself," said the man to the murmured agreement of his flock. "We have believed He would elevate the righteous and cast down the wicked, the purveyors and consumers of lies."

"Nikki," Rick said without moving his lips, "do not react to what I am going to tell you." He kept his eyes on the tall man. "I want you to reach under my seat. There is a gun."

Nikki gasped and opened her mouth to protest.

"Nikki," Rick grunted, doing his best impersonation of a ventriloquist, "get me the gun. I'm not going to hurt anyone."

"That time is upon us," said the tall man to a growing chorus of support. "The color of the heavens is proof."

Rick was stalling while Nikki fumbled underneath his seat. "Proof of what?" he called out of his window.

"We cannot let the nonbelievers pass," the tall man said. "We are sent here to meet those who would deny our Lord's dominion, His omnipotence."

The man stepped closer and the flock followed him.

"We're not denying anything," Rick called through the open window. Then he lowered his voice. "Nikki, hurry up."

"The Creator has given us the light in the sky. He has made useless our worldly possessions and devices."

The crowd inched closer. Rick furiously cranked up the window.

"We cannot let you pass. You have forsaken Him at this unholy place."

"Dad!" Kenny squealed.

Rick snapped, "Lock your doors, everyone."

"They're getting closer," Chris said nervously.

Mumphrey shook his head. "They're out of their ever-loving minds."

"We have awaited this day!" the tall man bellowed, his nose curling down over his smiling lips. He planted his hands on the hood of the Jeep.

"Nikki!" said Rick. "Where is it?"

Nikki handed the 9mm to Rick. "Here!"

Mumphrey looked over at Rick. "You got a license for that?"

"Really, Mumphrey? This is Texas. Of course I have a concealed handgun license. Everybody has a license. Plus, I don't need it to have it in my car."

The crowd surrounded the vehicle and started rhythmically thumping on the hood with their fists. *Thump. Thump. Thump.*

The Jeep was swaying now.

"Dad," said Kenny, "do something."

Rick revved the engine. It did nothing to deter the swarm. It only agitated them like bees and they thumped against the hood faster and faster, chanting.

"These people are psycho," said Nikki. "Like Branch Davidian psycho."

Rick held the titanium-colored 9mm in his lap. It was a TP9 and held eighteen rounds. It had a double-action striker mechanism and was Century International's version of a Smith and Wesson 99.

"Get out of the vehicle," said the thin man above the din of the chanting. "We cannot let you pass."

"There must be sixty of them," said Mumphrey. "At least. We can't—"

"Step away from my Jeep," said Rick. He was glaring into the unflinching eyes of the tall man. He leveled the four-inch barrel of the TP9 directly at him. "Do it now. Tell your people to do the same."

The man raised his hands in surrender, his unnerving smile stretching his face. "They are not my people." He pointed a finger upward. "They are His people." The chanting grew louder—Latin, Rick recognized now—and a chill ran along his spine.

"This is like the freaking *Omen*," said Nikki. She braced herself, planting her hands on the inside edges of both front seat backs.

Kenny and Chris whimpered. Rick felt Kenny gripping his headrest, catching strands of his hair with his fingers.

"Kids, get down," Rick said.

The Jeep rocked harder, like it was caught in a raging river. The flock had them surrounded. The looks in their eyes were vacant, as if they weren't even aware of what they were doing. It was the most frighteningly bizarre thing Rick had ever seen, and he'd gone through a divorce with a woman he'd scorned.

Rick leaned forward in his seat, emphasizing his aim. "Get them off the car and let us pass," he said. "I will use this."

The man's smile dissolved into a sneer. His fingers pressed down on the hood of the Jeep as though he were playing piano. "We cannot let you leave," said the tall man. "You have failed the Creator. Now is our time. The skies tell us so."

"These are doomsdayers, no doubt," Mumphrey said. "We gotta get away."

"That's it," Rick said.

"Wait!" urged Nikki. "Don't shoot them."

Rick caught her worried eyes in the rearview mirror. A deep crease cut across her forehead. Keeping the gun aimed at the tall man, he used his left hand to crack open the window.

"What are you doing?" Nikki barked. "Why —"

Pop! Pop! Pop! Pop!

Rick had the barrel wedged between the glass and the frame. Aiming into the sky, he quickly pulled the trigger again.

Pop! Pop! Pop!

The percussive rounds echoed in the cloudless sky, cracking across the rolling terrain like thunder. The rocking stopped. Most of the flock was running. The gunshots had awakened them from their trance. Some were stumbling head over heels down the grassy embankment that led to the museum. Others were backing away, their hands pressed flat against their ears.

One of the boys was crying in the backseat. Rick wasn't sure which one. "It's okay, boys. We'll be out of here in a second."

The tall man, though, was unmoved. He stood there, his fingers planted on the Jeep and his eyes affixed to Rick. The man tilted his head from one side to the other, flexing his neck. The smile returned. He pulled his hands from the Jeep and balled them into tight fists, whitening his knuckles.

"Back away," Rick said. He pulled the 9mm through the window and then shouldered open the door.

Nikki reached for his arm. "Rick, just back up. Go around. There's room."

He was already out of the Jeep, standing behind the half-open door, adrenaline coursing through him. He held the 9mm with both hands and aimed it at the man's head, his finger pressed against the trigger. He wanted to blow the smug, nasty glare off the man's face. The man recognized Rick's resolve. Or perhaps he wasn't quite as ready to meet his Creator as he professed to be. Whatever the reason, he took two steps away from the Jeep. Then two more.

The man sneered. "He sees you," he growled. "He knows what you've done. He is here and will have His vengeance."

Rick lowered the weapon, dropped back into his seat, and pulled the door shut. He put his foot on the brake, ripped the Jeep into gear, and hit the accelerator, swinging the Jeep around the tall man with a screech of the tires.

"He sees you!" the man shouted. "He knows your transgressions."

Rick blinked past the sting of salt in his eyes. "He sees me when I'm sleeping," he said. "He knows when I'm awake. He knows when I've —"

"Sheesh," Nikki cut in. "That was ridiculous."

Rick barreled past the red traffic light on Highway 67. He swung the wheel hard to the left without decelerating enough and fishtailed the Jeep. Then he punched the gas again to head east.

"Boys? You guys okay back there?"

Kenny and Chris climbed from the floorboard and into their seats. Neither of them said anything; both buckled their seatbelts.

"Boys," Rick said, "you were both brave. Really brave."

Kenny shook his head. "I wasn't. I cried."

Rick searched his son's face in the rearview mirror. Kenny's eyes were red and swollen and his nose was running.

"That doesn't mean you weren't brave, son," said Rick. "Brave people cry."

Kenny took a deep, ragged breath and exhaled, nodding at his dad.

Mumphrey looked like he'd seen a ghost. He had a death grip on the dash, beads of sweat blooming across his bald head.

Still holding the TP9 in his right hand, Rick offered it to Mumphrey. "Could you take care of this?"

Mumphrey took the gun without saying anything. He wiped his forehead with the back of his arm. "Doomsdayers," he said, shaking his head. "That ain't good."

Nikki put her hand on Mumphrey's shoulder. "What do you mean?"

"I'm just thinking out loud here," he said, finding a place for the TP9 in the glove box. "I gotta think those folks were just a sign of a bigger problem. Something more widespread."

"How so?" Nikki sat back and patted her hand on Kenny's leg, obviously trying to reassure him they were safe now, despite the direction of the conversation. "Those were just creationist freaks. They were a cult or something. I don't get how that means anything."

The old man shrugged, drawing his shoulders close to his ears. "I'm just thinking out loud. But if they weren't at the camp and they got some idea, somehow, that cars and phones and whatever else isn't working anymore, then they think the end of the world is coming."

"I don't know about that," Rick said. "They walked there. They were close. This could be isolated and they're just predisposed to want to see the end of the world in anything out of the normal."

"The aurora wasn't isolated," said Mumphrey. "I'm telling you, and I don't mean to frighten the boys or nothing, but like I said, I think there's a bigger issue. I think we might run into—"

"Holy—" Rick instinctively extended his arm across Mumphrey's chest as he slammed on the brakes. "Hold on." The Jeep's tires screamed to a stop inches from the back of a Toyota minivan.

Ahead of them, blocking both lanes of traffic, was a parade of stalled vehicles. Some of them were stopped dead in the right of way, others in the steep culverts framing both sides of the highway. Some had crashed into each other.

"Maybe you were right," said Nikki.

Mumphrey sighed.

CHAPTER 7

MISSION ELAPSED TIME:
72 DAYS, 10 HOURS, 55 MINUTES, 32 SECONDS
249 MILES ABOVE EARTH

The Orlan felt tighter with every passing minute. Clayton wanted nothing more than to rip it off and throw it through the airlock.

When he'd first put on the suit hours earlier, he'd felt a rush of claustrophobia that washed over him and then was gone as quickly as it came. During the entirety of his spacewalk, he'd felt comfortable in the suit, relatively speaking. It was different now.

He was in the airlock. Two dead men were floating alongside him in their suits. He'd failed to save them, but at least he'd recovered their bodies. If all went well, he'd be able to return them to their families. "If all went well" seemed like a pipe dream given his current circumstances.

Clayton fixated on Ben's reflective visor. Heat coursed through him at the memory of Ben's lifeless eyes glaring back it him from behind the gold-coated plastic bubble of the Extravehicular Visor Assembly.

A familiar knot swelled at the base of Clayton's throat. "I'm so sorry," he said for himself as much as to Ben.

Ben Greenwood was single and never married, though both of his parents were alive. They'd want to bury their son. He was sure of it. He'd met them once. They were from Nebraska and seemed like kind people. They'd raised a brilliant son.

It was Ben who'd first given Clayton the confidence to apply for the astronaut corps. Clayton met him at an engineering conference in Houston. Ben had given a brilliant speech about mechanical dynamics in low Earth orbit. Clayton approached him with some questions after the presentation. They'd grabbed overpriced cups of coffee, exchanged emails, and kept in touch.

Ben was among the senior astronauts. He'd flown on the shuttle before it was decommissioned. He was a fantastic ambassador for the program. He was an old-school astronaut: fearless and cocky, sharp and methodical.

Jackie had often teased Clayton he was "fangirling" over Ben. "Ben this, Ben that," she would say. "He's your hero, isn't he? He's Superman and you're Jimmy Olsen."

The truth was Ben *was* Clayton's hero as far as space exploration was concerned. He practically idolized him.

So when an email titled "Wanna be an astronaut?" popped up in Clayton's inbox, he'd opened it with ridiculous excitement. His fingers fumbled to click it open, his eyes darted wildly, searching the message for the key words.

Ben had forwarded a link to a NASA press release with the note, "You should do this." Clayton had clicked the URL and a fresh page had opened in his browser:

BE AN ASTRONAUT: NASA ACCEPTING APPLICATIONS FOR FUTURE EXPLORERS

NASA is looking for the best candidates to work in the best job on or off the planet. The astronaut candidate application is now live. Those chosen may fly on any of four different US spacecraft during their careers: the International Space Station, two commercial crew spacecraft currently in development by US companies, and NASA's Orion deep-space exploration vehicle.

That was all it had taken. That and a long conversation with Jackie. That, a long conversation with Jackie, and a rigorous selection process. It had been a nerve-racking twenty months.

First there was the application. NASA pored through them, weeding out those who weren't serious from those who were, selecting those deemed highly qualified. Questionnaires went out to Clayton's supervisors and references. Ben had been one of those references.

Clayton waited another three months until the highly qualified applicants were winnowed to the smaller pool of interviewees. Clayton went to JSC for the initial interview, a thorough medical evaluation, and an orientation.

The questions a panel of astronauts had asked him during the interview were simple and complex at the same time.

Why do you want to be an astronaut?

Can you fix things?

Who are you as a person?

Are you a team player?

The medical examination was thorough. They'd checked his sight, hearing, teeth, and his heart. He'd undergone MRIs and a VO2 max stress test.

Two months later finalists had been announced.

From that incredibly elite group, NASA selected its class. More than eighteen thousand people had applied. Half of one percent made the final cut. Clayton had been at the gym when he'd gotten the call. His Apple watch had buzzed against his wrist and displayed a blocked number.

He had stopped mid leg press and answered with his wrist, holding the watch close to his mouth.

"Yes?"

"You're in, brother," Ben had said with no preamble. "You're in. You're an astronaut. You're an explorer. You're part of the most select club on or off the planet."

Clayton had thought he was joking. "Riiiight," he'd said. "You're not supposed to have that info. The head of the corps is the one who tells me."

"Seriously," Ben had said. "I got some inside intel. Not a joke. You're in. Just act surprised when you get the official call."

Clayton had thanked Ben, still not quite believing him, and finished his set. His legs had felt like rubber. He thought back to that moment. He was never sure whether the weakness was from the set of presses or the phone call.

It had taken years to become flight certified, learn enough Russian to keep his job, earn an assignment, and then train for it. It had been years of work and stress and strain for him and for his reluctantly supportive family.

Now Clayton wondered if he ever should have applied. He wondered if he should have opened the email offering him the chance. He wondered if he should have even approached Ben at the engineering conference in the first place. If he hadn't done some or all of those things, Ben Greenwood and Boris Voin would somehow be alive. Another, better astronaut would have saved them. A better astronaut would have known what to do or would have fought harder to prevent or stop the EVA.

If he hadn't done any of those things, he'd be home right now. He'd be with Jackie and the kids. They wouldn't be alone coping with whatever the CME had done to their part of the Earth. He wouldn't be alone in an airlock, contemplating what he could have done differently, how his need for the ultimate rush had put everything that really mattered at extreme risk.

Clayton checked the pressure. It was getting close. He'd be able to leave the airlock and start the process of getting off the ISS. He closed his eyes and went through a checklist of things that would need to happen before he undocked and separated from the station in the Soyuz.

It was a long list and Clayton had no idea how long the computer systems would continue to function. He couldn't be sure how much time he had to do what he needed to do.

He opened his eyes and looked again at the reflective helmets velcroed to the wall of the airlock. He resolved that regardless of how much time he had and what other tasks he needed to complete, taking care of his crewmates was atop the list. He would make sure they returned to Earth with him. And if they didn't, it would be because he died trying to make it happen.

He wasn't sure what protocol might be. He didn't know what Mission Control would advise, although he could guess.

As far as the brass at NASA was concerned, he'd saved two very expensive EMUs. He'd heard they cost anywhere from ten to fifteen million dollars each. He'd return them to Earth if he could. So there was that.

Two hours later, Clayton pushed himself through the Zvezda Russian service module and into the Soyuz habitation module, squeezing past the large silver and black docking probe, lowering himself into the spacecraft. Before he began loading up the spaceship to go home, he needed to be sure he could make it work.

The Soyuz was a classic design, a ship in three parts. At the top was the hab, on the bottom was the instrumentation module, and in the middle the crew module.

Clayton squirmed through the hab and into the crew module, easing himself into the center seat, the seat reserved for the commander. It sat lower than the engineer seats on either side. It was Boris's seat. He strapped in.

In front of him were a series of buttons and levers and a periscope with exterior cameras. There was a pair of control sticks at his knees for if he had to manually control the ship. He prayed he wouldn't need them.

It was the first time he'd been in the module since they'd arrived as a trio two and a half months earlier. Clayton looked to his left. That had been his seat on the way up.

He stared blankly at the panel of buttons and knobs and switches in front of him, his mind drifting to the day they'd launched.

He'd eaten most of his breakfast of kasha and boiled eggs. His stomach was dancing with nerves, and he'd not been hungry. Boris had insisted he eat, telling him he'd need the energy later in the long day.

They'd laughed and joked on their way to the launch pad. Boris had talked about his wife and children, imitating their voices and mannerisms. He was joking about his daughter's first date with a boy when they'd pulled up to the pad. It was the same spot from which Yuri Gagarin, the first human in space, had launched into orbit aboard a Vostok and traveled around the Earth in April 1961. His trip had lasted one hundred and eight minutes.

Once at the pad, they'd climbed a narrow set of stairs to the gantry and then ascended an elevator to the top of the rocket and the entry to the Soyuz capsule. Clayton remembered thinking the rocket hadn't looked that big from the ground. From the top of it looking down, however, it seemed massive.

He'd been the first to climb into his seat through the habitation module, followed by Ben, then Boris.

"You ready?" Ben had asked Clayton with a big smile plastered to his face. "I'm not sure who's more excited about you flying into space, me or you."

The launch crew had closed the hatch and they'd begun their system checks. Clayton replayed the sequence in his mind, reminding himself of some of the tasks he'd have ahead of him when he was ready to leave.

Once they'd checked their communications, turned on the various systems and confirmed they worked, they did suit checks. Only then did they relax.

For close to an hour they sat there in the tight quarters, three men locked in cramped quarters, awaiting launch. Ground control piped in music to pass the time.

"Louis Armstrong," said Boris in his thick accent. "I like his music. Satchmo, yes?"

The strains of American jazz filtered through the capsule. Clayton had closed his eyes and let the music move through him. It had been a surreal moment.

He was a regular guy, a math whiz who was good at problem solving. He lived in a normal middle-income neighborhood with a wife and two kids. He drove a Ford F-150.

He wasn't a hero. He didn't think of himself that way. He was Clayton. Good ole Clay.

Yet he was about to blast off into space, as so few people had ever done. He was set to "boldly go" as James Tiberius Kirk would have said. He was risking his life for the betterment of mankind. In some small way, he'd believed the things he'd study and learn while in orbit would help future pioneers and generations of scientists.

He'd been drawn from his daydream and the beauty of Pop's trumpet with thirty minutes to go before the launch. They'd rechecked all of their systems at least twice.

He'd flinched at the heavy thump that rocked the Soyuz as the gantry was pulled back from the rocket. Boris had laughed at him. Ben had reached across Boris, patted his leg, and smiled.

"This is it," Ben had said and the capsule started vibrating, building into a rumble as the engines started. There was the countdown and the final clearance.

"*Tri…dva…odin…*"

Clayton had felt an enormous, heavy push, sinking him into his seat as the engines engaged and the rocket lifted off from Yuri's pad. The rumble had pulsed through his entire body. His pulse had quickened. His breathing had been rapid and shallow, his helmet plastered to the back of his seat.

It had been exhilarating and frightening all at once, as if he were on a roller coaster without a harness. He'd wanted to scream with excitement. He couldn't help but laugh as the adrenaline had coursed through his trembling body. For eight and a half minutes they'd rushed skyward. It had felt like five seconds. As soon as it had begun, it had been over. They were in orbit.

Clayton had wanted to talk about the launch, the childlike giddiness tickling his senses, but he'd resisted. He'd known the other men had been to space more than once. This was nothing for them.

And then Ben had thrown up his fist and cheered into his mic. "That was awesome." He'd laughed. "It never gets old."

"I love the launch almost as much as the landing," Boris had added. "What did you think of it, Clayton?"

Clayton's cheeks had been sore, but he couldn't be sure if it had been from the gravity bearing down on him during the launch or the smile glued to his face. He'd given his friends a thumbs-up.

"I'm speechless," he'd said, beginning to notice the lack of gravity. A whole new sensation filled him. He'd experienced weightlessness before. This was different. This wasn't like the C-9B Skytrain II in which he'd trained using parabolic maneuvers to give him moments of zero g. It was the real deal.

Now, seventy-two days later, he was in Boris's seat. He knew the trip back wouldn't be as fun as Boris had predicted.

He'd have to delicately maneuver Boris's and Ben's bodies into the crew module one at a time. He'd had the grim task of removing them from their suits. They'd not been able to fit through the PMA between Node 1 and the Russian segment. He'd done everything he could to avoid looking at their faces. He'd closed their eyes, at least. That had helped. They were still in the airlock, dressed in their undergarments. They didn't need their Launch and Entry Suits, called LES, or the Russian equivalent called the Sokol.

He did need to wear a Sokol, and he'd have to change into the pressurized, thermal suit before he pulled the trigger and returned to Earth. That suit could save his life if there was a pressure leak or any number of other problems.

Before he did that, however, he'd need supplies. The Soyuz was supposed to land in Kazakhstan. *Supposed* to. Given the endless number of variables and no communication with the ground, Clayton couldn't know for sure where he'd land. Plus, he had no concept of what the world might be like when he did return.

The capsule contained a survival kit, a newer version of the original Soviet NAZ-3 gear; the gear was exhaustive. The Russians hadn't forgotten anything.

Stored in a myriad of white Nomex bags and strapped into the sides of the capsule were the pieces of the kit. Aside from a snowsuit and a wet suit for each of the three men on board, they'd included a Makarov pistol and ammunition, a wrist compass, waterproof matches and a fishing kit, whistle, screwdriver, sewing kit, double-edged switchblade saw, granulated ethyl alcohol, strobe light with a spare battery, flare, fire starters, a knife, an antenna, a signal mirror, medical kit, canteen, hoods, gloves, cold suits, knit caps, boots, a penlight, a pair of radios, and vacuum-packed food rations.

The Soviets designed them to provide emergency supplies for landing in any environment. There was enough in the kit to sustain three men for seventy-two hours. As the lone survivor, that kit would last Clayton nine days.

Still, despite the Russians' forethought, he'd need more. He pulled himself upward through the habitation module and back into the Zvezda service module. He needed to search the crew quarters and take whatever he could find that might be useful once he landed back on solid ground.

He started with Boris's compartment, which the Russians called a *cayuta*. It was the closest to the Soyuz. He positioned himself above it and pulled open the single padded door.

It was the size of a phone booth but so much more personal. Clayton kept his hand on the door, afraid that letting go of it would allow the boiling guilt to overwhelm him.

Boris was dead. These belongings weren't his anymore. Not really. Still, Clayton took a deep breath of filtered air and pulled himself inside the cramped space.

Against one wall was Boris's sleeping bag strapped to the wall. Boris, like Clayton, needed to simulate sleep on Earth as much as he could. Some astronauts liked floating free in their quarters as they slept. Clayton had tried it and didn't like it. Boris must not have either.

Across from the bag, photographs of the Voin family were tacked to the wall, a sad gallery of a life that no longer existed as they had in those happy, frozen moments.

There was Boris with his arms around his wife, Albina. He was dressed in his military uniform, his shoulders pressed back with pride. Albina was on his arm, a genuine smile on her face, a deep spray of laugh lines emanating from the corners of her eyes.

Another photograph was of the entire family: Boris, Albina, their daughter, Nadia, and son, Alexei. They had their arms around each other, shouldering backpacks on a bluff. Behind them were the Ural Mountains. Clayton recognized the jagged black peaks from his time training in Kazakhstan. They were as stark as they were beautiful. The Urals were a metaphor for the people of Eastern Europe. He touched the photograph with a finger and swallowed against a dry throat.

"Focus," Clayton told himself, blinking back from the fantasy of what had been. "Find what you're looking for."

The problem was, he didn't really know what he was looking for. He only knew he'd find it when he saw it. Neither of the laptops affixed to wall-mounted arms were functioning.

On what passed for a floor, there was a trio of two-by-two-foot metal boxes held down with bungee cords. They were latched closed but didn't appear to have locks. Each was labeled with a piece of white electrical tape and Boris's name written across it. Clayton pulled himself lower in the space, his legs sticking out into the module, and unlatched the first case.

Inside he found some extra white socks, a blue and gold Russian Orthodox Bible, some mission patches and pins, and a red Aeroflot Airlines T-Shirt. Clayton pilfered the socks and closed the box. He reattached the bungee and opened the second box.

In that box there was a rectangular package inside plain brown wrapping. Clayton remembered Boris receiving the package on the last Space X supply delivery. Boris hadn't been excited about it, instead choosing to rifle through the candy treats and handwritten letters from home.

Clayton ran his finger along the Cyrillic script on the box, trying his best to read the scribbled letters. *"Avar-riya-noh-yay rah-dee-yoh."*

Emergency radio.

His eyes widened. A smile spread across his face as he ripped into the package like an eight-year-old on Christmas morning.

The shreds of brown wrapping separated and floated above him as he held the black cardboard box firmly in his hands.

The radio was a Yaesu FT1DR digital/analog transceiver. The box indicated it came with a lithium ion battery. He opened up the cardboard flap and pulled out the limited warranty card. It was valid in the US and Canada only.

"What?" Clayton joked aloud. "No ISS warranty? What a piece of junk."

Underneath the thick operating manual sitting inside the box's lid were all the needed components still covered in their original plastic. He unwrapped the antenna, the pre-charged li-ion battery, the AC adapter, and the transceiver itself.

It was squatty and fit comfortably in his palm. He flipped it over, finding the charging port and the other important features. He snapped the battery to the back of the radio. It was attached to the radio's rear outer shell and had a belt clip, which Clayton used to attach it to the pocket of his jumpsuit. He slipped the charger into the pocket and went for the third box.

He didn't think he could find anything better than a HAM radio. He was wrong.

Inside the box was a relic of the Russian space program. Clayton didn't even think they were allowed in orbit anymore. He didn't care how Boris had managed to smuggle the device on board, he was merely thankful that he had.

He gently pulled the Soviet TP-82 into his hands. He held it there, staring at it for a moment as if he were looking into the Ark of the Covenant. The TP-82 was a triple-barreled combination firearm and ax. It was a survival aid for cosmonauts who risked being stranded in the Siberian wilderness after landing and before recovery.

The pistol, which could fire two different gauges of ammunition, had a detachable buttstock and was also a machete. It was a brilliant and brutal weapon used for more than twenty years. By 2007, the remaining ammunition designed for the TP-82 was deemed unstable and the elegant dual-use relic was replaced with a standard semiautomatic pistol.

Clayton ran his hand along the woodgrain forestock wrapping the barrel of the weapon and then strapped it back into the box. Next to it, carefully folded over onto itself, was an ammunition belt.

He stuffed the socks into the box alongside the weapon and ammo belt, pulled several of the photographs from the wall, and carefully set them inside the container, underneath socks. He closed the box and grabbed it with both hands before tucking it awkwardly under his left arm. He maneuvered his way back to the Soyuz, glided into the crew compartment, and strapped it into his seat.

Still giddy from his finds, he quickly floated back to the Harmony node and his own crew quarters. Unlike the single-door Russian cubbies, the four crew quarters in the American side of the ISS had thinner French doors that gave them their privacy.

Clayton fingered open the doors and floated into his quarters. Despite lamenting the end of the shuttle program, one benefit of hitching a ride in a Russian rocket was the PPK allotment. The PPK was the Personal Preference Kit. It was limited to twenty personal items. Whereas a shuttle crew could only have brought one and a half pounds with them in the PPK, the Soyuz allowed for more than two pounds.

Clayton had used every ounce of his allotment for the PPK and for the OFK, the Official Flight Kit. He'd even worked the system by getting some of his favorite sweatshirts and ball caps labeled as "necessary supplies." But as he fished through his quarters, he didn't find anything practical to take with him other than a box of energy bars.

He spun himself using the pole mount for his laptop and grabbed photographs off the wall behind it. He didn't take the time to look at them, to think about them, to worry about the people in them. He couldn't do that. Staring at Boris's family had been enough.

He stacked the photographs on top of one another and tucked them into a crease at the edge of the box of energy bars. Clayton gave the space another cursory glance and pushed himself out of the space toward Ben Greenwood's, which was directly across from his in Node 2.

He floated in the doorway to Ben's quarters. His space was relatively empty. He liked living a Spartan life on the ISS. The less he had with him, the more he'd appreciate those missing things when he got back to Earth.

There was one thing Clayton took: a photograph of Ben and his parents. It was taken in Kazakhstan before they went into quarantine preflight. Ben had proudly affixed it to the wall next to his sleeping bag. It was the last photograph of the three of them.

Ben was in the center, his arms around his parents' waists. Ben and his father wore matching smiles. Clayton could see the older man in the younger one and vice versa. Father and son no doubt. They even shared the same receding hairline.

Ben's mom was smiling too, although it was different. Clayton could tell it was forced. Her teeth were pressed together as she might show them to a dentist. In her eyes, instead of beaming pride, he saw worry.

He'd never noticed it in the photograph before. Maybe he was transposing his own emotions, manipulating her gaze with what he knew now to be her son's fate.

Ben's mother had never liked his chosen profession. She understood it, she was proud of him, but she didn't like it. She'd told Clayton once that she'd had a recurring dream her son would die in space and that she wouldn't get to bury him. She'd confided in Clayton that the nightmare would wake her up drenched in sweat.

"No American has ever died in space," Clayton had tried to reassure her. "Ever."

"There's a first for everything," she'd replied, sadness in her voice. It was like she knew. A mother's intuition or something.

Clayton stuck the picture into the power bar box with his other photographs. He'd return it to the Greenwoods. It was the least he could do for them.

He backed out of Ben's quarters and flew out of the Harmony module, making his way back through the maze to the Zvezda service module. He found an outlet with a North American adapter in it and plugged in the AC charger for the radio, unclipped the radio from his belt, and connected it. Even if the li-ion battery had a charge, he'd need it fully juiced.

Clayton left the radio plugged in and floating while he pushed himself from Node 1 through the Russian FGB Module into the service module. He maneuvered to the rows of sealed plastic bags clipped to one of the four walls. He picked through the labeled bags, looking for his favorite dehydrated and ready-to-eat foods. "Favorite" was a relative term, as so many things were in space. Although he wasn't in love with any of the foods, there were some that were more tolerable than others. He held a half dozen in his hands and spun to the opposite wall. There he found red containers, which held Russian food. He plucked a couple of the Russian meals and added them to his haul, stuffed all of the food into a trash bag, twisted the top, and tied it into a knot.

Floating in the middle of the node, holding a sack full of food, Clayton realized he couldn't remember the last time he'd eaten.

Breakfast? Dinner the night before? No. It was breakfast.

He wasn't hungry though. There was too much to do. Nonetheless, he knew he'd need the energy to think straight. He let go of the sack and took an energy bar from the station's stash on the wall. Quickly, he gobbled the dry nutrition, grabbed the food sack, retucked his personal box of energy bars and photographs, and pushed himself back to Node 1 and the Zvezda.

He floated into the module and strapped the box and the sack to the wall. Then he checked his new toy, the radio. If there was any chance of communication with NASA, Roscosmos, or ESA, this would be it. He had no Internet, and the comms used to connect with any of the mission control centers had failed. This handheld radio was possible gold.

Clayton was a ham. He had a technician's amateur license, which allowed him to communicate with people on Earth through the high-powered frequencies reserved for those allowed to use them. Despite all of his other accomplishments, he was especially proud of his FCC-issued HAM call sign KD5XMX. His wife teased him he should have spent less time on the radio and more time learning Russian. Or better yet, she'd joked, he should have spoken Russian on the radio.

NASA had suggested, though not required, he get his license while he was in training for the mission. He'd taken on the task more seriously than he took to learning Russian, and at this moment was thanking himself.

The radio was seventy-five percent charged. He'd keep it plugged in while he tried connecting with any of the ISS's earthbound handlers.

It was a last-ditch effort to get help before he attempted to manually bring the Soyuz back to Earth, and it was his best hope at finding out how dire the situation was before he landed and found himself in the middle of the Dark Ages.

He unplugged the radio and took a deep breath before pushing himself through the maze and to the Columbus module. Once there, he rechecked the three HAM radios permanently installed in the ISS. None of them worked.

Clayton disconnected the antenna connection to one of the installed HAM radios and attached it to the antenna connection for the Yaseu. Even though the installed radios were dead, the CME wouldn't have had any effect on the external antennas.

Fidgeting with the buttons on the portable transceiver's face, he pushed the variable frequency operation and memory input and programmed an analog frequency of 146.52 into the A bank. He switched to the B bank and programmed 145.80.

He'd chosen the two frequencies because the first was a common calling frequency, especially in the United States and Canada. The second frequency was a common one they'd used during their seventy-two days in orbit. He hadn't checked a window to know where over Earth he was flying. It didn't really matter. Wherever he was, he'd have only a short window to connect and communicate. It was a literal shot in the dark.

Clayton said a prayer and keyed the transmit button. "Calling any station, anywhere. Calling any station, anywhere. This is Kilo Delta Five X-ray Mike X-ray on the International Space Station. I'm calling on one forty-six dot five two. Calling any station, anywhere. Please reply. Over."

He waited a moment and then switched to the other frequency and tried again. He was looking for anyone, anywhere in the world. One. Single. Person.

Clayton fiddled with the volume, hoping that would somehow help. He received no response. He tried again.

He alternated between the two channels, repeating his call. Each time he repeated the words, the desperation became more audible to anyone who might hear him.

"Calling any station, anywhere. Calling any station, anywhere. This is KD5XMX on the International Space Station."

Nothing.

Then…something.

At first it was a crackle-laced whisper, only a fragment of a word or phrase. Clayton couldn't make out what the person was saying. He couldn't even be sure it *was* a person.

He pressed the radio closer to his mouth and more quickly repeated his call. "Calling any station, anywhere. Calling any station, anywhere. This is KD5XMX on the International Space Station."

After a long moment, a single crystal-clear word came that almost made Clayton wish he'd heard nothing at all. It was a weak voice, maybe a child's, perhaps a young woman.

"Help."

CHAPTER 8

SATURDAY, JANUARY 25, 2020, 8:37 AM CST
CLEAR LAKE, TEXAS

The sunlight cascading into the bedroom woke Jackie. She squinted, blinked until her eyes adjusted, and sat up in bed. She hadn't slept much, and what little sleep she did get was pronged with a nagging worry. It was a dread that clouded her dreams.

Like so many moms, Jackie had lost her ability to sleep soundly once she'd had children. She was always on the edge of consciousness, listening for coughs or cries.

This was different. This was the uneasy sleep of a woman who knew sleep was a luxury and that whenever she awoke, she'd find herself living more of a nightmare than her subconscious could ever conjure. Her son was somewhere in North Texas. She had no idea whether or not he was okay. A nagging uneasiness dogged her every time she drifted toward sleep. She kept reaching for her phone on the bedside table, checking it to see if it worked. It didn't. Even the landlines were dead.

Jackie lay awake picturing Chris in the park. She imagined he'd slept buried in his sleeping bag. He called it his cocoon. He often asked to sleep in it at home, on his bed.

She trusted Rick. He wasn't the best husband, nobody would argue that. He was a good dad though, and Chris liked him. When Kenny had asked if Chris could go camping with him and his dad for the long weekend, she'd agreed. It would get her son's mind off his father's absence.

Clayton's adventure had been rough on all of them, but especially Chris. He missed his father. He needed his father. The video chats and emails weren't enough.

She hoped Chris wouldn't connect the problems on Earth with potential problems in orbit. There was too much to worry about. Just. Too. Much.

Her room reeked of stale smoke. Her stomach churned. The taste of vomit coated her tongue. She needed to shower, put on some fresh clothes, and brush her teeth. She'd feel a world better if she did those things before tackling whatever came next.

Marie was still asleep, a deep line of worry running vertically between her eyebrows. Her mouth was curved in a frown.

Jackie reached out toward Marie's shoulder but stopped and pulled her hand back, deciding to let her sleep. She planted her feet on the floor and walked to the bathroom.

She cranked on the shower but kept the water at a temperature not quite as hot as she'd like. Hot water was a commodity now.

She undressed, tossed her clothes into the hamper, and grabbed a towel from the linen closet. She caught a glimpse of herself in the mirror above her sink and stopped.

Jackie hardly recognized herself. She leaned in to the reflection, her attention drawn to the deep purplish circles that ran around her sunken eyes. There was a trio of deep creases running across the length of her brow. Her face was gray with smudges of soot accenting her cheeks.

It hadn't even been twelve hours and she looked as though she'd been struggling for weeks. She took a deep breath, filling her lungs, and exhaled. Her breath fogged the glass.

Her shower was quick, only long enough to wash away the grime of the previous night and give her a shot of much-needed energy.

She slipped into clean undergarments, which felt like heaven, and then found a well-worn long-sleeved Gators T-shirt and some yoga pants. She was going for comfort.

Jackie brushed her teeth and then the excess water from her hair. She looked again at the mirror. While she still looked exhausted, at least the grime was gone.

She crept out of the bedroom without waking Marie. Reggie and Candace were in the kitchen, eating breakfast. They'd made themselves at home.

"Morning," Jackie said. "How are you?"

Candace shrugged. Her eyes were puffy and red, her chin and forehead smudged with soot. Her mousy brown hair hung limply onto her shoulders.

Reggie scratched the gray stubble on his chin. "Okay, I guess," he answered between bites of an energy bar, "considering the circumstances."

Jackie pulled open the refrigerator. A soft blast of slightly cooler-than-room-temperature air blew onto her face. She grabbed a half-full gallon of milk and set it onto the countertop.

She found a glass and poured it full of milk. "Where's everyone else?"

"Sleeping, I think," Reggie answered. "Lana tossed and turned most of the night."

"You seen Betty or Brian?"

"Not yet."

Jackie turned to her new neighbor. "Candace?" she asked, drawing the woman's attention. "How are you?"

Candace's eyes glistened. Her lower lip and chin quivered. She buried her face in her hands and whimpered softly.

Jackie put down her glass and hurried to Candace. She wrapped her arms around the woman. Candace couldn't have been more than twenty-five. It was hard to tell. She was overweight. Not fat, but not thin either. That, combined with the stress etched into her tired face, made her appear older than Jackie thought her to be.

"I know," Jackie said, rubbing her hands on Candace's back. "You miss Chad. You did everything you could, Candace. You really did."

Candace gently pulled away and nodded. "I know." She sniffled. "I know. I can't get the image out of my mind. The sight of him there on the ground. Dead. We were going to get married, you know." Candace's voice warbled. "We'd picked out a ring and everything. He was going to propose on Valentine's Day in Cancun."

Jackie looked over at Reggie. His eyes were welling too.

"I'm not sure where I go from here," said Candace. "What do I do?" She looked Jackie in the eyes, searching for the answer.

Jackie tried to smile. "That's what we're going to figure out today. We're going to take stock and formulate a plan. Right, Reggie?"

Reggie cleared his throat and wiped his eyes with his knuckled fist. "Right," he said. "We'll figure out a plan. Together."

Candace smiled. The shift in her features pressed the tears from her eyes and down her cheeks. "Thank you."

Marie's voice broke the silence. "Morning." She trudged into the kitchen, her eyes still half shut with sleep.

"Morning," Jackie said. "I didn't expect you up so soon."

"I couldn't sleep," she said. "I want to go see the neighborhood." Her eyes widened as they adjusted to the light streaking in through the large kitchen windows.

"I don't know, I'm not sure we—"

"I think it's a good idea," Betty interrupted, walking down the stairs. Her right hand glided along the wrought-iron bannister, guiding her down the steps. "We shouldn't wallow inside. We should survey the neighborhood. Look for other survivors. Check the damage to our homes."

Jackie pressed her lips into a straight line. She resisted the urge to tell Betty to parent her own child and instead smiled. "Maybe you're right," she conceded. "It would be good. But first I think—"

"I think it should be the first thing we do," said Betty. "We need to see what's out there." Betty sidled up to the kitchen island and pressed her palms flat against it. Her gray hair was pulled back into a messy bun. She was wearing the same smoke-stained clothing from the night before.

Jackie's expression flattened, as did her tone. "We need an inventory," she stated purposefully. "We can't eat, drink, bathe, or do much of anything until we know how far our rations will go. We've got seven people in this house. Seven, Betty."

Betty rapped her fingers on the island, her false nails clicking rhythmically on the granite. "Well," she huffed, "I—"

"You're both right," Reggie interrupted. "We need an inventory, which I've started. And we *should* survey the neighborhood. We can do both at the same time."

Jackie eyed Betty from messy bun to bare feet. She'd never much cared for the woman but had always been neighborly. She knew Betty had her hands full. A single mother of a child with special needs was bound to have sharpened elbows.

While Jackie could bite her tongue at block parties or in passing on the jogging path, having the acerbic woman in her home was another matter. She took a deep breath and nodded in agreement with Reggie. When the others awoke, they'd split up into two teams. That would appease everyone.

Reggie shot Jackie another knowing glance. His lips were pursed, his brow knitted. Jackie figured he was thinking the same thing she was: It wouldn't be long before people were a bigger challenge than the lack of power.

SATURDAY, JANUARY 25, 2020 9:00 AM CST
CLEAR LAKE, TEXAS

The odor hit Jackie first. She couldn't place it, but it was awful. It was pungent and sour and made the hair stand on her neck.

She was standing at the end of her driveway, surveying what was left of the homes and the aircraft that crashed into them.

She tried breathing through her mouth in small sips. It didn't help. The overwhelming odor that choked the air only intensified as she stepped closer to the charred pile of wood and metal and fabric and bodies.

Bodies.

That was it. She smelled death. Amidst the sting of remnant smoke was the stench of burned flesh and hair.

"Nothing's left," Marie said. She was standing behind her mother. Somehow the two of them had convinced Betty it was best if she stayed home with Brian. She'd reluctantly acquiesced.

Jackie was doing her best not to gag. "Nothing," she whispered. Tears rolled from her eyes as she thought about the horror of the previous night. "Those poor people."

Marie tugged on her arm. "C'mon, Mom," she said, pulling her away from the carnage. "Let's go look around. We should find out what other people are doing."

Jackie followed her daughter up the street toward the circle that encompassed their neighborhood. When they reached the end of their street, Jackie's mind flashed to the night before. She'd cut the corner and run right to the other cul-de-sac, sprinting across the grass into what had resembled a war zone.

Marie stepped ahead of her mother and started walking backward. "You okay?"

Jackie offered her daughter as close to a smile as she could muster. "That's relative, isn't it?"

Marie shrugged and lowered her eyes, slowing to walk alongside Jackie. They turned right.

Jackie silently chastised herself. That wasn't the right answer to give her daughter, even if it was the truth. Marie needed a confident, strong mother. She draped her arm around Marie's shoulder. "I'm fine," she said. "We will all be okay. I was just thinking about the poor people who didn't survive last night."

A look of relief washed over Marie's features. Her eyes brightened; the corners of her mouth turned upward.

Jackie turned her attention to what lay before them. There were a dozen houses on the straightaway before the circle curved to the right. The driveways were littered with camping chairs, folding tables, and coolers. It looked like a block party. However, the faces of her neighbors weren't festive. They bore the wrinkles of concern and the frowns of worry. If they were standing, their shoulders were hunched. If seated, they were slouched, their chins against their chests.

It was a neighborhood defeated.

Jackie approached the first house on the left. Sitting side by side was an elderly couple, the Vickerses. They'd lived in the neighborhood longer than anyone. Pop Vickers, as everyone called him, was a retired NASA engineer. He'd worked on the *Mercury* and *Apollo* programs. Clayton loved talking to him about the space program's "glory days."

Pop waved. His wife, Nancy, smiled, almost. She was the shier of the two. Always polite, Nancy tended to keep her distance and let Pop flutter about as the social butterfly.

Jackie stopped at the end of their driveway and planted her hands on her hips. "How are you both doing? Can I do anything for you? Do you need anything?"

Groaning, Pop pushed himself from his chair and shuffled down the drive to Jackie and Marie. He was wearing a blue Adidas jogging suit and bright orange Crocs.

"I think we're okay," he said, his voice raspy with age. "We've got food and water. Thank goodness we didn't put in one of those tankless water heaters. You know they don't work if the power's out?"

Jackie smiled. "I didn't. I'm glad we didn't do it either, then."

Pop's wiry eyebrows arched high above his pale blue eyes. "You see the fireball last night?"

Jackie nodded. "I did. Very sad."

"I heard there were other crashes," said Pop. "Other planes, I mean. This wasn't the only one."

Jackie's heart quickened. "What do you mean?"

"You know I'm a HAM operator," he said, sticking out his white stubbled chin. "HAM radio. I keep it in my gun safe in the master bedroom. Whenever the power goes out or we get a hurricane coming this way, I play around with it."

"I think I knew that," Jackie said.

"So I was on it last night and again this morning," he said. "There was talk about other planes going down. People think this is one of those electromagnetic pulses you hear so much about nowadays. I don't think that's it, though."

"What do you think it—" Jackie cocked her head to one side. "Wait. Did you say your radio worked?"

Pop smiled proudly. "Yep. If it was an EMP or anything else that caused a power surge, the radio survived because it was in that safe."

"So if it wasn't an EMP, what was it? Some kind of storm?"

"There are all kinds of conspiracy theories floating around on the radio," Pop said. "Who knows? Everything from a legitimate terror attack, to government false flags, to the Chinese hacking our electrical grid. I don't buy any of those."

"What do you buy?"

"Space weather," he said. "Solar storm. That's why we had that aurora. It's red 'cause it's so far south."

Jackie heard the word "space" and her gut tightened. Her fear must have shown on her face, because Pop's eyes widened and he stuttered through a more comforting explanation.

"I-I'm sorry," he said. "S-sorry. That sounded crass. I know Clayton is up there." His eyes drifted to the sky as he kept talking. "Just so you know, the ISS does have protection against magnetic storms. Plus its life support and electrical systems have redundancies for their redundancies. I'm sure he's okay."

Jackie licked her lips. "Please keep me posted if you hear any more on the radio, okay?"

"I'm sure he's okay," said Pop, his voice straining. "Even if it's space weather, he'll be fine."

Jackie put her hands on Pop's shoulders and then pulled him to her for a hug. "I know," she said. "Clay is a survivor."

Pop's eyes glistened. She knew Pop didn't believe what he was saying. "I'll be back to check on you."

She led Marie away from the driveway and heard Nancy scold her husband for his lack of discretion.

"For a man who's supposed to be so smart," she said to Pop, "sometimes you're a total idiot."

Jackie took Marie's hand and led her further down the street and past the cul-de-sac that ran parallel to theirs. She looked to her right, taking it in as they walked by it. There was a yellowish haze that hung low in the air at the dead end. She could see the backpack still in the street. Jackie swallowed hard.

"Mom," Marie asked, letting go of her mother's hold, "was Mr. Vickers telling you the truth?"

"About what?"

"That Dad's okay."

Jackie nodded. "Yes."

Marie sucked in a deep breath. "I hope so."

"Jackie?" came a woman's voice from a driveway two houses ahead on the left. "Jackie Shepard, is that you?"

Standing at the end of her driveway was Rebecca Fulton, a fellow NASA spouse. Her husband, Mark, worked in Mission Control at Johnson Space Center.

Mission Control.

Jackie instantly picked up her pace to Rebecca's driveway. The two women met at the curb and embraced.

"Oh God," said Rebecca. "I saw the fire. The flames. Smoke. I didn't know…I should have… But I didn't. I'm so glad to see you."

"It's okay," said Jackie. "We're okay. We've got some others at our house. We'll be fine. You?"

Rebecca stepped back from Jackie. She folded her arms, hugging herself. She motioned to the window above the garage with her head. "The kids are upstairs," she said. "They're already going stir-crazy."

"What about Mark?"

"He's stuck at work, I guess," she said. "I haven't heard from him yet. He's got a long-range two-way radio with him he uses when he hunts. I've tried him on it. No answer. I'll keep trying. Mine's working. I pulled it out of an old Coleman aluminum cooler. It's about the only electronic thing that isn't dead. No other radio, no television, no phones, no news."

Jackie's eyes welled again, surprising her. She'd thought she was dry of tears. "If you do talk to him, and he mentions Clay..."

Rebecca's brow furrowed sympathetically. "Of course," she said. "The second I hear anything."

"Thanks," Jackie said. "It's hard not knowing..."

"Of course."

"I have half a mind to go up to JSC myself." She laughed.

Rebecca smiled. "I don't blame you. I'm worried about Mark and he's only a couple of miles away. I can only imagine..." Her eyes shifted toward the sky. "If that were my husband..."

It *wasn't* Rebecca's husband up there. It was Jackie's. She knew Rebecca couldn't imagine what it was like. Nobody could. Clayton was in space, one of fewer than six hundred people ever to leave Earth's atmosphere. She was one of fewer than six hundred spouses to watch their soul mates strap into a tube with an explosive device attached to it and rocket off the planet.

True, it wasn't like she was Alan Shepard's wife, Louise, or Neil Armstrong's first wife, Janet, or even Annie Glenn, John's wife. They were true pioneers in every sense of the word. They were badass women with adrenaline-junkie husbands. Still, Jackie was in an elite club and Rebecca had reminded her of her unique, unenviable situation.

While she appreciated Rebecca's kindness, she also wanted to scream at her and tell her that her husband being two miles away was in no way, shape, or form comparable to where Clayton was.

Jackie said goodbye to Rebecca and again took Marie's hand. "I've seen enough," she said. "We can go back to the house."

"We haven't walked the whole loop, Mom," Marie protested. "We haven't seen everything."

Jackie was flooded with a confluence of conflicting emotions she didn't like. She was worried, angry, afraid, resentful. Her husband had left her alone to cope with whatever madness had befallen them. She didn't like that last emotion. It came from nowhere and felt like acid in an empty stomach.

"We don't need to see everything, Marie," she snipped, looking at the helpless, vacant faces of the neighbors sulking with worry in their driveways and yards.

Jackie marched home with purpose. She had no real concept of how dire their situation might be even if she believed it to be life-altering. She was certain, though, walking around the block wouldn't change whatever the truth might be.

She needed to act as if the end of the world had happened and her husband was never coming home. That was a possibility with which she needed to cope, for which she needed to prepare. No more feeling sorry for herself. It was pointless.

There were a half dozen people in her home who would depend on her strength to weather the coming days. Her son would be home soon, she hoped. The people under her roof needed a leader. They needed someone who stopped worrying about what had happened or what might happen.

They needed a badass woman who was married to an adrenaline junkie. That was what they'd get.

She wasn't taking crap from Betty, and she wasn't deferring to Reggie. It was her house. *She* was in charge. She would lead her crew out of the rabbit hole.

Jackie marched down her street, Marie in tow, and neared her home. She took deep breaths in through her nostrils as she walked with long, purposeful strides. The dank, nauseating odor returned. The smell of death was as unmistakable as it was rancid.

Jackie closed her mouth, pressing her lips into a tight, straight line. Instead of trying to avoid the smell, however, she welcomed it. She took it in, recording it with her senses. It would make her tougher.

She could not avoid what lay in front of her. The more she accepted the reality as she believed it to be, the more prepared she was to survive it.

SATURDAY, JANUARY 25, 2020, 11:01 AM CST
CLEAR LAKE, TEXAS

The household, as it now stood, was gathered around the kitchen's granite island. Betty and Brian were seated on barstools; Reggie, Lana, Candace, and Marie were standing; Marie was leaning on her elbows, her cheeks smushed in her hands. Reggie was going through the lists of supplies, suggesting how they should ration food and water.

Jackie wasn't listening to the conversation. She was thinking about her son, Chris. She'd convinced herself he was safe. He was camping in a familiar place; he was with Rick Walsh, a capable man. Most importantly, he was earthbound.

The more she thought about him, though, the more an uneasy ache settled in her gut. After hearing others complain about their cars, she'd tried to start hers. It was dead.

If her car was fried and others in the neighborhood were too, how was Rick going to get Chris home? Were they stuck at the park with only a couple of days' worth of food?

She took a deep breath and tried to clear her mind. She couldn't be the leader she needed to be if she was focused on what she couldn't control.

"Jackie," said Reggie, waving his hand in front of her face. "Jackie?"

She blinked back to attention. "Sorry. I was just thinking."

"We need to talk about self-defense," Reggie said. "What is our plan?"

Betty grabbed hold of the conversation. "If we're talking about guns, I'm not comfortable with that. It's an accident waiting to happen. I've never been a fan of guns. Nope." She slammed her hands flat on the granite.

Brian was rocking in his seat. His arms were folded and he was picking at the dry skin on his elbows.

Jackie sighed. "I think we are talking about guns, Betty," she said. "I have my Concealed Handgun License. I've got a couple of handguns in the house. Reggie?"

"I've got a rifle and a revolver. They're in your garage, along with the ammo."

Betty pushed herself to her feet. The barstool squeaked along the floor as she stood. "I'm not okay with this. I don't like the idea of guns in the house. Not with my son here."

Jackie bit the inside of her cheek. "I understand your concer —"

"Do you?" Betty asked, her words dripping with derision. She planted her hands on her hips, her brows arched high above her eyes. "Do you really 'understand my concerns'?" She made air quotes with her hands.

Jackie clamped her teeth onto the other side of her cheek. There was no point in poking the bear yet.

Betty's face reddened. "You can't understand my concerns, Jackie," she said, her arms flailing. "You don't *have* a child like Brian. You aren't raising your kids *alone*. You didn't lose *your* house in a fire last night. *You* still have your granite countertops and stainless steel refrigerator. *You* still have window treatments and area rugs. You *can't* understand!"

Brian's rocking had intensified. "Six days, eight hours," he chanted, his eyes closed. "Six days, eight hours. Six days, eight hours."

Her anger immediately softened and Betty placed her hand on Brian's back. Tears streamed down her face. "What is it, Brian? Mom is sorry for upsetting you."

Brian kept his eyes closed but maintained the steady, even pace of his rocking. "Six days, eight hours."

Betty used a fingertip to swab the corners of her eyes. "What is? Tell Mom."

"Food and water," Brian said. "Food and water. Six days, eight hours."

Reggie stepped around the counter to Brian. "I calculated we have seven or eight days," he said. "I added the fresh food, canned food, and bottled water. I'm pretty sure we can last more than a week. If we conserve even more, we can go longer than that."

Brian shook his head. "Seven people," he said. "Seven people. Six days, eight hours."

Reggie's lips moved as he silently recalculated the numbers in his head. Then his eyes grew wide with the recognition he was wrong. "Wow, Brian, you're right. I only counted six people. I didn't account for Candace."

A strained smile brightened Brian's face. "Seven people. Seven people. Six days, eight hours."

"And when Chris comes home," Jackie said, "that's —"

"Five days, thirteen hours," Brian said. "Eight people, five days, thirteen hours."

Betty laughed through her tears. "Do you see?" she said to the group, her eyes dancing across the room from person to person. "Do you see? He's not like us. He doesn't process information the same way. I don't want guns in the same house as my son."

As a mother, Jackie couldn't imagine the difficulties Betty faced on a daily basis, let alone in the midst of a crisis. Betty was at the breaking point. She was fragile and needed handling with kid gloves.

Jackie braced herself, knowing that what she was about to say would infuriate Betty and might alienate her from the others. However, it had to be said. This was her house. No matter how unique Brian might be, she had to do what was best for the group.

"Betty," she said softly, "I cannot empathize with you or understand the difficulties you face every day. I don't pretend to know your life."

Betty bristled. "I sense a 'but' coming."

Jackie inhaled through her nostrils, taking a beat before dropping the hammer. She eyed Betty, holding the woman's sharp glare. "But this is my house."

Betty rolled her eyes. "Here we go. I knew this was coming."

Jackie maintained her gentle tone. "It's true, Betty. You are here at my invitation. I am happy to have all of you here as long as you need to stay. You have a place here. All of you. But you'll need to abide by my rules. If that's not okay with you, then we can find another place for you to go. I'd rather you not leave. That's your call."

The room was quiet for a moment. There was no immediate dissent. Betty was fidgeting with her fingernails. Brian was sitting still, picking at his elbows.

"I think that's fair," Reggie said, breaking the silence. "It's more than generous, really."

Lana nodded and echoed her husband's sentiments. Candace agreed.

"Don't look at me," Marie muttered. "I already live under her rules."

That elicited chuckles from everyone but Betty and Brian. Betty's face wore an exaggerated frown, the downward curve of her mouth etched into jowls.

Jackie stepped around to Betty, placing her hand on her neighbor's shoulder. "We're not engaging in a shoot-out in my living room," she said. "I don't want that either. I want to defend this house from outsiders who would…"

"Hurt us," said Reggie. "We don't want anyone hurting us."

Betty sucked in a deep breath and exhaled. "I don't have a choice. I really don't."

"Thank you, Betty," said Jackie, her hand still on Betty's shoulder. "I'm glad you're staying."

"We should really talk about the guns," said Reggie. "It's part of our plan. It may only be another day or two before people start getting desperate."

Lana shot Reggie a look. He'd opened the can of worms too quickly.

Betty pulled away from Jackie and rolled her eyes. "I need some air," she huffed and marched toward the front door. "I'm allowed outside, aren't I?" she asked without turning around.

Jackie didn't answer. There was no point.

Betty unlocked the door and swung it open. She shrieked and jumped back at the sight of Rebecca Fulton standing in the doorway, her hand poised and ready to knock. Betty brushed past her without saying anything and bounded out the door.

"Was it something I said?" Rebecca asked, peeking her head into the house.

Jackie noticed Rebecca had a radio in her hand. "No," she said and waved her into the house. "Please, come on in."

"I have some news," she said. "I heard from Mark."

Jackie's heart leapt. Her mouth went dry and she swallowed hard. "And?"

Rebecca held up the radio. "We only talked for a couple of minutes on the radio, so I only got basics."

Jackie's hands were trembling. "Okay," she said expectantly.

Rebecca took a deep breath and then unleashed what she knew. "He said MCC-H lost power. All of their primary systems went down." Her words were like boulders rolling downhill, accelerating as they spilled forward. "It was chaos in there for hours."

Jackie felt the energy sucked from her core. The conversation wasn't heading where she'd hoped, where she'd initially assumed it would go. The weight grew heavier on her chest. She found it difficult to breathe.

She managed a question through quick, controlled breaths. She was trying to keep her wits about her. "What are you saying, Rebecca?"

Rebecca held up her hands in defense. "I'm just telling you what happened. They lost power, but they have backup systems. Mark says its 'double-redundancy' or something like that."

"So the power's back on?"

Rebecca nodded. "Yes. They have all of their critical systems back up. They're working on communication."

The now familiar slug of nausea hit her stomach. "Working on it? What does that mean?"

"I don't know exactly," Rebecca said. "He can't talk about it. Especially on the radio. He did say they haven't talked with the ISS since the event."

"The event?"

"That's what he called it. I know I'm not bringing good news. But it's news. They are working to reestablish communication. That's the best I can do."

Jackie sighed. She flexed her fingers, trying to stop the trembling. "I know," she said. "I appreciate it."

She stepped to Rebecca and gave her neighbor a hug. It couldn't have been easy for the woman to come over with what was essentially bad news. It was kind of her.

Rebecca held onto Jackie and whispered in her ear, "He'll be fine, Jackie. He will. We're all praying for him, and the team is doing everything it can. Mark said that."

Jackie thanked her again. "If you need anything, let us know. We're here." She led Rebecca back to the door and saw her out. She looked to the street and saw Betty standing in the middle of it, staring at what little was left of her house. "I'll be right back," she said to Marie.

Jackie was struggling. She was flexing her will, exuding strength and leadership. She was also crumbling inside. Her thirteen-year-old son was somewhere in North Texas and possibly unable to get home, and she now definitely knew her husband was incommunicado. Nobody on Earth, not a single person, knew if he and the two other men with him were dead or alive.

She didn't even know for certain what "the event" was. She suspected Pop Vickers down the street was right. It was a solar storm. Space weather.

Jackie swallowed past the thought and balled her hands into fists. If she was going to keep it together, she'd have to focus not on her needs, but those of others. The people in her house, every one of them, had to see her attending to them. If they believed she had their best interests in mind, that she would do anything for them, they would do anything for her when the time came.

She stepped from her driveway and into the street, sidling silently up beside Betty. Betty was crying softly. Jackie could hear the ragged breaths that came with loss. She resisted the urge to put her arm around the woman or offer her any physical comfort, not wanting Betty to sense her own fear.

She stood next to Betty for more than a half hour. The two of them surveyed the smoldering char together but alone. When Jackie sensed the moment was right, and she'd managed to control her own emotions, she reached out for Betty's hand. Betty took it and the two women walked back to the house.

It was time to move forward.

CHAPTER 9

SATURDAY, JANUARY 25, 2020, 12:05 PM CST
HIGHWAY 67, RAINBOW, TEXAS

They hadn't moved much in twenty minutes. Rick had meticulously maneuvered the Jeep past the initial pileups only to find himself stuck on Highway 67 at the Brazos River. The bridge over the river was bifurcated. The eastbound lanes were narrow and blocked by half of a mobile home set atop the bed of a tractor trailer. The westbound lanes were narrow too and were obstructed by a three-car pileup halfway along the span. There was no going around the river and he'd worked too hard to risk backtracking west.

There was a cluster of seven cottages on the north side of the highway. The longer they sat in the cramped Jeep, the more inviting they looked with their bright green roofs and taupe siding. The rental cabins faced each other in a large circle on a sloping green hill that rolled gently to the river's edge. Rick imagined they had soft, comfortable mattresses and kitchenettes stocked with snack food and hot coffee.

"How long are we going to wait?" asked Nikki. "We can sit here waiting for the earth to spin, or we could make something happen."

Rick unhooked his seatbelt and shifted his weight to look back at her. "I already went up there once," he said, pointing at the mobile home. "There's no moving that thing."

"You didn't really look. You checked it, made a snap decision, and came back here," she countered. "I'm tempted to cross the river on foot. We're sitting ducks in this Jeep. Somebody is eventually going to—"

"We have kids in the car," said Rick, shooting daggers at her.

Kenny was asleep, his head awkwardly leaning against the window behind Rick's seat. Chris was awake.

"What does that mean?" Chris asked, his eyes wide with fear.

Rick sighed. There was no point in lying to him. "Nikki thinks we shouldn't be sitting here. She thinks it'll attract bad people."

Chris swiveled his head in both directions, looking for bad people. "Is she right?"

"Maybe," Rick acknowledged. "Let's go check again and see if we can find a way around that mobile home."

Chris's eyes lit up and he reached for the door handle without waiting for an answer.

Rick looked at Mumphrey and then back at Nikki. "You wanna come?"

Nikki nodded. "Yep."

"Sure thing," said Mumphrey. "Always happy to help."

"Let's all go, then," said Rick. He woke up his son, who groggily joined the others outside the locked Jeep. He retrieved the handgun from the glove box, tucked it in his waistband underneath his shirt, and climbed out of the Jeep, stuffing the keys in his pocket.

They trudged up the bridge. It was eerily quiet. The trees bordering the highway were still. The skies were empty. No clouds, no airplanes, no birds. It reminded him of the days after 9/11, when he was in college. This was different though.

The enemy was unseen. In fact, they didn't really know what had happened. Some fanatics thought the biblical end of days was upon them. He was of the opinion that an electrical charge had killed just about everything. His Jeep survived because it didn't have any computers. Who'd have thought having an old-fashioned distributor instead of electronic ignition would be a lifesaver? It was EMP-proof.

They walked between the white concrete rail and the outer edge of the wide road. Rick dragged his hand along the thick Visqueen sheeting that covered the open half of the mobile home. They reached the cab of the red Kenworth truck hauling the half-home. Rick knocked on the door. Nobody answered, so he knocked again.

"Hang on," a voice grumbled from inside the cab. "Hang on."

Rick stepped back. "Guess somebody's there."

A young man with at least a week's worth of patchy scruff appeared at the window. His hair was short but matted on one side. He had a long red crease down the right side of his face as evidence Rick had awoken him. The man knuckled the corner of his eye and blinked a couple of times before cracking the window.

"What do you want?" he said through a yawn and a thick East Texas drawl.

Rick motioned to the trailer. "You're blocking the road, so—"

The man scratched his chin and laughed. "Really?" He slapped his cheeks with his hands and opened his mouth to feign surprise. "I had no idea. Thanks so much for letting me know."

Rick clenched his jaw but smiled through it. He needed the man's help. "You're welcome. Now that you know about your truck, you think there's any way we could help you move it?"

The man ran a hand through his hair and eyeballed the group, his gaze lingering uncomfortably on Nikki. He kept his eyes there, licked his lips, and addressed Rick. "I don't think so," he said, a crooked smile worming across his face. He winked at Nikki. "Looks to me like you can just keep walking. I'll be happy to watch you from behind as you leave."

"We're not walking," Nikki said. "We're driving."

The man rolled down his window halfway and then leaned on it with one arm. "That so?"

"Yep."

"You got a hitch or something?" asked Mumphrey. "Maybe a winch even? I was thinking, if you did, we could disconnect the —"

"Hold up there, old man," said the man. "You're not commandeering my rig here. I mean, unless the lady here —"

A hand appeared from behind the man's head and slapped it. Then it popped him again.

The man grabbed the side of his head and turned back into the cab. "Dad," he whined, "I was just having fun."

An older man, a vision of how the younger one would look in twenty-five years, appeared at the window. He wore a sweat-stained, tan-colored Stetson and a white ribbed tank top.

"I apologize for the boy," he said. "He's a moron. I mean, straight-up idiot. I think I dropped him on his head one too many times as a toddler."

The younger man rolled his eyes. His demeanor had changed in an instant. His shoulders drooped, as did his head, and the crooked sneer was gone.

The older man shoved his way past his son and climbed out of the cab. He hopped from the step to the ground and offered his hand to Rick.

"I'm Frank," he said. "That's Junior the Moron up there."

Rick shook Frank's hand. "Rick."

"So you got a truck that's working?"

"A Jeep."

"It's the darndest thing," said Frank. "We were plugging along, Junior at the wheel, and the engine up and quits." He snapped his fingers. "Just like that."

"Dangerous," Rick said. "Glad we weren't on the road at the time."

"We're lucky we didn't wreck," said Frank, motioning across to the westbound lanes to the three-car collision. "Like them cars over there."

"You think you can help us?" Rick asked.

The man tilted the Stetson back on his head and rubbed his forehead. "I don't know. I'd like to help. But this Kenworth here is eighteen thousand pounds. We're pulling another thirty thousand. Ain't no moving that with a Jeep even if we had a winch and the right hitch."

Rick looked again at the three-car pileup. From this perspective he could see the wreck better than before. None of the cars were that big. None of them looked to be totaled.

"What do you think about moving those cars?" he asked Frank.

"Possible, I guess," he said. "Slip them into neutral. Move 'em a bit. You might creep by. I'll get Junior to help you out. We'll meet you over there."

Rick smiled. "Thanks, Frank. I appreciate it."

Frank climbed back up onto the cab step and started arguing with his son. Rick waved the group to follow him back down the bridge toward the Jeep.

"So what exactly are we doing?" asked Nikki. Her tone told Rick she knew the answer but didn't agree with it.

"We're going to try to move those cars over there," said Rick. "I think if we can move even two of them out of the way, we can make it across the river."

Mumphrey tripped on his cuffs and yanked up his pants after regaining his balance. "I think it's a good idea. Sure beats trying to move that mobile home. Like he said, that was too heavy even with a winch. I thought maybe—"

"Maybe it's a good idea," said Nikki. "But I feel like we woke a sleeping bear back there."

"How so?" Rick asked.

"A feeling," she said. "Junior didn't learn to be jerk from a saintly father, that's all I'm saying. We'd have been better off checking out the other side alone and letting those two sleep."

The boys marched quietly alongside the adults. Both of them had the looks of teenagers headed home with a bad report card. Kenny had his hands stuffed deep into his pockets and was chewing on his lower lip. Rick veered toward his son and planted his open hand on top of the boy's head. "You okay?"

Kenny looked up at his dad. He nodded, but his eyes were wide with worry, searching for reassurance.

Rick smiled, hoping to ease his son's concern. "You're doing great," Rick said. "I know it's scary. I'll get you home to Mom. I promise."

Kenny's chin trembled, but he managed to smile back. "I know." He blinked back tears and looked down at his feet.

Rick wondered if Nikki was right. Maybe he'd created more of a problem by asking for help. "Nikki," he said. "You take the boys in the Jeep. Drive west a block or two, cross over to the westbound lanes before the road splits, then drive up to the wreck. You mind doing that?"

"I can do that."

"Dad," Kenny said, "I wanna go with you."

"It's better if you're in the Jeep," Rick said. "You ride shotgun next to Nikki. Chris can ride in the back. Meet us up on the bridge."

Kenny grunted his disapproval but didn't argue. Nikki and the boys kept walking to the Jeep while Rick and Mumphrey headed north toward the cabins.

"Those cabins look nice," said Rick, trying to ease the tension.

"I was gonna say that," said Mumphrey. "I always pass them on my way to the park and I wonder what it'd be like to rent one. I've been coming to Dinosaur Valley for years. With the pop-up to lay my head, it never made sense, you know?"

Rick nodded. "This whole thing is crazy, isn't it?"

"It is," Mumphrey said. "We're only getting a taste of it here. I can't imagine what it's like in the cities."

Rick didn't want to think about it. He was worried enough about getting back on the road and delivering the boys to their mothers. The idea of metropolitan chaos was more than he could handle.

The men slogged along the bridge until they reached the wreck. It looked as if a Chevy pickup had veered into a Mercedes C280. The 280 then hit the guardrail on the inside lane before a Honda Accord slammed into it from behind.

Rick checked each of the vehicles. They were all empty. The Chevy's driver's side door was open.

"So weird," he said. "Nobody's here. Everything's empty."

Mumphrey peeked over his glasses at the Chevy. "My guess is people headed back to the hotels in Glen Rose outside the park. That's what I'd do. I mean, if I didn't have the pop-up."

"Good point," Rick said. "There were a fair number of people hanging out in the hotel parking lots."

"I think if you put the truck into neutral, you'll be good," said Frank. He was approaching quickly from the west, Junior at his heels. "Junior can help me push it backward."

Rick surveyed the wreck and nodded. "I think you're right. Once we move the truck back, we might be able to slide the Honda forward."

"Then we can move the Mercedes," Mumphrey added. "It's like a puzzle. We move one piece and then the other."

Junior gave Mumphrey a disapproving glare as he walked past him and planted his hands on the hood of the Chevy. He snorted and spat onto the highway.

"You gonna put her in neutral?" he asked Rick. "Or you just gonna watch me stand here?"

Rick climbed into the Chevy without responding to Junior and yanked the door shut. The truck had a manual transmission, making the job even easier. Rick put his right foot on the brake and engaged the clutch with his left. He freed the emergency brake and eased his foot off the brake. With the truck already in neutral, it was free to move.

Frank joined Junior at the front of the truck and they started pushing. Rick kept his left hand on the wheel and braced his right against the passenger-seat headrest, turning to look over his right shoulder. He guided the truck back, cringing when it ground against the side of the Honda. Mumphrey was behind him, guiding him like an air traffic controller.

Once Mumphrey held up his hands, Rick pressed on the brake, released the clutch and reengaged the emergency brake. One down, two to go.

They repeated the process with both cars, disentangling them from one another, until they'd cleared enough of a path in the left lane for the Jeep to pull through. Nikki and the boys parked the Jeep a few yards back and joined Mumphrey on the bridge next to the cars.

Rick hopped out of the Mercedes and walked over to Frank. "I don't know how to thank you," he said. "You're a lifesaver."

Frank took Rick's hand and shook it more firmly than he had before. "I wouldn't go that far."

Rick tried to pull free of Frank's grip, but the man wouldn't let go. He held Frank's hand, tightening his grip. His eyes went cold, his expression dark.

Rick jerked free of the handshake. "What are you doing?"

"We're gonna have to take that Jeep."

Rick pulled the TP9 from his waist and aimed it at Frank. His hand wasn't trembling this time. "I don't think so."

Frank eyed the gun and then looked past Rick. He winked.

"Dad!" Kenny's voice cracked with fear.

Rick swiveled to see Junior standing behind Nikki. He had one arm tight across her chest, his hand wrapped around her side. He was holding a knife to her throat with the other hand, his face close to hers. The reptilian smile had slithered its way back onto to his face.

"I'd put down that gun," said Frank, tilting the brim of the Stetson over his eyes. "Otherwise people are gonna get hurt."

Rick backed up, taking quick short steps so he could widen his field of vision between Frank and Junior. He held the gun's barrel even with Frank's chest.

"Boys," he said, "run over to Mr. Mumphrey."

"Do it slow, boys," Frank counseled. "Do it slow."

The boys walked toward Mumphrey. The old man put his hands around their shoulders when they reached him. Both teens were pale. Kenny was taking deep breaths in and out through his flaring nostrils. Chris couldn't peel his eyes from Rick and the TP9 in his hand.

Junior tightened his grip around Nikki, who remained silent and whose face gave away nothing. "You didn't think we were good Sumatrans for nothing, did you? If you did, you're bigger idiots than I thought."

"It's Samaritans, Junior," corrected Frank. "You're the idiot, boy."

Rick weighed his options, playing out scenarios as quickly as his cluttered mind could calculate them. If he shot Frank, Junior would kill Nikki. If he shot Junior, he'd have to be a crack shot or risk hitting Nikki. He kept working to find different solutions. None of them ended well. He even considered shooting the front tires of the Jeep. That, though, would leave everyone stranded and anger Frank and Junior.

He looked over at the boys. He had no choice but to put away the gun and let the men steal their only way home.

"All right," he said, lowering the weapon to his side. "Take the Jeep. Let her go."

"You gotta put down the gun," said Frank, "and you gotta do it slowly. Nothing fast or jerky. Otherwise, Junior cuts the lady's throat and it would be on you. Your fault. You understand?"

Rick leaned over to lay the gun at his feet. As he was about to place the weapon on the highway, he heard Nikki talking.

"Okay," she said. "Okay, Junior. Just hang on."

She was raising her right hand above her head as though she were surrendering.

"You're hurting my back," she said. "Can you ease up a bit?"

That was when she struck.

Nikki grabbed across his wrist with her right hand, rolled his knife hand down across her chest, and pinned it there with surprising speed. She then raised her right arm even higher and moved her fingers across his face, blocking his view.

Junior grunted a curse. He'd already lost his advantage.

Nikki opened her mouth wide, then bit down viciously into Junior's forearm. He cried out in pain with a high-pitched squeal that sent a chill along Rick's spine.

She tore at his flesh with her teeth until he released his grip, at which point she spun inward and underneath his blood-soaked arm and leveraged her motion to reverse the hold. She now had her right arm around his neck and the knife pinned behind his back.

Junior's eyes widened and his jaw dropped open. Instead of a grunt or a wail, the sound coming from Junior's mouth sounded like air leaking from a balloon. His wide eyes blinked rapidly and he dropped to his knees. His knife hand was crippled and his arm hung oddly from the elbow.

Standing there with the knife in her hand, Nikki picked up her foot and kicked her heel into the back of Junior's head. He dropped forward onto the highway with a sickening crack.

Rick hadn't let go of the TP9. Still crouched low, he spun to retrain the weapon at a dumfounded Frank. The man was speechless. His mouth was moving, but he wasn't talking.

Nikki had moved so swiftly, so surprisingly fast, everyone stood silently for a prolonged beat. She stepped over the dying man and marched defiantly toward Frank.

"Give me the gun," she said to Rick. He handed it to her without question. She leveled it at Frank's face and moved to within a couple feet of him.

Tears streaked down his sallow face, his lips trembled, and his feet seemed cemented where he stood. He was in shock.

"Give me the hat," she said to Frank. "Now."

Frank was frozen.

Nikki closed the distance, pressed the gun against his cheek right under his rapidly blinking eye, and pulled the hat from Frank's head. She flipped it over and put it on.

Frank swallowed hard. "Is Junior dead?" he asked sheepishly, his voice barely above a whisper.

"No."

Nikki backed away from Frank, the gun steady in her hand. She was fearless. She walked up to Rick and handed him the weapon.

"Here you go," she said.

Rick studied her emotionless gaze. Mesmerized, he blankly took the TP9. She spun the knife, folding it over into the bolster with one hand, then offered it as well.

Rick shoved the knife into his pocket and the two of them started walking back to the boys. They were nearly there when a loud, guttural roar from behind shook him. He turned back in time to see Frank running at them. His face was twisted into an angry red mess of teeth and bulging eyes. A deep purple vein strained across his forehead. His hands were outstretched like talons as he pounded the highway.

Rick raised the TP9, but knew he wouldn't be able to get off a shot in time. Frank lunged at him. Rick pulled the trigger and a shot ricocheted with a snap off the pavement.

Frank grabbed at Rick's gun hand, but as he did, Nikki had somehow turned, dropped to the ground in front of Rick, and forcefully punched her fist into Frank's groin. Like a pneumatic drill she repeated the jab three or four times, vocalizing a loud grunt with each powerful release.

Frank's momentum was stalled with that first punch. The following blows doubled him over before he fell to the ground, curling reflexively into a fetal position, gagging and coughing.

Nikki looked up at Rick. "That oughta do it. Let's get out of here."

Rick held out his free hand and helped her to her feet. He leaned over and whispered in her ear, "That was the sexiest thing I have ever seen in my life."

She smirked and tipped the hat. "Thanks. Told you I could handle myself."

Mumphrey had already led the boys back to the Jeep and was sitting in the backseat with them.

"You can be in the front," Nikki said.

"You earned it," Mumphrey said in admiration. "I ain't never seen anything like that."

Rick put the TP9 back in the glove box, started the engine, and rolled past the two injured men in the street. He eased past the wreck and pressed the accelerator. There was a clear path across the river and closer to the interstate.

The boys sat in the backseat quietly. Both looked haggard. They'd seen things in the last couple of hours no child should see.

"We're getting you home, boys," Rick said. "Don't worry. We'll be okay."

Rick couldn't tell whether they believed him or not. He wasn't sure if he even believed himself. They were only a few miles from the park and already they'd survived two life-threatening situations. It was surreal. How could people have grown so desperate in a matter of hours? What would happen if the power was out for good?

He shook off the thought. He couldn't let his mind wander. It didn't do anybody any good.

He looked over at Nikki. "Where'd you learn that?"

She shrugged. "My dad was a cop. He made me take self-defense classes."

"That was more than a self-defense class. That was…"

Mumphrey leaned forward. "Incredible. Like I said, I ain't never seen anything like that."

"Agreed," said Rick. "It was like you were a pro or something."

Kenny snapped his fingers. "Wait a minute. I *do* know you."

Nikki shook her head. "I'm sure you—"

Kenny's face lit up with recognition. "You're Deep Six Nikki!"

Rick pressed on the accelerator, speeding past a pair of stalled cars. "Deep what?"

"Deep Six Nikki," said Kenny, his voice energized with the excitement of a new discovery. "She's one of the best MMA fighters in the world!"

Rick glanced over at Nikki, who was avoiding his eyes. "MMA as in mixed martial arts? Like the WWE?"

"That's wrestling, Dad," said Kenny. "MMA is like kickboxing but better. It's UFC, actually. Deep Six Nikki is famous for her sleeper hold. She calls it the 'Shut Off Valve.' If my phone worked, I'd show it to you on YouTube."

Nikki fidgeted in her seat and adjusted the shoulder strap on her seatbelt. She looked out the window.

Rick thumped her on the thigh with the back of his hand. "Is that true? Are you Deep Six Nikki?"

"Yes."

Nikki's glare dared him to laugh or chuckle or make any sort of joke about her alter ego.

"That's amazing," he said with a tone he hoped conveyed the sincerity with which he meant it. "It's like you're a superhero or something."

She ignored him.

Rick's eyes moved between the road ahead and Nikki. "Seriously," he said. "All superheroes have hidden identities. I'm not joking."

"It sounds like a joke."

"Sensitive?"

She shrugged.

"It's cool," said Kenny. "So cool. Can I have your autograph?"

Nikki's cheeks flushed. She half turned to face Kenny. "I don't have a pen or any paper. Later maybe, okay?"

"Nikki Six," said Rick. "I like it."

She playfully punched his shoulder. "Shut up and drive."

CHAPTER 10

MISSION ELAPSED TIME:
72 DAYS, 13 HOURS, 59 MINUTES, 58 SECONDS
249 MILES ABOVE EARTH

Help? The person on the other end of the radio needed help? A jolt of anxiety rippled through Clayton.

"This is KD5XMX on the International Space Station on one forty-six dot five two," he said. "I am monitoring. What is your QTH?"

There was a crackle. The voice returned. Clayton was certain it was a woman this time. She had an accent he couldn't quite place.

"Help, please," she said. "We're trapped."

The crackle returned and Clayton knew he wasn't talking to someone who was a HAM. She didn't understand "QTH" or the other HAM shorthand. Clayton knew he had no more than ten minutes. The radio pass was short because of Earth's curve. The ISS was moving too fast to keep the connection any longer than that.

Foregoing his training, he said, "My name is Clayton Shepard. I am an astronaut on the International Space Station. Who is this? Where are you? Over."

A pause.

"Astronaut? In outer space?"

"Yes. But close to Earth."

"You can't help us. Power is not work — "

"Where are you?" Clayton asked. "What is your name?"

"Calcut — " said the woman, her transmission stopping short.

"Calcutta?" Clayton asked. "Are you in Calcutta?"

There was no response.

"Are you in Calcutta?"

Clayton swore and turned his chin to ease the stiffness in his sore neck. The tension radiated from his shoulders. He yawned to release the pressure in his ears.

He keyed the radio again. "This is KD5XMX clear with unknown transmission with Calcutta. Any other stations monitoring please call now. Over."

He switched frequencies. No response. Clayton pinched his nose and popped his ears again.

"This is KD5XMX," he said wearily. He was ready to give up and fly blind. The brief but bothersome communication with Calcutta had both raised his hopes and elevated his concerns for what lie below.

The power was out, people were stuck in something or on something, and whoever's radio it was, they clearly weren't able to operate it. None of it was good news.

Clayton was about to switch frequencies again when the radio crackled.

"This is KH6XZ," said a deep male voice through the static. "I hear you, KD5XMX. What is your QTH? Over."

Clayton thumbed the radio. "This is KD5XMX. I'm aboard the International Space Station. You? Over."

The response was immediate. "This is KH6XZ. Did you say the International Space Station? I'm in Honolulu. Over."

Clayton smiled. "This is KD5XMX. That is affirmative, KH6XZ. My name is Clayton Shepard. I am alone aboard the ISS. Please provide your situation. Do you have power? Over?"

There was a long silence before the man returned. "This is KH6XZ. Not sure I believe you. Can you prove it? Over?"

Clayton's smile evaporated. Prove it?

He opened his mouth to clear the pressure that had again built in his ears. He was beginning to feel pressure around his eyes.

"This is KD5XMX," he said. "Check QRZ.com and input my call sign. You'll see it was registered six months ago. I have a tech license. The address is NASA, Johnson Space Center, Houston. Also, if the ISS radio was working, the call sign would be NA1SS. Over."

Another pause. "This is KH6XZ. I can't check. No Internet. No electricity. No transportation. Something happened here. It's nighttime. Everything is pitch black. No cars on the roads. No parties. How is it where you are? Over."

That was a complicated question with an even more complicated answer. "This is KD5XMX. I'm alive and working on a plan to get back to Earth."

"This is KH6XZ," said Honolulu. "What happened? Why did the power go out? When is it coming back?" The signal crackled.

Clayton paused with the radio in his hand. "This is KD5XMX," he said. "It was a solar storm. A big one. I don't know when the power's coming back."

"This is Kilo Hotel," the radio crackled. *"When – I – this – "*

Clayton started to respond, then decided better of it. Honolulu couldn't hear him. He opened his mouth wide to release the pressure building again in his ears.

"Wait," he mumbled, clearing his ears. "That's not right."

Clayton pressed his fingers to his sinuses beneath his eyes. There was pressure building again.

A rush of panic leapt through him. He disconnected the radio from the antenna and pushed himself free. He needed to get back to the service module. There was a leak. Somewhere on the station, a seal was leaking. The pressure was dropping. It could kill him.

"Where's the alarm?" he mumbled. "There should be an alarm."

Clayton knew the intermodule ventilation would shut down if there was a leak. That hadn't happened, which meant the automatic response system wasn't functioning as it should.

The Caution & Warning system should have produced an emergency alarm for a depress, or rapid depressurization. It was a repeating beep that would have appeared on the laptops. Clayton hadn't heard it.

"The computers," he said, pushing himself frantically through the ISS, maneuvering as quickly as he could in the microgravity environment of low Earth orbit. The CME must have damaged components he couldn't immediately determine by checking the basic systems in Node 1 or giving the Zvezda a cursory check. He hadn't taken the time to do a thorough systems analysis as he should have.

"Stupid, Clayton," he muttered breathlessly. "It ain't brain surgery. You lazy, single-minded..."

He stopped the verbal self-flagellation as he neared the Zvezda. He remembered distinctly from their safety training that protocol instructed he close, but not lock, hatches manually and head straight for the Soyuz until he could be sure there wasn't a catastrophic failure. That was the smart thing to do.

He wasn't going to do that.

Clayton wasn't going to launch without Ben and Boris. It wasn't going to happen. He couldn't leave their bodies behind. Something deep in his psyche compelled him to take them back to Earth. There was no negotiating that in his mind. He'd already risked his life once to save them. He would do it again to bring comfort to their families and honor the sacrifice both men had made.

Instead of doing what he was trained to do, he decided without pause to do what conscience demanded of him. He needed to find the leak and stop it. He prayed he had enough time as the pressure built again in his ears. Clayton knew what would happen if he couldn't find and isolate, or fix, the leak. He'd die. It wouldn't be pretty.

"Under pressure," he hummed. "Under pressure."

He'd always liked Queen. He liked David Bowie too. It seemed appropriate to offer his best version of their collaboration as he tried manipulating the computer in the Zvezda. Plus, he was trying to maintain his sanity. He felt like the little Dutch boy who kept sticking his finger in a leaking dyke.

He yawned to alleviate the relentless pressure building in his ears and sinuses.

"How Vanilla Ice ever thought he could get away with copying the beat," he said aloud, "is beyond me. But the dude knew what he was doing, I guess. Was he Canadian?"

He mouthed the unmistakable syncopated beat of the tune and found the data, which brought him back to the moment. The ISS software was designed to trigger Caution & Warning alarms if the pressure dropped too low. They hadn't worked, so Clayton was manually searching the data to learn what he could.

He knew that as the pressure slipped lower and lower, he'd be closer to unconsciousness. At fifty percent of the needed pressure, he'd start experiencing hypoxia.

He'd get confused, which he feared was already happening, as his mind floated from the merits of rock and roll to saving his life. His skin would change color. He'd cough. His heart rate would increase and so would his breathing. He'd sweat. He'd wheeze.

At fifteen percent, he'd have about ten seconds before he lost consciousness. Then it was over. His blood would essentially freeze and his organs would expand.

Clayton's mind flashed to Schwarzenegger's disgusting scene in *Total Recall*. He looked at his hand. It wasn't a normal flesh color, having faded to a bluish gray.

"I look like a Smurf," he said, poking at his skin. "A Smurf running out of time."

Under normal circumstances, the protocol was definitive. He'd stick to it as close as he could without abandoning Ben and Boris. First and foremost he needed to know how much time he had left, how long he could cheat death again.

The Reserve Time, also known as Tres, was the time left before the station reached its minimum habitable pressure. If the ISS hit that number, he'd have to evacuate. The reserve time populated on a device called a manuvacuumeter.

Clayton cursed the display and thumped it with his finger, hoping the readout was wrong. He had twenty-two minutes.

Twenty-two minutes. Thirteen hundred twenty seconds. Shorter than an episode of *Family Guy* without the commercials. Less time than it took to bake a pizza. He could listen to "Under Pressure" five times. During the sixth play, he'd be dead.

"Better than nothing, I guess," he said, popping his ears again. If the leak was coming from the Soyuz, that was a problem. Regardless, twenty-two minutes would evaporate before he knew it.

Clayton hurriedly pushed himself from the display, which he hoped was providing accurate information, and moved to the opposite end of the module. Strapped against the wall with Velcro was a white Nomex cargo transfer bag. He pulled the bag from the wall and carried it with him to the Soyuz.

The bag contained an ultrasonic leak detector. Once he found the leaking module, he could use the detector to better find the exact location before using an O-ring, self-adhering patch to stop the leak.

He reached the Soyuz, drew himself into the orbital module, and let go of the bag. He positioned himself behind the hatch and shoved it closed.

Floating in the module, he pinched his nose to even the pressure in his ears. If the pressure returned, he'd know the leak was in the Soyuz.

He closed his eyes and started humming again. "Under pressure," he mumbled. He floated there in the module, his hands pressed against the hatch. Waiting.

Thirty seconds. A minute.

Clayton exhaled. He was good. No leak in the Soyuz.

Still, he was losing time. Less than twenty minutes. Maybe eighteen.

Fighting the building panic, he opened the hatch and moved back into the ISS. The next step was isolating the modules. He needed to know if the leak was coming from the Russian or US side of the station. The pressure immediately built in his ears. He could feel it behind his eyes.

He flew to Zvezda and stopped his momentum at the monitor. His eyes scanned the data. Fourteen minutes. The pressure was dropping fast.

"Fourteen?" He coughed. "Mother—"

Clayton's vision was blurring. He started the wrong way before turning around to find his way to the American side of the ISS.

Toting the case, he pushed himself toward the spot where the American and Russian modules joined. He stayed on the Russian side, let go of the case, and closed the hatch joining the two sides. He coughed again.

He released the pressure in his ears and waited. He was having trouble breathing. His heart pulsed against his neck. His chest felt heavy.

If the pressure returned, he'd know the leak was in the Russian side and he'd have to isolate it and fix it in whatever little time he had remaining. An increasingly unlikely possibility.

If it was on the American side, he could isolate the modules by keeping the hatch closed.

He cleared his ears one more time for good measure.

Ten seconds. Thirty. One minute.

His ears were good. He gleefully pounded on the hatch with his fist.

"Thank you, Torricelli," he said, referring to the seventeenth-century Italian scientist who discovered vacuum and invented the barometer. His work, along with Galileo's, was critical to understanding air pressure.

Clayton checked the hatch, making certain he'd secured it. He spun and pushed off the hatch with his feet, propelling himself back toward the Zvezda. He centered himself at the display. The pressure was steady. The timer was frozen at eleven minutes.

"Plenty of time," he said. "No problem."

Still, he was short of breath. His vision was better, but not clearly focused.

He blinked rapidly. It didn't help.

Then he felt it.

The pressure. It was building again in his ears and beneath his eyes.

He looked at the monitor, nosing closer to the display. It was stalled at eleven minutes. The pressure indicator wasn't moving.

He popped his ears. Immediately the thickness returned. He hadn't fixed it. The leak was in the Russian module.

He was running out of time to find it and fix it.

He took a bungee strap from the wall and looped it through the case's handle. Then he found the patch kit next to the spot on the wall where he'd found the ultrasonic case.

He pulled the strap through the handle of the patch kit and then wound the bungee around his waist like a belt. He pulled it taut and ushered himself back to the airlock.

Clayton didn't know how much time he had. He needed to get his crewmates into the Soyuz.

He pulled Boris first, clumsily dragging him through the module until he carefully maneuvered the Russian's body through the orbital capsule and into the crew capsule. The cases strapped at his waist kept Clayton from fully entering the crew capsule. He left Boris in there floating; he'd strap him in later.

His heart beat against his chest, hard and fast enough that Clayton thought he could hear it behind the expanding wall of pressure in his ears. He tried breathing evenly, but it was nearly impossible. He quickly floated back to the airlock to retrieve Ben's body.

He pulled his friend from the airlock and then spun to move the short distance to the Soyuz. He was pushing Ben from behind, moving his body closer to the Soyuz and a trip home. As he neared the hatch, he stopped moving. There was something tugging at him and drawing him backward.

Clayton looked over his shoulder and saw the patch case was caught against a module wall. He popped his ears and tried focusing on the bungee. He didn't have time to go back and free the case. He made the snap, not altogether clearheaded decision to lose the bungee. He fumbled with the strap around his waist, confused by the way he'd wrapped it around himself. The more he untied it, the more tangled it seemed to become. There was a tingle in his head, behind his eyes. His deep breaths were becoming ragged.

He coughed and then wheezed as he tried to fill his lungs with air. Clayton floated in the module like a man tied to weights in the deep end of a pool. He struggled to free himself from the simple belt he'd constructed moments earlier.

For a split second, he found some clarity among the static and realized what was happening. That eleven minutes might have only been three or four. That pressure he thought was well above the fifteen percent threshold might be on the verge of dipping below it. Clayton considered he might have only seconds to live. The Soyuz, which he knew was safe, was his only option.

He sucked in another noxious breath and changed his mind about the bungee. Instead of undoing the mummy wrap, he slipped out of it. He tucked his thumbs inside the cords at each hip and tugged downward, pushing the cords down his legs as he would a wet swimsuit.

He drew his knees up and pulled down until he freed himself of the cords, kicking them loose into the module. He spun around to find Ben. The dead astronaut's body was stuck against the module wall above the hatch.

Clayton reached up for Ben and pulled him downward. Despite the microgravity of low Earth orbit, Clayton's body felt heavy. His head throbbed.

Somehow, he managed to direct Ben's body past the narrow hatch opening and then wormed himself into the capsule behind Ben. Once he was completely through the opening, he grabbed the hatch and pressed it closed with what little strength he could muster. Even the minor task of pushing a virtually weightless hatch forced him to grunt as he shut and locked it.

Clayton was winded. Nausea crept into his gut and throat. He coughed again and nearly puked. He floated in the cramped capsule, his hands flat against the hatch as they'd been when he pushed it closed. He needed a minute.

As he regained his wits, his mind searched for the humor. He wanted to laugh. He couldn't find anything funny about it.

Then he thought of David Bowie. Of "Major Tom."

His circuits were dead. He was feeling still. He hoped his spaceship knew which way to go.

He'd listened to Bowie's "Space Oddity" countless times. He'd never really thought about the lyrics until that very moment.

"I really am an idiot," he said. "I need to get home."

CHAPTER 11

SATURDAY, JANUARY 25, 2020, 1:37 PM CST
CLEAR LAKE, TEXAS

The car wouldn't start. Not that Jackie thought it would. Neighbors had complained about dead batteries or fried engines in all of the vehicles. Still, she had hope. The hope died when the push-button start wouldn't even click.

"Great," she said. "Absolutely great."

Her worry shifted to Chris. Was he stuck hours north of home? Would Rick be able to bring him home safely, or was his Jeep dead too?

"Mom?"

Jackie turned to her daughter, who was sitting in the passenger seat.

"I was talking to you," Marie said.

Jackie smiled weakly. "Sorry."

"So we're walking?"

"I'm riding my bike. You're staying here."

"You're not going alone, Mom."

"I'm not leaving my house in the control of strangers."

"But you'd leave your teenage daughter with strangers while you bike to Johnson Space Center?"

Jackie rolled her eyes. "That's not what I meant."

Marie unbuckled her seatbelt. She'd been hopeful too. "Our neighbors aren't strangers, except for Candace. She seems nice enough, even though she keeps crying every few minutes."

"Her boyfriend died in her arms," Jackie said. "She's allowed to cry."

"I wasn't judging…"

Jackie lifted her right hand from the wheel and brushed it against her daughter's cheek. "I know."

"So leaving me at home," said Marie, "what's that going to do?"

Jackie pursed her lips. "Really," she said, "I just don't want you going with me."

"Why?"

Jackie sighed. "I don't know what I'm going to find when I get there."

Marie shifted in her seat, turning toward her mother. "What is that supposed to mean?"

She felt her daughter measuring her. Her daughter was intuitive. Jackie had always had trouble hiding her emotions from her firstborn. Even the way she'd greet her on the phone would elicit concern if she didn't strike the right tone.

"Mom," Marie pressed, "what are you not telling me?"

"Our neighbor Rebecca stopped by the house."

Marie's chin quivered and her eyes welled. "Mom..." she whimpered.

"Oh, honey." Jackie knew she'd hesitated too long. "Your dad's okay."

Marie's shoulders sagged with relief. She let go of the breath she'd been holding in her lungs.

Jackie corrected herself. "Actually, I shouldn't say that. I don't know how he is. I don't know exactly where he is. That's the reason I'm heading over to JSC. I want to know what they know."

"What exactly did Rebecca say?"

"She said the ground lost contact with the ISS," Jackie replied. "They're working to reestablish communication with the crew," she said, barreling through the explanation. "They're doing the best they can. The good news is that they don't have any indication anything is wrong up there. As far as we know, they're floating around as they usually do, playing with experiments and taking pictures of the pyramids."

Tears leaked from the corner of Marie's eyes. "But if we lost power down here, they probably lost power up there. They can't live without power, Mom."

Jackie leaned into her daughter and took one hand with both of hers. "NASA is smart. They've never lost an astronaut in space. They have backups for their backups."

Marie frowned and pulled away. She shouldered the door open. "Are you trying to convince me or yourself?"

Jackie shuddered against the slam of the passenger's side door and watched her sulking, worried teen huff into the house. Under normal circumstances she'd have shouted Marie's full name and ordered her back to the car, delivering a lecture on manners and respect.

These weren't normal circumstances.

Jackie shoved open her door and went into the house. She was met with the smell of cooking sausage.

Candace was in the kitchen at the island. Her eyes were red and puffy. Reggie was cooking on the gas stove top, working a large pan skillet, and had it covered in sausage links. Lana was standing next to her husband, leaning on him as he worked a spatula. She seemed mesmerized by the sizzle.

"Where's everyone else?" Jackie asked.

Lana looked up from the skillet. "Betty and Brian are out back, sitting by the pool," she answered. "Marie went into your room and slammed the door. Everything okay?"

Reggie glared at his wife. "That's personal," he said. "Plus, you could guess everything is not okay, what with Chris and Clayton not here."

"It's okay," said Jackie. "I know you're being thoughtful."

Lana smiled. She rubbed her husband on the back. "We're a little stressed."

"I'm riding my bike up to JSC," Jackie told them. "I want to know what they know. I can't keep looking up at the sky blindly, wondering what's going on with Clay. And there's nothing I can do about Chris. So..."

"I get it," said Candace. "You want to feel like you're doing something."

Jackie nodded. "Yes."

"Let me go with you," offered Candace. "If you have a second bike."

Jackie glanced over at her closed bedroom door before answering Candace. "I think I need to go alone."

Candace frowned. "Please don't make me beg. I need something to distract me. I can't keep sitting here crying."

"I've got another bike," Jackie said. "You can go with me."

Candace's face lit up like a child. "Really?"

Jackie shrugged. "Sure."

Candace pushed herself from the island. "Thank you, Jackie. I need this."

Jackie told Candace where to find the bike in the garage and told her she'd be there in a minute. She crossed the great room to her bedroom door and started to turn the handle. She hesitated. Instead of opening the door, she knocked.

Marie barked, "What?"

"Can I come in?"

"It's your house. You can do what you want."

Jackie opened the door and found Marie sitting on her bed, her legs crossed. She was picking at her manicured nails. She'd only had them painted at the salon three days earlier. Jackie eyed the chipped blue polish on Marie's fingers and wondered if she'd ever again have a day at the salon with her daughter.

"I'm taking Candace with me."

"Of course you are."

"I need you here."

"Why?"

"A lot of reasons."

"Like?"

"This is our house. You know where things are. You have privacy in my room. You're safe."

Marie chewed on her index finger at the cuticle, knowing it was one of Jackie's pet peeves. Jackie ignored it.

"Also, I don't know what's out there beyond our neighborhood. Until I do, I don't want you leaving our street."

Marie rolled her eyes. "I drive into downtown Houston all of the time, Mom. I can handle myself."

"That's different," Jackie said. "You know it's different."

"Whatever."

Jackie curled her hands into fists and sat on the edge of the bed. She stared at Marie until her daughter looked back her.

"Listen," she said, "I'll cut you a lot of slack. The world sucks at the moment. I get it. But enough with the teenage angst. Enough with the disrespect. I am your mother. You'll do what I tell you to do. If I tell you to stay here and guard the fort, that's what you do. Got it?"

Marie's jaw tensed and she opened her mouth to say something but must have thought better of it. Instead she nodded. "Got it."

Jackie reached over and rubbed Marie's knee. "I love you, Marie. I'll be back before you know it. Just don't let Betty take over the house while I'm gone."

Marie smirked. "I'll try."

Jackie slid off the bed and blew her daughter a kiss. She shut the door behind her and strode to the garage.

Candace already had the garage door open and two bikes in the driveway. She was bent over at her waist, pumping air into a front tire.

"You didn't have to do that," Jackie said, grabbing two bottled waters from the slightly below air temperature refrigerator. "But I appreciate it."

Candace kept pushing and pulling on the pump. "It needed air. Figured I'd go ahead and do it so we could get a move on."

"Sounds good," Jackie said. "I got some water. It's less than a five-mile ride, but it's better to stay hydrated."

Candace pushed the tire with her thumb and disconnected the pump. She recapped the valve and took the bottle. "Thanks. I didn't see any helmets."

"Chris has one somewhere," Jackie said. "I don't know where he keeps it."

"No biggie," said Candace. "We'll be okay."

Jackie pulled the garage door shut. "Ready?"

"Ready."

They hopped on the bicycles and rolled down the driveway, gathering speed as they pedaled along Jackie's street before turning left to leave the neighborhood. Neighbors watched them as they sped past. Some of them waved. Most of them stared with blank looks.

Everyone was still in shock. Jackie figured they were processing the plane crash, the death, the loss of power, the lack of certainty about what might come next. Instead of being proactive, they were passive. They were sitting around waiting for Godot.

Jackie pedaled harder to escape the loop that encircled her neighborhood and then sped from the development closer to Saturn Lane. The chilly breeze was liberating.

She sucked in a breath of the air less rank with smoke and decay than on her street. The muscles in her calves and thighs worked to push her forward.

Candace kept pace with her, drafting on her right side. They were moving at a surprisingly good clip. Then they turned onto the boulevard.

It reminded Jackie of what the town looked like after a hurricane or flood. Cars were stopped in the middle of the road, perched on the edge of curbs. Some were smashed together from collisions.

Jackie dropped her feet from the pedals and skidded to a stop. Candace braked alongside her.

"It's like a moment frozen in time," said Candace. "Like when the Earth stood still."

Jackie scanned the bifurcated street. She was glad the car hadn't started. There'd have been no way for her to navigate the obstacles.

What struck her most of all was the relative quiet. There was no whoosh of passing cars or the low rumble of air traffic. The only noise she could hear was the distant hum of gasoline generators.

People who lived in Southeast Texas were used to losing power in predictable storms. They had generators strong enough to run refrigerators or a few fans. Some of the wealthier people had built-in natural gas generators that would power entire houses.

Jackie had neither. She cursed Clayton under her breath for leaving her unprepared and immediately sought forgiveness by looking up at the cloudless sky.

"Hey, look at that." Candace pointed across the street.

There was a group of teenagers, maybe a half dozen of them, huddled together on the opposite side of the road and fifty yards or so in the direction they were planning to travel.

They were stopped at a pair of dead cars. One of them, with a thick mop of brown hair and hands stuffed deep into his loose-fitting pants, stood as a lookout. The others were trying the doors. None of them had noticed she and Candace were watching them.

When none of the doors opened, one of the boys, whose head was nearly bald, pulled off his long-sleeved T-shirt and wrapped it around his arm. He motioned for the others to step away, reared back, and punched his elbow through the glass of the passenger's side door.

He moved to the next vehicle while another boy reached inside the car and opened the door. A couple of them disappeared into the front seat, no doubt rifling through the owner's belongings.

The shirtless thug repeated the glass break on the other car. He shook out his shirt and slipped it over his head while another pair of his friends broke into the second vehicle. Jackie was mesmerized by the looting.

Candace thumped her on the arm. "He sees us," she said. "We need to go."

Jackie's eyes darted to the lookout. He'd pulled his hands from his pants pockets and was pointing directly at her. The others were too busy thieving to notice at first. But the bald one who'd taken off his shirt, the one Jackie thought might be the leader, followed the lookout's finger across the street until he apparently saw Jackie and Candace watching them.

The boy yelled something to the others. Jackie couldn't make out what it was. But it was aggressive and angry. The others pulled themselves from inside the cars, and like a pack of lemmings, they all snapped their attention in unison.

"Should we go back?" Candace asked.

"No," Jackie said emphatically. "That would lead them into our neighborhood. We don't need that."

"You think they'd come into the neighborhood?"

"Candace, they're breaking into cars in the middle of the day on a major street. They'll loot neighborhoods next. Ours doesn't need to be the first."

"So what, then?"

Jackie put one foot on a pedal, stood tall to push it forward, and propelled herself forward. "We're on bikes. They're on foot. We speed right by them."

Candace followed Jackie's lead and started pedaling to keep pace. "I don't know, Jackie," she said.

"We don't have a choice. I'm finding out what's up with my husband. These punks aren't stopping me."

Jackie stood from her seat and pedaled with purpose. She gripped the handlebars, steering around stalled cars and trucks.

The boys were huddled behind the cars they'd burgled. A couple of them pointed and looked in her direction. She tried to ignore them and pressed harder, moving the bike faster and faster as she zigged and zagged along the boulevard.

Candace was at her side, breathing heavily, exerting herself to propel the bike as fast as she could. If it hadn't been for the slalom course in front of her, Jackie knew she'd zoom right past the thugs without a problem. As it was, she worried they'd take the right path and knock her from the bike. She prayed they'd flunked geometry and physics.

Thankfully the four-lane road was split with a large grassy median running along the center of it, providing a little extra distance between her bike and the boys.

She was ten yards from being directly across from them when they started running at her. A couple of them bolted straight for her. Another two ran for Candace. The bald one and the lookout ran ahead to try to intersect their path.

The boys were smart, Jackie thought as she pedaled harder, jerking the bike from side to side as she gathered more speed. They were surrounding them. If the first two stopped or slowed them, the trailing boys would close ranks. This wasn't good.

The bald boy and the lookout were sprinting across the median a few yards ahead of her. Jackie tried to swerve to the left. A minivan blocked her path. It was too late.

"Go around the van!" she called to Candace, who'd slipped a couple of bike lengths behind her. "To the left!"

"Got it!" Candace huffed.

Jackie looked at the two boys running straight for her. The bald one's teeth were bared. He looked like a rabid dog. He was fast — faster than Jackie had calculated. He was mere feet from her, his arms outstretched and his hands balled into fists. He was yelling something at her. She was too focused on avoiding him to comprehend it.

At the last moment, she swerved right. She split the narrow space between his outstretched left arm and the lookout, who couldn't control his body enough to redirect his momentum.

Jackie bounded onto the median, rumbled onto the grass, and almost lost control of the bike as she rapidly decelerated onto the uneven turf. She dropped her right foot from the pedal and dragged her toe along the ground to catch her balance just enough to prevent herself from falling forward over the handlebars or losing complete control of the bike.

Her heart was pounding. Her legs burned. She looked over her left shoulder. The boys were still coming at her. She tried to find the pedal with her foot but couldn't find her footing.

"Gimme the bike!" growled the baldheaded teen, spit flying from his mouth and sticking to his chin. "Come back here and gimme the bike."

Jackie didn't understand his anger. She stared into his narrow black eyes. There was depravity there in someone so young. He couldn't be more than sixteen or seventeen. He might not even be shaving yet. But he was lean and muscular; the veins in his arms pressed against the pale skin on his forearms and biceps.

She found the pedal and pushed herself away from him and his trailing pack. The bike bounded onto the pavement and the rear tire skidded. She turned the handlebar sharply left to straighten her path.

Quickly she regained her rhythm and was pedaling away from the boys, who couldn't keep pace. Up ahead, still on the other side of the road, was Candace. She was still standing, working the bike as she propelled it farther away from the threat,

Jackie checked over her shoulder. She was safe. For now.

"Keep going!" she called ahead to Candace.

Candace responded by throwing her a thumbs-up. She kept pedaling without looking back.

Jackie weaved between the stalled cars, SUVs, and trucks. Once she was sure she was far enough away from the boys, she dropped onto the seat and glided.

Despite the chill, she was sweating, her legs heavy with exhaustion. Her mind was racing. They'd not even been without power for a full day and the looting had begun.

There were kids roaming the streets as if they owned them. She saw no police, no firefighters. No authority at all.

She'd lived through so many storms before where the infrastructure was tested. It always felt temporary. It was an inconvenience. This, she felt in her gut, was different.

She pressed down on the pedals and pressed toward the front gates of Johnson Space Center, hoping she'd find answers once she got there.

She also hoped she wouldn't see the gang of teenage thugs again.

SATURDAY, JANUARY 25, 2020, 2:17 PM CST
CLEAR LAKE, TEXAS

The guard at the gate wasn't budging. "I'm sorry, Mrs. Shepard," he said without any emotion. "I cannot let you past the gate. We're on a lockdown."

Jackie affected her best "I-don't-care-what-you-say-I-want-what-I-want" voice, enunciating every word as clearly as she could without spontaneously combusting.

"It. Wouldn't. Make. A. Difference. If. The. Center. Was. Quarantined. For. Ebola," she said. "I want to see someone about my husband. You do understand he's one of three astronauts in orbit right now?"

It was a rare occasion Jackie would mention her husband's vocation. Other than her close friends and family, she never talked about his work. Most people who cared about it already knew.

This was that moment, though, when she calculated it was best to remind the man why she was being such a persistent pain. She had a right to information. She had a right to know her husband's condition.

"Yes," said the guard. "I am aware that Mr. Shepard is on the ISS. I can imagine your frustration, but—"

Jackie snapped, unable to contain her emotions. "Do you have a spouse in space right now?"

"No. I—"

"Then you *cannot* imagine."

"I have my orders."

Candace put her hand on the small of Jackie's back. "Can I make a suggestion?"

Jackie took a deep breath and exhaled through her nostrils. "Sure."

Candace stepped to the side, next to the space separating the guard and Jackie. She smiled and started talking to the guard.

"We both understand the sensitivity of the moment," she began. "I think my friend just needs information. She doesn't have to come onto the property if somebody could come to her."

"Everybody is extremely busy, ma'am. We—"

Candace held up her hands, stopping the guard before he again drew the wrath of Jackie. "Just let me finish, please," she said sweetly. "You could get someone on the phone or the intercom. Those are working here, right?"

The guard shook his head. "I can't discuss that. It's privileged information," he said and held up a finger before either woman could protest. "But I'm sure I could facilitate a situation report via phone."

Jackie and Candace thanked him. He disappeared into one of the guard booths that separated the lanes leading in and out of Johnson Space Center. To their right was a parking lot and a badging office. That was where official visitors, contractors, and the media picked up their temporary credentials whenever they were on the property. To the left, past the guard booth, was a rocket-length building and a cluster of standing rocket engines.

It was called Rocket Park and was a nice attraction for visitors who wanted to learn more about the space program's infancy. The standing rockets were a Gemini-Titan, a Mercury-Redstone, and Little Joe II. Inside the long building that resembled a closed airplane hangar was a Saturn V rocket. They were the machines that built the space program.

They were also fantastic museum pieces worthy of the Smithsonian. Still, Jackie always thought about the shuttle when she visited JSC. It was missing from the garden and from nearby Space Center Houston, the tourist attraction that drew a million tourists every year.

The Space Center had lost out on receiving one of the surviving orbiters when NASA retired the program. Instead, it got a mock shuttle and a real Shuttle Carrier Aircraft, the 747 aboard which shuttles made the cross-country journey from California to Florida when they couldn't land at Kennedy Space Center.

It was a crime. Houston and JSC were home to the manned flight program. The first word spoken on the surface of the moon was "Houston." Most of the astronauts and their families lived in the Houston area. They'd given their lives and lifestyles for the betterment of space exploration. Instead, New York City got a shuttle. *New York?*

Jackie sucked in a deep breath and blinked back tears, looking at the Rocket Park and thinking about how much she and her family had given up for the program and how much more she feared she was about to lose.

"Thank you, Candace," she said. "You pulled me back from the ledge. I was about to lose it."

Candace smiled. "Of course. You helped me last night. You're giving me a place to stay, feeding me. Trying to help you was the least I could do."

Jackie wrapped her arms around her new friend. Candace initially flinched, then relaxed into Jackie's embrace and reciprocated with her own hug. The split-second comfort of the embrace was interrupted when the guard emerged from the booth.

"Mrs. Shepard," he said and waved her toward the booth, "I have someone on the line for you."

Jackie held up crossed fingers to Candace and walked the short distance into the booth. There was a phone receiver on the desk. She picked it up and drew it to her ear.

Her heart was pounding. "This is Jackie Shepard," she said breathlessly.

The woman's voice on the other end of the line was vaguely familiar. "Mrs. Shepard, this is Irma Molinares. We've met before. I'm in the astronaut corps and I am the crew support astronaut."

"Yes," Jackie said. "I know who you are. Clay speaks highly of you."

"That's very kind of him," Molinares replied. "I wish I could be delivering you the information I have face-to-face, but it's all hands on deck, as you can imagine, and for security reasons we're on lockdown."

Jackie's stomach tightened. She grabbed the desk with her free hand and leaned over. "Is Clay…" She couldn't finish the sentence. Saying it out loud would make it real.

"Honestly, we don't know. We believe the crew is alive, but we haven't been able to reestablish communication with them since the event."

"What event? What actually happened?"

"The best I can tell you right now is that there was a solar storm. It interrupted our ability to speak to the ISS. We were in the middle of a transmission when we lost contact."

"Solar storm? Like a solar flare?"

"Similar," Molinares said. "Though not exactly. This was what's called a coronal mass ejection. To put it simply, it unleashed a tremendous amount of magnetic radiation."

"That's why we lost power?"

"Roger. As far as we can tell, most of the world is either functioning with limited or no electrical capabilities. The grids are fried. That's the unclassified information we're receiving from foreign space programs and our own military."

"How long will we be without power?"

"Nobody knows. Communication is so hit and miss that we can't determine the depth of the permanent damage to global electrical and communication capabilities."

"And you said it's radiation that caused it?"

"Roger."

"Is that dangerous to the crew?"

Molinares paused before answering. "Potentially," she said. "Not immediately. Maybe long term. It likely wouldn't have killed them."

"Likely?"

"Likely."

Jackie's knees felt like jelly. She found a chair and pulled it toward herself to sit down. She untangled the phone's cord and leaned back in the seat.

"The greater concern, and I'm just being as honest as I can be with you, is what the magnetic blast did to their life-support systems."

Jackie ran her hand through her hair and curled a finger through the ends of the strands. "You can't monitor that from mission control? I thought you could tell everything from those monitors and computers you have there."

"Normally we can." Molinares was speaking calmly. "Right now, we can't. We have redundant systems here that allowed us to recover power and revive critical systems across a variety of platforms. The ISS is not one of them."

"What does that mean? What are you not saying, Irma?"

There was silence on the other end of the line. Jackie then heard muffled voices before Irma Molinares answered her questions.

"We are able to monitor a couple of systems," she said, her words measured. "We know that there is currently limited power on board. We also know there is a pressure leak."

"A pressure leak?"

The guard appeared at the doorway to the booth. Jackie shot him a knife-edged glare and he stepped away.

"Roger," said Molinares. "It's on the Russian side of the ISS, which is a good sign. The crew was in the middle of an EVA when the CME hit them. Shep—your husband was in the Cupola, assisting Greenwood and Voin with their work. We think alarms, if they're functioning, would have alerted him to the leak. He'd be attempting to fix it or initiate the emergency evacuation protocol."

"Speak English, Irma."

Molinares sucked in a deep breath. "He'd know there was a pressure leak and he'd either fix it or get out of Dodge. Given that we see the pressure in the Russian side of the ISS dropping and not stabilizing, he's likely trying to leave."

"Leave how? A Soyuz?"

"Roger."

"Where's it parked?"

Molinares paused again as if caught off guard by the question. "Uh..."

"Irma?"

"It's on the Russian side."

Jackie laughed incredulously. "So you're telling me they may be on the American side, which is good. But to leave, they have to be on the Russian side, which is bad."

"Roger."

"And that's if they're even alive."

"Roger."

"Which you can't confirm."

"Unfortunately."

"So what are you doing?" Jackie asked, fighting the heavy weight of dread and fear that sank her deeper into the chair. "And how will I find out what you learn? I can't stay up here at the gate indefinitely."

"We're working on providing a space for you and your children here at JSC," she said. "That way we can keep you apprised of any new developments. Are your children with you?"

"No," she said. "Our daughter, Marie, is at our house. And my son, Chris, is...I don't know where he is."

"What do you mean, Mrs. Shepard?"

"He's on a camping trip in North Texas. I haven't heard from him yet."

"That complicates things," said Molinares. "I imagine you wouldn't want to be here with your son unaccounted for."

"Roger," Jackie said snippily. "I guess we'll come back once he's home. You'll hold a place for us?"

"Of course," said Molinares. "And if I learn anything before you come back, we will figure out a way to get someone to your house. We have the address."

"Good," Jackie said. It wasn't much, but it was something. As soon as anyone learned anything about Clayton, they'd let her know. "Thank you."

"I'm sorry to cut our conversation short," she said. "I've got to get back to work. We're all pulling triple duty here. If you could put the guard back on the phone with me, I'll give him instructions on what to do when you come back."

"Okay," Jackie said. She started to pull the phone away from her ear when she heard Molinares say her name.

"Jackie," she said, her voice more feminine and comforting than it had been the entirety of their conversation. "Speaking for myself now and not NASA," she whispered, "I am so sorry. I cannot imagine the worry and the stress with which you're coping. I wish there was more I could do or say to help ease both. I really do."

"You saying that is enough, Irma. It really is." Jackie pushed herself to her wobbly feet. She leaned on the desk and called the guard, handed him the phone, and walked out of the booth.

Candace stood yards away, her arms folded across her chest. Her eyes widened with expectation as Jackie walked toward her. "What did they say?"

"Not much good, really," said Jackie. "The ISS has a pressure leak. They can't communicate with the crew. They don't know if they're dead or alive."

"That's good news," Candace said.

Jackie furrowed her brow. "How so?"

"If they don't know he's dead," she said, "then I'm betting he's alive. He's a freaking astronaut, right? I mean, he must be pretty resilient, right?"

Jackie smiled. She liked Candace's optimism. And the young woman was right. Clayton *was* resilient. He was persistent. He was smart. She also knew that Clayton loved his family; he knew how important he was to their happiness and success. Jackie looked over her shoulder at Rocket Park and then up toward the afternoon sun. She decided to adopt Candace's bright outlook. Clayton would find his way to the Soyuz. He would drop back to Earth. He would make it home and be the one to take Chris on his next camping trip.

She picked up her bicycle and flung a leg over it. It was time to head home and await Chris's return. He wasn't in imminent danger as far as she knew. He wasn't at risk of dying in a vacuum.

Jackie chuckled nervously at the morbid thoughts racing through her head, at the contemplation of a life without Clay. He'd better be alive. If he didn't survive his midlife crisis, she'd kill him.

CHAPTER 12

SATURDAY, JANUARY 25, 2020, 2:25 PM CST
I-45 SOUTH NEAR CORSICANA, TEXAS

The strobing emergency lights surprised Rick almost as much as the speed with which they reached the outskirts of Corsicana. After the trouble at the bridge outside the park, the drive had been uneventful. He'd occasionally had to snake around stopped cars, though nothing major.

A police roadblock was the last thing he expected.

Nikki thumped Rick on the leg. "What do you think it's about?" she asked.

Rick shook his head. "I don't know."

There were two Texas Department of Public Safety patrol cars blocking the southbound lanes of the highway. It didn't look like a checkpoint. There was no going around them.

"Should we turn around?" asked Nikki.

"No," said Rick. "That would just cause more of a problem than whatever this is. Last thing I want is to end up in jail."

"True."

"I agree," Mumphrey chimed in. "Best not to tangle with the law."

Rick slowed to a stop but kept the Jeep in drive. There were two troopers manning the blockade, both wearing the standard-issue top to bottom tan uniforms and the requisite Stetsons.

The older of the two approached the driver's side, signaling for Rick to roll down his window. He had one hand on his holster.

Rick cranked open the window and planted both hands on the steering wheel. He waited for the trooper to speak first.

"Where you headed?"

"South."

The trooper bent over, eyed Nikki, and then scanned the trio in the backseat. "Where'd you get the Jeep?"

"It's mine," Rick said. "Do you need to see the registration?"

The trooper rapped his fingers on the open sill. "No, that's not going to be necessary."

Rick saw the other trooper ease from the front of his vehicle and start moving toward the passenger side of the Jeep. He too had a hand on his service weapon.

"What's going on here?" Rick asked.

The trooper ignored the question. "How far south are you headed?"

Rick clenched his jaw and gripped the wheel. He looked over at Nikki. She offered a glance that suggested he keep his cool.

"We're headed to Houston, sir."

"Huh," said the trooper, running his tongue along the inside of his cheek. "That's quite a trip. You have enough fuel?"

Rick checked the gauge. It was three-quarters full. "Yes."

"Well," the trooper said, "we've got a couple of options for you."

"Really?"

"The governor declared a state of emergency," said the trooper, working his thumb on the top of his weapon. "He's given us the authority to confiscate vehicles for emergency use. As you can imagine, most of our fleet is useless."

Rick thought about the gun in the glove box but immediately pushed it aside. He wasn't going to win. He wasn't going to give up the Jeep either.

"What's the other option?" he asked, sensing the other trooper was at Nikki's window.

"We siphon half your gas."

"So," Rick said, forcing a toothy smile, "let me make sure I understand your proposition."

"Go ahead," said the trooper, matching the faux grin.

"I either give you my Jeep, stranding me here with a woman, an older man, and two children, or I give you half a tank, guaranteeing I get stranded down the road."

"That's about right," said the trooper. "The grid is fried. Our vehicles are toast. Gas pumps aren't working. So…"

Rick checked his rearview mirror. There was nothing directly behind him. "How many other lucky citizens have won the lottery?"

"You're the third," he said. "A couple of old Ford trucks."

"How many other roadblocks?"

"Between here and Houston?"

"Yep."

The trooper shrugged. "I don't know."

"We passed a DPS station in Waxahachie," said Rick. "I didn't see any roadblocks there. We drove right past a couple of troopers. They waved at us when we went by."

The trooper glanced through the Jeep to his partner on the other side of the vehicle. His eyes darted to Nikki and back to Rick. He rolled his tongue around the other side of his mouth, poking out his cheek.

"I don't know what to tell you," he said. "I only know what my orders are."

Rick played the options in his head. He didn't like any of them. He didn't buy what the troopers were selling. He couldn't even be sure they *were* troopers. Even if they were, none of it made sense unless the government knew more about the outage than everyone else. Maybe this wasn't a state of emergency, but instead it was the beginning of martial law. It didn't matter. He was getting the boys home.

"What happens if I decline?"

The trooper laughed and then looked across the top of the Jeep at his comrade. "He asked what happens if he declines."

The other trooper laughed, his belly shaking. He leaned down and looked at Rick through his reflective sunglasses.

Rick chuckled. "Guess that's my answer. All right then," he said. "I'm guessing we're better off giving up the Jeep. You'll drive us to the closest rest stop or hotel, right?"

"Of course." The trooper smiled.

Nikki thumped him again. "What are you doing?" she mouthed.

The boys protested. Mumphrey gave Rick a knowing look and sat back against his seat to reaffix his buckle.

"Let me hop out," Rick said. "We have stuff in the back we'll need to take with us."

The trooper stepped back from the door. He relaxed his posture and pulled his hand away from the holster.

Rick opened the door and dangled his left leg out of the Jeep. Instead of stepping out, he stepped on the gas.

The Jeep jerked forward. The tires squealed. "Boys!" Rick said, yanking the door shut as he spun the wheel to the left to avoid the patrol cars. "Get down!"

Rick glimpsed the older trooper's wide, fear-filled eyes as he stumbled backward and fell onto the highway. In the side-view mirror, he saw the second trooper draw his weapon. Rick couldn't tell if he'd opened fire until the back window exploded.

Nikki screamed. The boys cried out. Mumphrey had his arms around both children, trying to keep them low.

Rick pushed the pedal to the floorboard and the Jeep fishtailed. The passenger side slammed into the front of one of the patrol cars, but Rick regained control as he drove onto the median, jumping the SUV into the northbound lanes.

He yanked the wheel back to the right, burning the tires against the roadway and driving into the skid. He pressed the gas again to straighten out. Rick turned to look out the passenger's side at the southbound lanes and saw the second trooper still firing his weapon. Bright muzzle flashes sparked each time he pulled the trigger.

Rick turned his attention back to the road ahead and checked his speedometer. The Jeep was rumbling south in the northbound lanes at ninety miles an hour. He took his foot off the gas and drifted.

Nikki punched Rick in the shoulder. "What the hell was that?" she said. "You could have killed us!"

Rick rubbed his arm. "I didn't," he said. "You guys okay back there?"

"Yeah," said Kenny. "I'm good."

"I'm okay," said Chris.

Mumphrey loosened his seatbelt and leaned forward, bracing himself between the front seats. "I knew you were making a run for it," he said, his voice shaking with excitement. "I could see it in your eyes."

Rick suddenly felt the weight of what he'd done. He felt dizzy and his stomach lurched. He thought for a moment he might vomit.

Mumphrey tapped Rick on the shoulder. "I knew you weren't giving up. I thought better to do what the law says. That wasn't right though. Nope. There was something fishy about that."

Rick adjusted the Jeep's path to avoid an eighteen-wheeler stopped in the left lane. "I don't know," he said. "Those guys were dead serious."

Nikki loosened her seatbelt and spun onto her knees to look out the shattered rear window. "At least they're not coming after us," she said and then plopped back into her seat. "That would have been bad."

"I think whatever event happened doesn't have a simple explanation," Rick said. "Or if it's simple it's bigger than dead cars and no power."

"Mr. Walsh," asked Chris, "what do you mean?"

Rick looked at the frightened boy in the mirror. He took a deep breath and checked his speed. "Police wouldn't act like that if they didn't have good reason. Police are good. They help us."

"Didn't seem like they were helping us," said Chris.

Mumphrey wagged his finger. "You make a really good point," he said to Rick. "Things must be bad out there. I mean to say, they must know how far the power outage stretches or how bad the grid is damaged."

"I thought Texas was on its own grid." Kenny spoke up. "That's what my history teacher told us."

Mumphrey nodded. "It is. Texas's electric grid is separate from the rest of the country. That doesn't mean more than Texas wasn't hit."

"Hit with what?" asked Chris.

"That's the million-dollar question," said Rick. "We don't know."

"You could have asked those troopers before you ran like a fugitive," Nikki complained. "Maybe they would've told you something."

Rick raised one eyebrow incredulously and glanced at Nikki. "Really? I don't think so."

"We'll figure it out if we get home," Mumphrey said.

"*When* we get home, Mr. Mumphrey," corrected Kenny. "*When*."

Rick smiled. "That's my boy." He adjusted the mirror to wink at his son before easing the Jeep to the side of the road. "We've gotta cross back over."

He turned the wheel toward a narrow strip between the north and southbound lanes and accelerated onto the median. The Jeep bounced, freeing hanging shards of glass from the rear windows as Rick found his way back onto the interstate. He maneuvered around a stalled minivan and pressed the gas.

"Just a few hours more," he said, "as long as we don't have any more problems."

Rick glanced at Nikki in time to see her avert her eyes. Her cheeks flushed. She lifted her eyes back to meet his.

"Thank you," she mouthed before turning back to look out the window. She leaned her elbow on the armrest and rested her forehead on the glass.

Rick assumed she was thinking the same thing he was. That he was stupid to run from the troopers. He was also brilliant.

He accelerated and switched into the fast lane to avoid a pair of stopped cars. He checked the rearview mirror. Nobody was following them. There were no flashing lights, no siren. His gambit had worked. He was almost as much of a badass as Deep Six Nikki. Almost.

CHAPTER 13

MISSION ELAPSED TIME:
72 DAYS, 14 HOURS, 35 MINUTES, 18 SECONDS
249 MILES ABOVE EARTH

For the second time in his life, Clayton didn't like the idea of flying. It was more like falling, really, and there wasn't a lot he could do to assure exactly where he'd land.

Although he wasn't the commander of the mission, he was a pilot. He'd had his license since he was seventeen. His father, an aeronautical engineer, had instilled a love of flight from the earliest days Clayton could remember.

The two of them had lovingly restored and updated an experimental RV-12 airplane. They'd spent more than one thousand hours putting it together and spent countless more flying in the side-by-side aircraft together.

Looking up through the clear canopy at the ink blue sky from eight-thousand feet above Earth, Clayton had first deeply contemplated what lay beyond it. His father had always indulged Clayton. Aside from the RV, they'd turned the two-car garage of the family home into a rocket assembly building.

They'd sanded, glued, and painted more model rockets than they could count. Some of the better ones hung from the ceiling in Clayton's bedroom, swaying on clear fishing wire against the breeze from the air vents.

The two of them had stopped building the rockets when his sister died. They'd stopped doing a lot of things when she died. However, they kept flying. It was an escape from the pain beneath the surface, the guilt that chained the entire family to its grief.

Then his dad got cancer and they'd sold the RV to pay the medical bills. Clayton was eighteen and heading off to college. He'd delayed his admission and gave up flying when the cancer won.

A boy with no father and a dead twin needed to be grounded. So he kept his eyes straight ahead, avoiding even an upward glance at the heavens that had become home to his father and sister.

Then he met Jackie. She restored his faith and gave new life to his dreams. If it hadn't been for her, he'd not have had the confidence to finish his degree, become a prized engineer, or apply to the astronaut corps, let alone look upward.

Clayton had always believed things happened for a reason. Even if he didn't understand what that reason might be, there had to be one.

A wave of happy memories floated in and out of his mind: the first time he landed the RV and the wide, beaming smile on his father's face, the moment he'd handed his college acceptance letter to his mother and the tears that poured from her eyes. She'd wet the collar of his T-shirt with her hug and stained it with her mascara.

He remembered Jackie's enthusiasm while making love to an "astronaut" for the first time. He'd laughed and told her it had better have been the first time.

Clayton blinked himself from the momentary daydream and looked at the familiar Soyuz controls. He'd practiced on an identical configuration in a simulator. Still, there was something different knowing this was the real thing and the stakes were as dire as they could possibly be. Before he ran through the checklist, he wanted to remind himself of the panel's configuration.

"Yesli by ya znal bol'she russkogo," he said. *I wish I knew more Russian.* "It would make this a lot easier."

Directly in front of the commander's seat was a circular periscope viewing window framed on either side by joysticks. They were similar to the thumb sticks on Xbox controllers.

To the left were the critical command indicators and the left seat audio controls. To the right were the center and right seat audio controls. Only the center seat mattered for this trip.

Working his way up the right side, he checked the suit fan switches and the cabin temperature selector. The circuit breaker panel looked intact and functional. His eyes scanned counterclockwise across the VGA display monitors. One of them was monochrome. The other was eight color. Neither was going to win tech prizes for clarity or resolution, but they'd work.

On either side of the right monitor, running vertically down the panel, was a series of status indicators. In the middle, at the center of the panel, like a webcam on a laptop, was the master alarm.

Clayton unscrewed, pulled forward, and then thumbed the left joystick, manipulating it in a circle. It controlled the ship's translation: its forward, backward, up, down, right, left movements. The right joysticks controlled the roll, the pitch, and the yaw. Together, the joysticks gave instructions to the Reaction Control System, a set of thrusters clustered around the Soyuz's exterior.

All of the buttons, controls, and displays were in Russian. He had a cheat sheet in English that helped, though in mid-flight — or mid-fall — it wasn't as if he'd have time to keep consulting the translation cards.

His most pressing concern, however, wasn't the Russian labeling. It was his ability to successfully undock the Soyuz at a precise attitude. If he was off by even a little, when he pushed the Soyuz free of the ISS, he could hit another part of the station.

Orbital mechanics was not his strength. Clayton wondered then if he *had* any strengths and reminded himself of an old joke he'd heard and often repeated. He pretended he was telling the joke to someone who could hear him.

"A mechanical engineer was removing a cylinder head from the engine of an expensive, high-end German automobile when he saw a neighbor walking past," Clayton said, checking the functionality of the status indicators. "The neighbor was a cardiologist who lived in the biggest house on the street."

He scanned the cheat sheet with his finger and glanced up at the corresponding button.

"He invited the doctor into his garage and showed him the work he was completing under the hood. Then he says, 'Look at this engine. I opened it up, took out the valves, fixed everything, and put it all back together. It's running like new.'"

He checked the alarm and then the left display. Both looked good.

"Then the engineer says, 'It's basically the same thing you do. So how come I barely make six figures and you make eight?'"

Clayton tucked the cheat sheet in between the seats and unbuckled his belt, floating free of the commander's seat and pulling himself toward the orbital module. He needed to step away before running through the final check and entering the proper commands into the computer.

"'That's easy,' said the doctor. 'You try doing it with the engine running.'"

Clayton laughed at himself. He knew he was smart, but he wasn't surgeon smart. He wasn't commander smart. He wasn't fly a Russian brick back to Earth without killing himself smart.

He was kinematics smart. He knew angular velocity and acceleration. He could calculate how they'd interact with relative velocity and fixed rectangular coordinates.

He was statics and dynamics smart. He could calculate how moving and nonmoving parts of a machine would interact.

He was law of energy smart. Clayton could predict the energy generated or conserved by machines based on design.

He was thermodynamic smart. He was good at calculating efficiency or lack of it.

Okay. Maybe this is in my wheelhouse.

Maybe he was good enough to get himself home.

NASA wouldn't have invested twenty-one million dollars in training him if he were a dope, right?

Clayton knew that he had to pick the right time and calculate the exact attitude at that time to detach from the ISS and start his descent. Some of it was automatic and computer controlled, but he had to feed the computer the right data at the right time. The thought of it was overwhelming. His mind flipped through a series of what-if scenarios like he was living his own *Choose Your Own Adventure* book. It was paralyzing.

If he uploaded the wrong information to the computer, there were infinite ways to die on reentry. If the engines didn't burn enough, the descent could be too fast and too high and cause the Soyuz to skip off the atmosphere. He'd be bounced deeper into space and float away like an untethered helium balloon.

If the engines burned too much, his reentry might be too steep with too much speed. He'd burn up.

Usually, the ground team would calculate the return trajectory. They'd find him the right path to Kazakhstan, where the recovery team would welcome him home and hand him an apple as a welcome home gift.

Clayton considered how different his return home would be. He prayed he'd find land and not water. The odds were against him. Two-thirds of the world's surface was water. If he landed himself in the middle of an ocean, he might as well have burned up in the friction of reentry.

He took a deep breath and fished through the gear stored in the orbital module then pushed himself to the airlock that separated him from the leaking Russian side of the ISS. He had to clear his mind. He thought back to building the RV with his dad.

Nothing about it was easy. Riveting at a precise speed and angle was challenging. Fitting that canopy just right was difficult. Cutting the holes for the instrumentation was a task. There was no room for error.

As they worked, Clayton's dad often reminded him the biggest obstacle to building the plane, or completing anything monumental, wasn't in the details. The obstacle was looking too far ahead. If they worried about what came next, they'd never finish the task at hand.

"How do you eat an elephant?" he'd asked his son one afternoon in the hangar while Clayton struggled with a fitting.

Clayton had frowned, wiping sweat from his forehead. "How?"

"One bite at a time."

Clayton had always been a planner. He'd enjoyed the mental gymnastics of calculating the end of one task to get to the next. It was good for some things and not good for others.

His dad was right. One bite at a time.

The first bite was uploading the proper information to the computer and an official system pre-check. Nothing else mattered if he didn't do that first. He gave himself a push into the crew module, making sure he hadn't left anything in the orbital module, and moved into the commander's seat again. It wasn't as comfortable as his own seat, now occupied by Boris. Each of the seats had been custom fit for maximum comfort on reentry.

Tucked between the seats next to his cheat sheet was an electronic tablet containing the commander's checklist. The commander, unlike the other crew members who used a paper checklist, had an iPad.

After calculating the best window for undocking and the correct trajectory, Clayton rechecked his math. He checked it a third time. He believed he was right, but he couldn't be sure. It was like navigating a plane at night with only the help of VFR and a partially cloudy sky.

Clayton unlocked the device and began swiping through the procedures. He used a stylus to punch buttons on the control panel and began the sequence indicated on the checklist.

"It's like Ikea put this thing together," he mumbled as he progressed through the tasks one at a time. "Just give me an Allen wrench and an unpronounceable Swedish name and we're good to go."

Clayton then apologized to the Swedish. "That was unfair," he said. "The Hemnes is a wonderful dresser and the Karmsund table mirror is the perfect accessory."

He swiped through the checklist again to make sure he hadn't missed anything. The last step was placing the Soyuz on autonomous power, giving over control to the craft itself. He wouldn't touch anything else until sixty seconds before it was time to undock. He was almost there.

Clayton gripped the command stick like a magic wand and initiated a series of commands that powered up the docking mechanism. Another series of pokes began the undocking, counting down from ninety seconds.

Ninety seconds. A minute and a half. That was it, and there was no turning back.

Clayton's stomach rolled. His tongue was thick in his dry mouth. He swallowed against a sandpapery dry throat.

He watched the numbers count backwards, one by one, getting closer to zero. His sense of dread, of base fear, was far more visceral than the sweaty anxiety he'd experienced seventy-two days and sixteen hours earlier when the engines had ignited and pushed him from the bounds of Earth.

Four. Three. Two. One.

Clayton leaned his shoulder forward and used the stick to push another command. It opened the hooks that held the Soyuz tight against the ISS at its connection to the Russian service module. He had another four minutes to wait.

He hummed the *Jeopardy!* theme song that swam in his head.

"I'll take Famous Explorers for a thousand, Alex," he said in his best Alex Trebek impersonation. It actually sounded more like he was impersonating Will Ferrell impersonating Alex Trebek.

"He is the first American astronaut to return to Earth alone in a Soyuz capsule," he recited.

Pretending it was a buzzer, Clayton turned the stick vertically and punched its top with his gloved thumb.

"Yes," said Trebek. "Clayton, go ahead."

"Well, Alex," Clayton said earnestly in his own voice, "who is…me?"

"You are correct," he said in the Trebek voice and checked the countdown indicator on the panel in front of him. "You have the board. But hurry, we have only two minutes left."

"I'll take People Who Are In Over Their Heads for two hundred."

"Very good," said Trebek. "Here is the answer: He started pretending to be a game show host in the most critical moment of his life, totally ignoring the stakes in favor of passive-aggressive avoidance behavior."

"That's a really tough one, Alex. I'll throw caution to the wind and take a guess. Who is me?"

"Oh," said Trebek, "I'm so sorry. The correct answer is 'Who is the psychobabbling idiot at the controls of a Soyuz capsule?'"

Clayton watched the numbers tick down.

"That's all the time we have for today," Trebek said. "Thanks for joining us for this deorbit edition of Jeh-par-dee."

Then Clayton remembered Trebek was Canadian. "Figures. Canada keeps saving me from oblivion one way or the other."

The countdown reached zero and the Soyuz detached using a set of pushers that slowly moved the Soyuz away from the ISS. Clayton checked the display for visual confirmation of the separation from an exterior-mounted camera and from a monitor. He wouldn't be able to feel it. He'd see it though.

The levity of the game show evaporated and Clayton focused. He licked his cracked lips, remembering he hadn't had anything to eat or drink since the CME hit the station. He wasn't hungry; he wasn't thirsty. He was determined to get home.

In the monitor he could see the full separation of the Soyuz from the ISS. So far, so good. The clock reset. He had three minutes until the Soyuz would fire its thrusters to increase the space between it and the ISS.

Clayton was struck by the silence of their movements, the disorienting float free of the space station. It was if he'd closed his eyes in the cabin of a plane as it began to pull away from the gate, only to open them, look out the window, and be confused as to whether the plane or the terminal were moving.

The three minutes ended and the burn began. For fifteen seconds the thrusters fired. Clayton counted those seconds in his head. When he reached fifteen, he pressed the panel to upload the data for the autonomous control descent.

Clayton and the Soyuz had two orbits around the Earth. Silent and alone they'd whoosh around the planet to more fully separate the distance between themselves and the ISS. At the end of the second orbit, they'd be miles from the station and ready for the deorbit burn.

Burn. Not a favorite word at the moment. Clayton shifted in the seat, adjusting the straps that held him there. Two orbits at five miles per second. Each orbit lasted about an hour and a half on the ISS. Three more hours. Given that his orbit would be below the station, it wouldn't take quite as long. Maybe two and a half hours. That was a trip from Houston to Austin, except there were no views outside. He couldn't watch Earth speed by as he could in the Cupola. Instead he was lodged between two dead men in a space smaller than a Volkswagen Beetle.

Clayton could play *Jeopardy!* again. He could avoid the obvious. Or he could take stock. He could relish the memories of his life. He could spend time talking to his wife and children, his parents, his twin.

He leaned his head back against the commander's seat and closed his eyes.

"Jackie, I love you." His voice cracked and he struggled to keep speaking. "I loved you when I met you. I love you more now. You are the one who holds onto me when I reach too high and lose my balance."

Clayton couldn't feel the inertia of the craft as it raced around the globe beneath it, but he was acutely aware of the tears pooling around his eyes, stuck there because of surface tension.

"I know you'll be okay without me," he said. "I'm the daredevil, but you're the strong one. You always have been." He blinked at the tears. "I remember that time we were driving across the desert. I think it was Arizona. Maybe it was Nevada. We were almost out of gas. I mean, we were on fumes. Just you and me in the middle of nowhere. The kids weren't even a thought then. I don't even think we were engaged yet."

Clayton blinked away the tears and sniffled. "We passed the last gas station while you were sleeping. You woke up and were so upset I hadn't stopped to fill up. I swear I could see your uvula flapping in your throat as you screamed at me. It got worse when I started laughing at you, promising you we'd be fine."

Clayton checked an indicator on the panel and made sure the orbit looked good. All was fine as best he could tell.

"I tried to make it into a game. Counting down the miles to the next gas station while the dial kept dropping lower and lower. You were sitting there with your arms folded across your chest, grumbling and calling me every name in the book."

Clayton opened his eyes and checked for any alarms or anomalies. The automated system was performing well.

"Then we ran out of gas," he said. "We had no cell service. I thought your head might explode. Instead, you got scary calm. I was a little freaked out. You told me later that once we'd run out of gas, once the threat was gone and the reality set in, the time for complaining was over. It was time to get to work."

Clayton let the notion soak for a moment. He hadn't thought about that story in years, not since the last time Jackie reminded the children of their father's brilliant idiocy.

It was the perfect story. He'd taken the risk without fear, bringing her along unwillingly into the abyss. She'd panicked at not having had a choice, but when the worst happened, she was the one who rose to the occasion. She was the hero.

"We walked three miles to the gas station. I apologized and tried to hold your hand. You rightfully resisted. You were the one who calmly filled the gas can. You were the one who arranged for the ride back to the car. You were the one who cleaned up my mess. When we got back to the car and I cranked the engine, you leaned over and planted a good one on me."

Clayton's heart skipped, thinking about that moment.

"I asked you why you kissed me when I'd left us stranded. You said it was because everything turned out okay. No harm, no foul. And you got in a good workout, so you could eat whatever you wanted for dinner. I think we had steak that night."

Clayton wanted to kiss her again. He wanted to hold her, smell her hair as she clung to him. He wanted her to yell and scream at him. He wanted to hear her tell the story of his brilliant idiocy again and again. He couldn't be certain of any of it as the Soyuz zipped silently toward its second orbit.

CHAPTER 14

SATURDAY, JANUARY 25, 2020, 4:00 PM CST
CLEAR LAKE, TEXAS

Jackie stopped pedaling and let her momentum push the wheels forward. It was a nice break from the hard ride back to the neighborhood. She hadn't stopped pedaling since leaving the front gate at Johnson Space Center.

"I'm glad we didn't see those punk teenagers on the way home," said Candace as she pedaled next to Jackie. "I don't think I could have outrun them a second time."

Jackie agreed with a nod and sigh. She leaned forward in her seat, leaning her weight onto the handlebars, and started pedaling again.

Candace cranked her bike to keep pace. "You think we'll see them again?"

Jackie wrung her hands on the grip. "Them or someone like them."

"Why do you say that?"

"Just a gut feeling. They were so…uptight at JSC. Everyone's so tense. It's like this isn't a temporary thing."

"The power?"

"The power, the cars, the frustration." Jackie leaned into a right turn, which brought her one street closer to home. "Everything. It's been less than a day and it feels longer than that. It feels…"

"Darker?"

Jackie stopped pedaling and glided next to Candace. Her new friend had picked just the right word. "Yeah," she said. "Darker."

Jackie prayed she'd get home and see Rick Walsh's Jeep in the driveway. It was a fantasy, she knew, but she could hope. She needed to have hope.

It was one thing to have her adult husband in space. It was another to have her young son incommunicado in what she believed to be a quickly devolving society. In such a short time, she'd gone from not worrying about her son's safety to focusing on it.

The pair turned another corner and Jackie slowed the bike as the familiar, bitter smell of lingering smoke stung her nostrils. She pressed the brakes with her hands and then rose from her seat and planted her feet on the ground, skidding to a stop.

On the main loop, the road that led to her cul-de-sac, there were easily three times as many people milling around as there were when she left. It looked like Halloween night without the costumes or the candy. Or the fun.

"What is that about?" asked Candace. "Who are those people?"

The sun was setting. It would be dark in a half hour or less. It was hard to make out faces. "I don't know," she said.

"I'm new to the neighborhood and all," Candace said, "but I don't think they live here."

"I don't either," said Jackie, flexing a leg and leaning the bike to one side.

"Should we check it out?"

"Probably wouldn't hurt." Jackie pushed forward on her bike and rolled past the entrance to her street. She looked to the end and her driveway where the cul-de-sac began. No Jeep. She pulled in a deep breath and turned her attention to the crowds ahead of her.

There were men there she didn't know, but most of the people were women and children. They were carrying bags and backpacks. The closer Jackie got, the more the crowds looked like solicitors. They'd walk up and knock on doors or approach homeowners sitting in their driveways.

Jackie slowed in front of the Vickerses house. Pop and Nancy were still sitting in their chairs. The crowds had moved past them.

"What's going on?" she asked, dismounting from her bike and rolling it up the driveway. "Who are they?"

Pop leaned forward in his chair and waited to speak until Jackie and Candace had gotten closer. Nancy's arms were folded across her chest.

"They're from the apartment complex a few blocks away," Pop said. "They're asking for handouts."

Candace glanced over her shoulder at the closest group of people and lowered her voice. "Handouts?"

Nancy nodded. "Food. Water. Gasoline. Diapers. Like we're a supermarket or something."

"Now, Nancy," Pop said, putting his hand on her knee. "They're frightened. They're unprepared. Like the rest of us, they don't really know for certain what happened. I don't blame them."

"I don't blame them," she snapped under her breath, "but it bothers me they'd think we could help. It's not as though we're swimming in produce and nonperishables."

Jackie watched a woman with two small children approach a neighbor across the street and three houses down. She was the last of the shoppers, as it were. Her bag was virtually empty. Jackie could tell by the way it easily swung back and forth on the woman's arm.

She couldn't hear the conversation, but she saw her neighbor hold up a finger. The woman knelt down as she waited, kissed both children on their foreheads, and then graciously accepted two cans of food. She almost genuflected with thanks before moving to the next house.

"It hasn't even been a day," said Candace. "They can't be out of food or other things yet, can they?"

"They're not out," Jackie said. "They probably won't run out for days. But they're smart."

"How do you figure?" asked Pop.

"With a hurricane or a flood, we know there's an end in sight," Jackie said. "We know we've got a week, maybe two, without power. Some of us can go to hotels. Others can go to shelters. Somewhere not far away there is power, and we know it'll eventually come back on."

Candace held up a finger. "There's the Red Cross."

Jackie nodded. "That's right. But here and now there isn't any of that. There's no support, and there's no end in sight. We don't even know what happened last night."

"It was a solar storm," Pop stated.

"Maybe," said Jackie. "It doesn't really matter, though, does it? Solar storm, nuclear attack, computer hack, Revelations…"

Pop bristled. "It does matter. And it was a solar storm."

Jackie softened. "Okay," she relented, "it was a solar storm. Let's go with that."

Pop folded his arms and sat back in his chair, a twin to his wife. "Fine. It's a fact."

"That doesn't change the uncertainty of everything else," Jackie continued. "Those families, the ones from the apartment complex, have no idea how long this will last. They know at some point they'll run out of baby formula, food, water, soap, and everything else. They also know we'll eventually run out. But we have more of everything, in their minds. So they're better to come hit us up now, while we still have a lot, than when our supplies have dwindled three days or three weeks or three months from now."

The others stood there silently, presumably absorbing what Jackie had suggested. She knew she was right. She looked over her shoulder at the crowds working their way along the street. Some neighbors were helping; others weren't.

"The problem will be," she went on, "when they run out of everything and come back in desperation."

"Like feeding a stray cat," said Pop.

Jackie frowned. "I don't really like that analogy, Pop. These are people like you and me. But, yes. The analogy fits."

Candace blinked through a stream of tears coursing down her face. Her eyes pleaded with Jackie for some modicum of comfort where she knew there was likely none. "I hope it isn't what you think," she said while catching her breath. "Desperation is a bad thing. It's a very bad thing."

Jackie was so engrossed in Candace's emotion she didn't hear the footsteps pounding the street behind her. She spun around, surprised to see Marie standing at the curb.

"Mom, I saw you down here. What's going on? I thought you went to NASA?"

"I did. I'll fill you in when we get home."

Marie appeared clearly frustrated by the nonanswer. Jackie noticed the bruise-colored circles surrounding her eyes. Her mouth was drawn into a resting frown, deep lines framing the inside edges of both cheeks.

"There's not much to tell you," Jackie added.

Marie looked over her shoulder toward their home. "I didn't come here to ask you about Dad anyhow."

Jackie frowned. "Oh?"

Marie turned back to her mother. "We have a new visitor at the house. She just showed up. She's waiting for you."

"Who is it?"

"Kenny's mom."

Jackie heart skipped. "Has she heard from the boys? Does she know if they're okay?"

Marie shook her head. "No. That's why she walked over. She's panicking."

Jackie excused herself from the conversation with the Vickerses and walked her bike back to her house. Marie and Candace flanked her. She tried to keep her attention away from the blackened heap of homes to the left as she approached the cul-de-sac, but they drew her eyes like a magnet.

In the mess, somewhere, she knew there were bodies: bodies of parents, children, babies. Her stomach lurched. Her gaze stuck to one large piece of charred wood. It was part of the home's frame. It was long and narrow, two by six or longer. The fire hadn't just burned it. It had cracked it in a way that made the solid wood look crinkled, like a freshly pulled straw wrapper dampened with a droplet of water.

"Jackie?"

She turned away from the char to see Kenny's mother in the driveway. She had her arms folded and was rubbing them as if she were cold.

Jackie walked the bike over the threshold of the driveway where it met the street. She stopped next to the woman, who appeared more fragile than normal.

Karen Walsh was a waif. She'd always been wiry, but now she appeared sickly. Her thin, ashy blonde hair was pulled tight into a ponytail, revealing a large, pinched forehead. There was a large vein running close to the surface from her hairline to her brow. A stain of mascara was thick under her eyes. Her cheekbones strained against her nearly translucent skin. The divorce had worsened issues Jackie imagined already existed.

"Karen," she said, popping the kickstand on the bike and offering the woman a wide embrace. Karen reciprocated and Jackie's fingers found the woman's rib cage. No doubt she was sick.

"How are you?" Jackie asked.

"Worried. Have you heard from Rick or from Chris? My phones aren't working. The power's out at the house. I don't know what to think."

Jackie pulled away from Karen and shook her head. "No, nothing so far. I was hoping you had news."

"I'm just sick," she said. "I can't sleep, I can't eat, and I couldn't sit in that house alone for a minute longer. I had to do something. I hope you don't mind I came here."

Jackie gave her a reassuring smile. "Of course not. Why don't we go inside and I can fix you something to eat."

"You've already got a houseful," said Karen. "I didn't know that when I decided to come over."

"Not a problem," said Jackie. "One more person won't make a difference. Plus, it'll make me feel better having you here. We can count down the minutes until we see the boys together."

Karen nodded and wiped her eyes with the tips of her fingers. She tried to smile, but it looked to Jackie more like someone showing a dentist their teeth.

Jackie led her to the house. One more. What was one more person? Until it was two more. Or three more. There was only so much she could handle. She calmed herself, telling herself to stay strong. She left the bike on the porch and walked into her home. The waxy, vanilla scent of candles greeted her and masked the odor of stagnant smoke outside. The eyes of her guests followed her from the foyer and into the great room.

They were all sitting there expectantly. Reggie and Lana Buck sat together. Betty and Brian Brown were there. Marie was already plopped at the kitchen island, leaning on her elbows with her head in her hands. Candace walked in from the garage and took a seat next to Marie. Karen was standing next to the fireplace, chewing on her fingernails.

Reggie leaned forward on the sofa, scooting to the edge of his seat. "What's the news?"

Jackie opened her mouth to answer, but she hesitated. She still had to tell her daughter what she'd learned, or hadn't, about Clay. She needed to do that alone, without everyone else hearing it at the same time. The conversation wouldn't be easy, not with Marie, not with the rest of them. Looking at the people depending on her, Jackie realized that nothing was easy now.

In less than a day, *easy* was a word she couldn't find in her vocabulary. The world had changed overnight. Something deep inside her gut told her it was true.

It was apparent on the faces of the people in her home. It was breeding in the feral gang of boys on the street. It was spreading through the throng of apartment families looking for help before they needed it. It ate at what was left of Karen Walsh's body.

Jackie's eyes shifted from person to person. She measured them measuring her. Perhaps it was just her world that had changed, but she doubted it. Whether Clayton came home or not, whether Chris walked in the door in a minute or in a day, things had changed. She found Candace at the island and thought about what the young woman had said minutes earlier.

"Desperation is a very bad thing."

CHAPTER 15

SATURDAY, JANUARY 25, 2020, 4:32 PM CST
I-45 SOUTH NEAR HUNTSVILLE, TEXAS

"Are we getting close?" Kenny asked for the third time in five minutes.

"Closer," said Rick. It had taken a lot longer to reach Huntsville than he'd anticipated. Driving at forty miles per hour saved fuel, but it made for a grueling trip.

There were less than two hours until sundown. Rick didn't want to be on the road in the dark, but he knew he wasn't going to have a choice. He was a good forty-five miles from Mumphrey's home in Spring and twice that distance from Clear Lake.

"I gotta go to the bathroom," said Kenny. "Really bad. Can we please stop?"

"I can pull over here in a second. You can hop out and —"

"I can't go on the side of the road, Dad."

"Sure you can. We'll turn our heads and —"

"Dad," Kenny stressed. "I. Can't. Go. On. The. Side. Of. The. Road."

"*Oh*," Rick said. "I get it. How urgent is it?"

"Urgent."

Rick scanned the horizon. There wasn't much but thickets of pine trees and sloping grassland. He'd seen a sign for an exit a half mile back, so he knew one was coming up.

"All right," he said. "We'll stop. If we find a bathroom, everybody needs to go." He drove into the right lane and approached exit 118. It was a good choice. There was a pair of truck stops on the southbound feeder road as soon as he pulled off the interstate.

There were easily a half dozen big rigs parked at both of the stops. At the first stop, men and women were sitting in folding camping chairs, guarding their livelihoods. One group of men was standing under an awning near the building, flicking ashes off cigarettes in between long, cheek-sucking drags. Another couple was grilling on a portable propane grill. The man had a handgun holstered to his denim-clad thigh. All of them turned their attention to the Jeep when Rick pulled into the expansive parking lot.

"I don't know that I like the idea of mingling with a bunch of truckers," Nikki said nervously.

"Why? That sounds classist."

Nikki rolled her eyes. "The last truckers we met weren't the greatest."

"That shouldn't be an indictment against all of them."

Mumphrey piped in. "I get both sides of what you're saying. That father-son duo was pretty awful. I follow you, Nikki. But the boy here has to go to the toilet. We gotta help him out."

Rick eased the Jeep into a parking spot and shifted the SUV into park. "Plus," he said, "I'm not worried. I've got Deep Six Nikki on my side."

Nikki shouldered open the door and hung her right leg outside. She turned back and smirked. "So you think."

She led the group toward the main building. Rick walked behind her, paying attention to the sway of her hips, until the man at the grill interrupted his fantasy.

"Hey, y'all," he said, a spatula in his hand. "Where y'all from?"

Rick motioned for the group to continue to the building and the bathrooms. He stepped toward the griller, gratefully inhaling the cooking odor from the grill. "Houston area. You?"

"Oklahoma," he replied. "We got stuck here, just like the rest of these drivers. Guess it's better than being stuck on the road."

"Guess so. Are there working bathrooms in there?"

"For now," said the griller. "Probably only a matter of time before they get too nasty to use. Can't buy any food in there unless you got cash. Credit card system is down."

Rick looked over at the building. The lights were on; people were shopping up and down the aisles. There were three people working behind the counter.

"They have power?"

"Generator."

Rick stepped closer to the griller and the woman sitting in front of the truck. She was engrossed in the pages of a romance novel. She hadn't looked at Rick yet.

The griller turned back to prod a burger on the grill. He had a filthy white towel draped around his neck like a scarf. The gun strapped to his right leg was semiautomatic, either a 9mm or a .40 cal.

The griller glanced over his shoulder. "I'm Gary," he said. "This here's Fran."

The woman peeked over the top of the book and smiled. "Hey," she said.

Rick waved a hello. "Have you seen any police since the power went out?"

Gary flipped a burger. "Not a one." He pointed with the spatula toward the highway. "We seen a couple speed by on 45. That's it."

"Your trucks won't start?"

"Nope."

"Any idea what caused it?"

"The Russians or the Chinese," said Gary the Griller. "No doubt in my mind. They dropped one of them EMPs, killed off everything."

"What are you going to do?"

"Wait here for now," he said. "We've got access to food, a place to sleep. We're good for a couple weeks at least. No sense in risking anything on the road."

"I get it."

"Your Jeep is good though, huh? I'm guessing it's because it's old school. No electronics for the EMP to hit."

Rick motioned with his head to the group of smokers near the entrance of the building. "What do the others think?"

Gary laughed. "Everybody knows it's an enemy. There's one fella who thinks it's a false-flag operation."

"False flag?"

"Yeah. You know, a government conspiracy. They make us think it's a convenient enemy, but it's really our own government that's responsible. Like 9/11 and Sandy Hook."

"Never heard of it."

Gary shrugged. "I don't buy into it. I wasn't a birther either. But that's just me."

"Rick!" Nikki called from the building, holding open the door. "We need you in here."

Rick waved at her. "I gotta go," he said to Gary. "I wish you luck. Hope everything works out."

"Nothing we can do about it," he said and then laughed. "Just make the best of it while we can. Then we fight like hell."

Rick offered an understanding smile then marched toward the building. Nikki stood there, holding the door for him. He was surprised at the dichotomy of the emotional reaction to the apocalypse. On one hand there was a group of "doomsdayers" bent on some sort of Revelations-style salvation. Then there were those, some of whom claimed to be cops, using the chaos as an excuse for violence and thievery. At the other end of the spectrum there were these truckers — salt-of-the-earth, hardworking men and women who were taking the punches as they came. They seemed unfazed.

He thought about where he fell along that spectrum. He wasn't sure. He didn't believe the conspiracy theorists. This wasn't a false flag. It wasn't the Chinese or Russians, at least he didn't think so. That undulating red aurora at the park made Rick believe it was a solar storm.

He couldn't know how long they'd have to live without power. Even if it came back at the snap of a finger, all of the cars and trucks littering the roads were dead.

What did that mean?

What would happen to his 401k? Would there still be money in his financial accounts, or would the surge have destroyed the banking computers that held all of his money?

He'd been so focused on getting everyone home, he hadn't really considered what they'd face once they got there. A chill ran along his spine and he shuddered involuntarily. He tried to shake the thoughts of what might still lie ahead. It was too much to consider.

He thanked Nikki for holding the door and started to move past her and away from the suffocating odor of stale cigarette smoke, then stopped in the entry when she whispered to him.

"Hey," she said, "I know you were looking at me when I was walking ahead of you. Your eyes were a little lower than they should have been."

A rush of heat rushed Rick's face. The blast of warm embarrassment replaced the chill still radiating through him. "I…uh…I…"

She winked, offering him a reprieve. "No need to apologize, I just wanted you to know I noticed."

Rick swallowed hard. "Still. Sorry. I'll try to keep my eyes up."

Nikki laughed. "Good luck with that. By the way, your son's shopping for snacks. You have any cash?"

"A little. Everyone finished in the bathroom?"

"Yep," she said, leading him to the candy aisle. "Except for you. What did that guy say? You were talking to him for a while."

Rick still couldn't look her in the eyes, or anywhere else, so he kept his gaze on his shoes as he answered. "He floated a couple of theories about the power loss. He said they haven't seen any police presence. He also said this place only takes cash and that the bathrooms are good for now."

"I knew the last two things already," she said. "I could have guessed about the police. Everybody seems pretty chill here, like they're okay with everything. You get that vibe?"

Rick nodded and raised his head. He looked off to the left as he talked. "I do. Kinda weird."

"What's their theory?"

"Most of them are pretty sure it was an attack. One guy thinks our own government did it."

"You buy that?"

Rick watched his son pick a fifth chocolate bar from the shelf. His arms were full. "No. I'm with Mumphrey. I think it's weather related. It doesn't change anything though."

"How so?" Nikki asked.

Rick finally looked at her, drawn into her eyes. She was searching him for an explanation, her mouth drawn tight with worry. Deep Six Nikki was a badass, but she was human.

"No matter how we lost power," he said, "we have the same issues facing us. When's it coming back? And if it does, what damage is left behind?"

"You think it's a long-term issue?"

Rick shrugged. He didn't know. He *couldn't* know. He imagined nobody knew. Even the government, which might know the extent of the damage, couldn't be sure how long it would be before the power was back.

"I think we need to be prepared for the long haul."

Nikki's eyes left his and she looked past him, her mind seemingly drifting with her gaze. She nodded slowly then blinked back to the present and led Rick to his son.

Kenny and Chris both clung to more candy than they could comfortably hold. Kenny also had a pleading look on his face, his brows arched high with the desperation of a child asking for something he knew his parent would likely deny.

"You don't need that," Rick said, playing his part to a tee. "You just ate this morning."

Kenny's face melted with disappointment. His shoulders drooped for emphasis. "Pleeease? This morning feels like it was last week."

Rick glanced at Nikki. She held up her hands, abstaining from the decision. He sighed.

"Fine," he relented. "Two each. That's it. You don't need too much sugar, especially because we're going to be in the car for a few more hours."

Kenny's face lit up and he thanked his dad. Chris thanked Rick too and offered him a couple of the bars he didn't choose. Rick took one and handed the other to Nikki.

"Where's Mumphrey?" he asked, realizing he hadn't seen the old man since walking into the store.

"Over by the radios," said Nikki. "He was hoping one of them might work."

"Do they?"

"Most of them," she said. "But they're all two-ways. They've got maybe a one- to two-mile range."

"Wouldn't be bad to have a couple of those," said Rick. "How much?"

Nikki shrugged and led Rick back to the electronics section. Mumphrey was playing with a couple of the radios, oblivious to their presence. He jumped and almost dropped the radio in his hands when Rick called his name.

"Mumphrey, how much are those things?"

"This one's forty-nine dollars," he said. "You need two. So it's ninety-eight. They've only got a one- or two-mile range though."

"Good enough for me," said Rick. "Are there four of them?"

"Yeah."

"Let's get four."

Nikki nudged Rick. "They only take cash, remember?"

"I've got it," he said.

"What about later?" she questioned. "If this is a long haul, as you suggested, won't you need as much cash as you can keep?"

"Good point," admitted Rick. "But I also need a way to communicate without standing next to the person. This is good."

Nikki eyed the radios. "Two hundred dollars good?"

"I won't pay that." Rick nodded toward the front counter. "Let's go," he said. "Mumphrey, could you carry two of the radios? I'll take the other two."

Mumphrey handed a pair of radios to Rick and grabbed two more from the shelf. Rick wove his way to the counter and the trio of clerks in various states of consciousness.

All three clerks were men. Two of them, neither of whom seemed interested in helping him with his purchase, hadn't shaved in a week or more. The third was younger and slightly more eager. His eyes were swollen and bloodshot. His hands jittered as he drew a swig from a large can filled with an energy drink. Rick guessed none of them had bathed in a while.

"How's it going?" Rick asked politely. The group helped him deposit the load of candy bars, bottled waters, and radios.

The two unshaven clerks grumbled their responses. Both sounded drunk or on the verge of collapse.

The red-eyed clerk at the register belched. "Cash only."

A waft of citrus-laced tobacco breath brought tears to Rick's eyes. He took a step back from the counter.

"I've got cash," he said. "I wanted to deal with you on the radios."

The clerk's face twisted into a knot. "Deal?"

"Yeah," Rick said. "Nobody else is buying them. You need cash, right? I'll give you a hundred for the four of them."

"No way," said one of the unshaven clerks. "They were already half off. Those are good radios."

"Yeah," said the register clerk. "They're good radios."

"One twenty, plus everything else here. The candy. The water."

"You know you've got fifty dollars in water, right?"

Rick laughed until he saw the blank expressions on the clerks' faces. "Ten apiece? That's gouging. It's illegal."

"You a cop?" asked the register clerk.

"No."

"Then it ain't illegal. It's fifty for the water. Twenty for the chocolate. Two hundred for the radios. I'll skip the tax."

"Thirty for the water. Ten for the chocolate. One twenty for the radios."

"We ain't dealing," said the register clerk. "You think—"

"Hang on," said the bearded clerk who hadn't spoken yet. He was the oldest of the three. His hair was receding against a scalp that had seen too much sun. The hair remaining on his head matched the mangy white stubble on his face. He stepped to the counter and looked down at the haul on top of it.

"One hundred sixty? What bills you got? I don't want big bills."

"Twenties. Fives."

"One eighty, you got a deal."

The register clerk narrowed his red eyes "But—"

"Shut up. I'm the assistant manager on duty. I get the say. One eighty."

Rick shook his head. "One sixty."

A sly smile snuck across the older clerk's face. He rubbed the scruff on his chin. "One seventy-five."

"Done."

Rick told the boys to grab the candy and pulled out his old, worn wallet. Nikki got the water and Mumphrey grabbed the radios without being asked.

He pulled out the cash and laid it on the counter one bill at a time before stuffing the aged billfold back in his pocket. "Thanks."

"Thank you," said the older clerk. He quickly tucked the cash into his hands and folded the bills in half.

Rick handed the keys to Nikki. "I'm going to the bathroom. I'll be right out."

Nikki took the keys, put her hand on the back of Kenny's head, and moved the group to the parking lot. Rick wound his way through the store, following the overhead signs pointing to the men's restroom.

He pushed open the door with his fists and shuffled onto the aged linoleum floor. He stopped at the ceiling-to-counter mirror above the row of sinks and looked at the nearly unrecognizable man staring back at him.

It hadn't even been a full day since the event, but Rick was already a shell of himself. Instead of appearing thin and fit, he was gaunt. His skin was sallow. His eyes were sunken and cushioned by thick, swollen lids. His five o'clock shadow had deepened, revealing the gray he worked so hard to hide on his head.

He leaned into the mirror and touched his face, pulling down on his eyes to reveal a riverbed of swollen red blood vessels. He was no better than the register clerk. He tucked his nose into his armpit and sniffed. At least he smelled like scented pine, even if he looked like death warmed over.

Having seen enough of his doppelgänger, Rick spun on his heel to find a urinal. He didn't really have to go, but thought it better than waiting until he did. He'd reached the first one when he heard footsteps behind him.

"Hey." It was the older clerk. The younger one who'd manned the register was with him. The younger one had a sawed-off shotgun at his waist, aimed at Rick.

Rick felt like wetting himself. He raised his hands above his head. "H-h-hey." He was as confused as he was frightened and immediately regretted leaving his handgun in the Jeep.

"You got more cash in that wallet?"

Rick stood silently, cursing his fortune. Three times in the same day he'd had someone trying to hurt him. He wondered if he had the word SUCKER tattooed on his forehead. What was it that had people willing and ready to take advantage of him? If he still wondered where on the apocalyptic response spectrum he stood, he now knew definitively where most of humanity likely did. It had taken no time for people to devolve to their basest instincts.

The register clerk nudged the shotgun toward Rick and stepped forward. "He asked you a question."

"I-I—"

The register clerk mocked Rick. "I-I-I. You got money in the wallet. Give it to us."

"This was your plan the whole time?" Rick said, stalling. "Bargain with me and then steal the rest?"

The older clerk halved the distance between the shotgun and Rick. "No," he said. "It wasn't until I saw all the extra bills in your wallet and you decided to go to the bathroom alone that I figured I'd take advantage of the situation."

Rick couldn't believe it. He'd set himself up without even knowing it. "And you're the manager?"

"Assistant manager," he smirked. "Now carefully reach into your pocket, drop the wallet on the floor, and slide it over to me with your foot. Then we'll watch you take a leak and escort you from the premises."

Rick stood still, his eyes darting from the gun to the older clerk and back.

The older clerk cleared his throat. "You understand?"

Rick nodded and lowered his right hand. He dipped it into his back pocket and withdrew his billfold. He raised the worn, overstuffed brown leather wallet and held it above his head before kneeling to put it on the ground. He kept his eyes on the shotgun, which was beginning to shake in the hands of its energy-drink-swilling operator.

The older clerk's eyes were bulging in anticipation. "That's it," he hissed. "That's it."

Rick looked down at his wallet for a brief instant as if to say goodbye. His arm tensed as he readied himself to give away his money, his identification, and the wallet his father gave him.

"C'mon," said the one with the shotgun. "Slide it ov—"

A loud grunt and the shuffling of feet called Rick's eyes up to the clerks. They weren't alone anymore.

Rick fell back on his heels, catching himself with his hands. The clerks were still there, one of them aiming a shotgun at him. But standing behind them were Gary the Griller and Deep Six Nikki.

Gary had his handgun at the back of the older one's head. Nikki had the TP9 from the glove box pressed to the shotgun clerk's temple.

"Drop the shotgun," said Gary. "Now."

The clerk knelt down and put the short-barreled blaster on the floor. He was cursing everyone and everything in the room.

"Kick it over to Rick," said Nikki.

The clerk started to turn in protest, and in a split second Nikki snapped her knee forcefully into his kidney. His body wrenched awkwardly and he gasped in pain, grabbing at his side.

"Do as the lady says," instructed Gary.

The clerk hunched over, drooling and huffing from the blast to his lower back. He shuffled weakly with his right foot and slid the shotgun most of the distance to Rick.

Rick grabbed the weapon by the buttstock before leveling the shotgun at the register clerk.

Gary thumped the barrel of his gun on top of the older clerk's head. "What do you want to do with these fellas, Rick? Your call."

The hunched-over clerk mumbled something and spat a thick yellowish gob of fluid onto the linoleum. He grunted and then laughed.

"What did you say?" Nikki asked.

The clerk, apparently undaunted by Nikki's first jab, suggested what he'd like to do to her. Before he'd finished with the vulgarity of it, she'd shoved him into the tile wall.

When he caught himself against the wall, she drove a foot, heel first, into his calf, twisted to the side, flicked her leg upward, and drove the toe of her hiking boot into his nose.

It exploded with a spray of blood and the clerk grabbed his face while crumpling to the floor in a heap. His nasal, gasping wails echoed off the walls of the bathroom.

Nikki shifted her weight to her other leg, jumped into the air, and caught the older clerk on the jaw with her heel. His head snapped to the side, carrying him into the row of sinks away from Gary. His forehead slapped against the counter before he dropped unconscious to the linoleum.

"Holy mother..." said Gary, his face ashen. He aimlessly waved the gun as he backed away from the mess in front of him. "Who in the world are you?"

Nikki twisted her neck and it cracked. She flexed her fingers in and out, relaxing the tightly balled fists she'd employed while kicking the clerks into oblivion.

She shrugged. "I'm nobody special. I just don't like crooks." She looked over at Rick. "You okay?"

Rick nodded. "How'd you guys know what was happening?"

"I saw them," said Gary. "When your friends walked past me and you weren't with them, I figured you were still in the store. Those clerks weren't shy about taking that shotgun through the aisles. I figured something was up."

Nikki stepped over the whimpering register clerk. He was in the fetal position, shivering in a growing pool of his own blood.

"He came and got me," said Nikki. "He thought you might be in trouble."

"And the boys?"

"They're with Mumphrey. They're okay."

Rick swallowed hard and reached for his wallet. He shoved it in his back pocket with one hand while still holding the shotgun with the other.

His eyes danced from Nikki to Gary and back again. "Thank you," he said. "I know that's not enough, but thank you."

"It's enough," said Gary. "Hell, I'd pay money to see missy over here do her *Crouching Tiger, Hidden Dragon* bit again." He kicked at the older clerk. "What do you want to do with them?"

Rick stared at the blood leaching across the linoleum. "I think that's up to you, Gary," he said. "You're staying here. We're leaving."

Gary sighed. "Makes sense. I'll take care of the clerk up front and make sure he doesn't have any designs on anything. The other fellas will be more than happy to figure out a plan for these two here."

"The smokers?"

"Them and a couple of the others," he said. "None of us are leaving. We'll figure it out."

Nikki motioned to the bleeding one. "He might need medical help."

Gary chuckled. "He might. You stomped the snot out of him."

The clerk whimpered. He tried lifting his head and whispered something unintelligible. It was too much effort, apparently, and he gave up. His eyes were swollen shut. His nose looked like half a sourdough pretzel.

"We should go," said Nikki.

Rick agreed and they moved from the bathroom into the store. Rick handed Gary the shotgun. He followed Nikki out of the building and into the sunlight. He trailed behind her for a few steps until she slowed her walk and strode next to him.

"That's twice," she said, smiling.

Rick raised his hands in surrender. "I wasn't checking you out. I swear."

She giggled in a way that belied her strength and disarmed him. "Not that," she said. "That's twice I've saved your behind."

CHAPTER 16

MISSION ELAPSED TIME:
72 DAYS, 18 HOURS, 34 MINUTES, 06 SECONDS
241.5 MILES ABOVE EARTH

"For not knowing Russian, I'm a regular Crazy Ivan," Clayton said. *"Pozdravleniya."*

He congratulated himself for having gotten as far as he had. He'd undocked successfully without hitting the ISS and damaging the Soyuz. He'd entered orbit and completed two passes around the planet. And now he was on the verge of the deorbit burn.

Clayton entered the final commands into the computer that enabled the main engine, known as the SKD. The cover for the propulsion system was open. He'd double-checked the parameters as best he could, and the SKD ignited.

The engine was, counterintuitively, a brake. It was intended to slow the Soyuz's speed as it reached the most vulnerable points of the reentry. It was on the rear side of the craft and fired for exactly four minutes and forty-five seconds.

Normally, days before reentry, the crew would have had a run-through with the ground team. The control instructors in Russia would have reminded them of important tasks and tested them on emergency procedures. They would have relayed to the crew a timeline and ground conditions. That hadn't happened. Clayton Shepard, first-time astronaut, was left to his own devices.

This was the critical moment.

He'd known from the instant he'd decided his only way home was to self-guide the Soyuz back to Earth, this was the point where he was most likely to screw up. It was also where he'd likely die if he had.

There were only three choices. He would live, at least until the next phase of reentry, he would die a quick but agonizing death, or he would slowly suffocate to death as he drifted into the abyss.

Clayton held his breath. He wiped sweat from his eyes. If the calculated burn wasn't enough he'd skip off the atmosphere like a pebble flicked across a pond. That was the abyss option. If it was too much, he could burn up. That, of course, led to the agonizing, if not relatively fast, demise.

The SKD stopped its burn; the indicators looked good. Clayton's entry was within the window, according to the data he could understand on the panel in front of him. He could be pretty certain he wasn't going to bounce off the atmosphere. However, he wasn't entirely sure his measurements and calculations had slowed the craft enough to prevent too much friction once he sank into the dense layers of the atmosphere.

Regardless, he acted as though he had fifty-five minutes until landing. He was on the final leg of his journey back to Earth.

Clayton reached up and grabbed his visor. He closed his helmet and depressurized the Orbital module. The next step was separating the crew module from the other two.

He looked over at Ben Greenwood then at Boris.

"I should have saved you," he said to both of them. "I could have saved you. If I'd ignored protocol, worried less about myself, and gotten out to you sooner, you might have lived."

Clayton didn't know why he was saying it. He couldn't reconcile the emotion that pushed the apology from his lips. He did know, rationally, there wasn't anything he could have done. Both of them were likely dead within a few minutes of the CME shutting off or damaging the critical systems in their suits. It might not even have taken that long.

There was something about sitting between them that turned the cramped but utilitarian space of the module into a confessional. For more than twenty minutes he talked to the men. He told them about his fears. He opened up about his selfishness, how he never should have become an astronaut. It wasn't what his wife had wanted, he admitted to them. He knew she was against it, but he manipulated her into going along with it. He played on her guilt and her love for him until she relented, until she supported his application.

Now he'd left her alone in a dark world. He had no way to talk to her, no way to know if she and their children were okay. The idea of never seeing them again was overwhelming. It was driving his efforts to get home, to survive what should have killed him.

As bad as it was in orbit, it could be far worse below. In space he had to worry about physics and chemistry and biology. Those were the forces acting against him unless he used them to his benefit. On Earth, he'd have to worry about people on the other end of a fulcrum; he'd need to protect his family from forces he couldn't master with his wits alone. His journey might not truly begin until he landed. He hadn't considered that until now. What a lousy time for the thought to fill his mind.

He was contemplating the rough road ahead when he felt a percussive explosion outside of the Soyuz. It sounded like somebody was clinging to the outside of the craft and was slamming it with a sledgehammer. The Soyuz was shaking from the force.

Had he miscalculated? Was he not on the right trajectory? Was he coming in too fast? Were the heat shields compromised?

An instant later there was another explosive shock to the craft and the Soyuz shook violently. The blows felt as if they were hitting all sides of the crew module.

Clayton's teeth rattled. His heart pounded against his chest. He could feel the pulse in his ears as he frantically scanned the instrumentation for some sort of warning, some kind of alert.

There was nothing.

CHAPTER 17

SATURDAY, JANUARY 25, 2020, 7:31 PM CST
SPRING, TEXAS

As tough as the first part of the trip was for Rick and his group, the last fifty miles were uneventful. Sure, they'd taken twice as long as normal, but he was getting close to dropping off the first of his passengers. He was that much nearer to being home, and more importantly, his son was nearer to the arms of his mother.

He loved his son unequivocally. Kenny loved him too. Their male bonding time was good, but Kenny's mom needed her son. After the divorce, after Rick left her emotionally ruined, Kenny had become her purpose.

She was a good mom before the divorce. She'd become a great mom after it. Rick knew Kenny sometimes rolled his eyes at his mother's attentiveness or concern, but the kid loved it. Kenny needed her too.

Rick had stolen a part of both of them when he'd cheated on them. He'd had their unadulterated trust…until he didn't. Rick had offered his ex primary custody without a fight. It wasn't that he didn't want to have his son with him, it was that he knew his mother needed the boy. It was the least he could do for them after causing as much pain as he had.

Rick could only imagine how Karen was coping. No power, no phone, her son not home. Getting Kenny home to his mother was the most important thing he could do. Despite his occasional fantasies about Nikki, Rick truly was focused on getting his son home.

He knew Chris's mother would be just as worried, especially with her husband, Clay, the astronaut, orbiting around the planet. He hadn't talked about it with Chris. He didn't want to worry the kid any more than he already was. It would be good to get the Shepard boy home too.

Rick weaved around a stalled Mazda SUV. "All right," he said, "Mumphrey, we're here in Spring. Tell me where to exit."

Mumphrey was looking out the window. He didn't say anything. His gaze was distant. His mouth was turned down into a vacant frown.

Rick repeated himself. "Mumphrey, we're in Spring. What exit do I take?"

The old man blinked and smiled. "That's the thing," he said. "I probably should have told you sooner. I mean, I know I should have told you sooner."

Rick glanced at Mumphrey in the rearview mirror. "Told me what?"

"I don't live in Spring," he said. "I mean, I used to live in Spring, right off the exit. But I don't now."

Rick checked his mirrors. There was no traffic in either direction. He slowed the Jeep to a stop, unfastened his seatbelt, and spun around to look Mumphrey in the eyes.

"What do you mean you don't live in Spring? Where do you live?"

Mumphrey looked down at his lap. His hands were clasped together and he was nervously rubbing his thumbs across one another. "In the pop-up."

"What?"

Mumphrey looked up at Rick, his eyes glistening. He swallowed hard. "I live in the pop-up. I go from camp to camp. Been doing it since I lost my home. Bank took it when I got sick."

Nikki reached for Mumphrey's hands. "I'm so sorry, Mumphrey. I had no idea."

Rick softened his tone. "Why didn't you tell us?"

Mumphrey shrugged. His eyes welled. "I dunno. Haven't you ever had a secret that was too embarrassing to tell? You know, like if you told someone, it would change what they thought of you?"

Rick glanced at his son and then back to Mumphrey. "I have. I get it."

Mumphrey squeezed his eyes shut, pressing the tears down the sides of his face. "I live in the pop-up, but I keep moving. I was afraid if I stayed there by myself…"

"You don't owe us an explanation," Nikki said. "We're in this together." She looked over at Rick. "Right?"

"Of course," said Rick. "You've been a big help with the boys. I'm glad you're with us."

Mumphrey swallowed hard and nodded. A grateful, crooked smile spread across his face. "Thank you."

Rick turned back around and buckled himself into his seat. He planted his hands on the wheel and shifted into gear. "All right," he said. "Let's get these boys home."

He accelerated and swerved around a stalled eighteen-wheeler. It was dark, which made the going even slower than it had been in the daylight. Rick's neck ached. His shoulders were sore. But he felt good.

"So I guess you're gonna tell me you don't live in Galveston," he said to Nikki.

She laughed. "No," she said. "I do. I'm living on the beach at the moment."

"At the moment?"

"Yeah," she said. "I'm a nomad. I can't ever stay in one place too long. I get bored. I think it's from spending the first eighteen years of my life in one spot. Now that I'm free to roam, I do."

"So you're not from Texas?"

"Nope."

"No hint?"

"I'm not from Texas."

Rick flipped on the high beams, avoided a collision between two pickup trucks and glanced over at Nikki for a split second. Then it hit him. "Nikki's not your real name, is it?"

Nikki didn't say anything. Rick could sense her shifting uncomfortably in her seat.

He pressed. "I bet your dad wasn't a cop either."

"My dad was a cop," she said. "That's the truth."

They rode for a half hour in silence with the boys and Mumphrey asleep in the backseat. It was cold in the Jeep, with the temperature having dropped and the back window blown out.

They were getting close to downtown Houston. It was odd. There was no evidence of the tall towers that hugged the eastern edge of the interstate. It was too dark. There was no moon. The skyscrapers that dotted the center of the nation's third-largest city were powerless, just like everything else.

Rick finally broke the silence. "I guess I could just Google you," he said. "I mean, I could if my phone worked."

Nikki was staring out the window into the darkness. Her forehead was leaning against the glass.

"What would I Google, though?" he wondered aloud, trying to bait her. "Deep Six Nikki? Nikki UFC? Shut Down Valve?"

"Shut Off Valve," she said without turning her head.

"What?"

Nikki turned and rolled her eyes. "It's the Shut OFF Valve," she said. "Why would it be the shut down valve? There's no such thing."

The interstate curved south around downtown. The unlit skyline was to their left now.

"What's with the attitude?" Rick asked. "I'm just trying to make conversation."

"You're prying."

"Prying?"

"I told you I don't put down roots," she said. "I don't discuss my private stuff. Not with anybody."

"You have to make an exception."

"Why?"

"You've saved my life twice," he said, smiling. "I have to know who to thank in my will. If I don't know your real name, the trustee is going to keep the riches for himself."

"Don't you have an ex who gets everything?"

"She already got everything," he said. "Deservedly so."

"So if you're a bad guy, why would I want to let you in?"

"I didn't say I was a bad guy."

Nikki turned back to the window. "Riiiight."

Rick enjoyed the banter with Nikki. She was a challenge. She was smart. She could also murder him with her bare hands if she was so inclined. There was also something dishonest about her. He liked that too.

It wasn't just that she had a pseudonym and wouldn't divulge her real name. It wasn't that she kept everything close to the vest and was borderline misleading about who she was and where she'd been. Sure, that was part of it, but there was something more.

It took a poser to know one. That was it. Rick could see through her because he saw himself in her. There was a good person in there somewhere, someone who wanted to do good but was always battling demons who'd have her slide toward the unethical or immoral. It was something only damaged people could see in one another.

The undamaged wouldn't see it, or if they did, they'd spend all of their energy trying to change it. There was no winning. Rick's ex was a good woman bent on changing him from the very beginning. She was attracted to his dark side, to his pliable view of the world. With that came the risk.

"I'm no more a bad person than you. I think we're the same, actually," he said and immediately regretted his choice of words. "Wait," he said, stopping Nikki before she could answer. "I didn't mean it that way. That sounded like a villain talking to a superhero at the end of a really bad movie."

Nikki folded her arms across her chest. "I was gonna say —"

Rick raised a finger to silence her. "Hang on. What I'm saying is I think you hide things for the same reason I hid things. There's something you're battling within yourself."

Nikki laughed the kind of chuckle that told Rick he'd dug the hole deeper. "Okay," she said. "You don't know me. You don't know anything about me except what I've chosen to tell you. So don't presume anything and stop with the deep psychoanalysis. It's all crap and it's unattractive."

Rick gripped both hands tightly on the wheel at ten o'clock and two o'clock. He fixed his eyes to the high beams illuminating the road and checked the speedometer. He was doing fifty. It was a little fast for the conditions, but he wanted to get the boys home. Chris first, he decided as he whizzed past the south loop. He knew Gulfgate Mall was to the right, although he couldn't see it. Beyond the triangular beam of the lights was darkness.

It reminded Rick of looking out the window of an airplane on a clear night. He could always tell when they were hugging a coastline. The dots of yellow and white lights would end at the shore, giving way to the never-ending blackness of the ocean. It always freaked him out, thinking about the vastness of the sea. It made him think about crashing, about surviving alone in the cold, wet dark.

As he drove south, he wasn't worried about the cold or the water. The dark, however, sent a chill along his spine he felt in his legs and arms.

"I don't pretend to know you," he said to Nikki without turning to look at her. "I hardly know myself, despite a lot of crap-filled psychoanalysis."

He changed lanes. The Jeep rumbled and stuttered when he accelerated again. The gas gauge showed a quarter of a tank. It was enough for now.

"I'll be honest with you, Nikki," he said, despite believing that whenever someone said that, they were lying. "I don't really care what your real name is. Your childhood, good or bad, doesn't matter to me. I'm interested in getting my kid home to his mom. I'm concerned about what's gonna happen when I run out of gas or if what little food I have in my refrigerator is halfway to spoiling."

Rick changed lanes again and rolled past Broadway, the exit for Hobby Airport. He was less than ten minutes from the South Beltway and maybe fifteen or twenty from his exit. The yellow high beams cut a path along the concrete highway. He'd driven this interstate countless times, but it was a foreign trip right now. It was the darkness, the fear that at any moment another nut job would stop them or attack them or worse.

"That's pretty harsh," said Nikki.

Rick glanced at her. "What is?"

"What you said."

"Sorry."

"No, you're not."

"Look, Nikki," Rick said. "I think you're attractive. I think you're smart. Normally I'd be relentless. Truth is, I don't have the energy for it."

He drew his right hand from the wheel and wagged his finger between himself and Nikki. "This sexual tension, or whatever it is between us—"

"It's not sexual tension."

"Whatever it is, I can't do it. It's stupid. The world is dark. There's no power. We've almost died three times today."

"*You've* almost died."

He rolled his eyes and corrected himself. "I've almost died three times."

He checked the gas gauge again. It hadn't moved. His speed was steady.

Nikki tugged on the seatbelt across her chest. She turned toward Rick and put her hand on his leg.

"I appreciate the honesty," she said, "and I'm sorry for saying you were full of crap. I just don't like talking about myself. It's a me problem."

"I like a girl who can admit her faults."

Nikki turned back toward the window with a roll of her eyes. "Of course you do."

Rick steered through the darkness, driving in silence until he found his exit and slowed onto the ramp. He instinctively flipped the turn signal before realizing he didn't need it.

He looked over and Nikki's eyes were closed. Her head bounced against the window as the Jeep navigated the rough-hewn feeder road. Rick couldn't be sure what time it was, but he knew it was late. Without a moon, he couldn't accurately guess the time, but he figured it was close to nine o'clock.

He turned off the feeder road and rolled through the obstacle course on Bay Area Boulevard. For the first time since the truck stop, he saw groups of people gathered together. Some were on street corners, others in parking lots. He'd only catch a glimpse of them in the ambient light of the high beams. He could feel the people watching him as he passed. Rick wondered how many working cars or trucks had driven the road since the event the night before.

He turned off Bay Area Boulevard onto a less traveled street. He was only a few minutes from Chris's house. Finally.

"Hey, guys," he said to everyone in the Jeep. "It's time to wake up. We're almost there." He rolled to a stop at an intersection. Just beyond the spray of the headlights were the shadowy outlines of a group of people. They were walking toward him.

From the backseat, Kenny sat up straight and mumbled groggily, "Are we home?"

Rick smiled at his son in the rearview mirror. "Getting there."

"Did I sleep?" asked Nikki.

Rick kept his foot on the brake, anxious to see who was approaching his Jeep. He could see their basketball shoes, the low sling of their jeans. "For a minute," he said to Nikki.

"What are you waiting for?" asked Chris. "Why are we stopped?"

"No reason," said Rick, his attention on the group of teens waving their hands at him. They were alternately shielding their eyes and motioning for him to move toward them. One of them, the one in the front, had a shaved head. Another had a mop of dark hair covering his eyes. His pants were baggy and loose fitting.

"Looks like they want something," said Mumphrey. He cleared his throat. "I wouldn't give it to 'em. I'd keep moving. I don't like the look of 'em."

Rick lifted his foot from the brake and pressed the accelerator, turning the wheel to the right. He watched them as he picked up speed and then shifted to the side-view mirror once he'd completed the turn.

The boys had picked up speed. They weren't walking. They were running. They were yelling at him. He couldn't understand what they were saying over the rev of the Jeep's engine.

"Punks," he muttered and then turned his attention to Chris. "I turn up here, right?"

"Yes, sir."

Rick turned into Chris's neighborhood, which was only two and a half miles from his ex's house. He'd be quick at the Shepards' house. His ex would be worried until the second he put Kenny into her arms.

As Rick turned onto the main street that looped around Chris's neighborhood, groups of people appeared from the dark like ghosts. They looked like families. They were carrying bags and boxes. Some of them were carrying their sleeping children. They eyed the Jeep like zombies. Rick punched the accelerator to speed past them.

"They look like refugees you see on the Discovery Channel," said Mumphrey. "You know, the ones forced from their homes and they take what they have and they keep walking to another country? I was watching this documentary about it…"

Rick tuned Mumphrey out and found Chris's street. He turned right and drove to the house at the end of the street, rolled into the driveway, and shut off the ignition.

Nikki wrinkled her nose. "Anyone else smell smoke?" she asked, interrupting Mumphrey's description of the Syrian refugee crisis. "Like a forest fire?"

"I smell it," said Mumphrey. "Definitely."

Rick swung open his door. The air was bitter and sour. Something had burned. It was more than that, though. There was the odor of something else, something foul. He couldn't place it.

Chris hopped out of the Jeep and ran to his front door. He tried opening it, but it was locked. He knocked on the door, calling to his mother.

The front door swung open and Chris disappeared into the yellow glow of the interior. Rick heard the happy cries of Jackie Shepard and he smiled. He'd done something right.

He turned to shut his door when he heard a familiar voice coming from the house. *Karen?*

"Rick? Is that you? Kenny?" she called, running toward the Jeep. Kenny jumped from the backseat and bolted past his dad to his mother. She cloaked him with her arms and buried her face in his head.

Rick walked toward them, his hands stuffed into his pockets. He lowered his eyes as he approached his ex.

"Rick," she said, looking up from Kenny while clinging to him, "what happened?"

"Long story," he said.

"Rick," she said, drawing his eyes to her, "thank you."

Rick looked at Karen and hardly recognized her. She was a shell of the woman he'd seen less than forty-eight hours earlier. "No thanks necessary."

Karen started to smile and then stopped. Her eyes left Rick and moved past him, over his left shoulder. "Who is that?"

Rick turned to see Nikki standing outside of the Jeep. Mumphrey was behind her, stretching his arms.

"They're campers," Rick said. "We met them at the park. They've been a great help."

"Why does she look familiar?"

"I just have one of those faces," Nikki said, walking toward them with her hand extended. "I'm Nikki."

Karen kept her hands on her son. She gave Nikki the once-over.

"Nikki," Rick said, "this is Karen, Kenny's mom. Karen, this is Nikki, and that's Mumphrey."

Mumphrey stopped mid-stretch and waved. "Hi, ma'am."

"They were stranded at the park. We offered them a ride. They were a big help in getting us home."

Karen pursed her lips. "I'm sure they were."

"It's not like that," Rick said.

"It's not like that," Nikki echoed, stepping back.

Jackie Shepard emerged from the house. "Rick," she said, "thank you so much."

Saved by the bell, Rick thought.

Jackie bounded toward Rick and stopped next to Karen. Her eyes were wet and swollen. "Thank you for getting Chris home. I can't imagine what it took."

"It was nothing," Rick said.

"That's Nikki," said Karen.

"And I'm Mumphrey," said the old man. "We're tagalongs, ma'am."

Jackie greeted them and put her arm around Karen. "Are you hungry?"

"We're—" said Rick.

"Starving," Mumphrey finished.

"You must come in," said Jackie. "I've got a houseful, but you're welcome to a late dinner. In fact, I suggest you spend the night. It's too dangerous out there at night with no streetlights and all of the stalled cars."

Rick waved his hands in protest. He didn't want to spend the night under the same roof as Karen and Nikki, apocalypse or not. "Thanks, but that's not—"

"I think that's a great idea," said Karen. "We can all get to know one another. Then Rick can take Kenny and me home in the morning."

Rick smiled. "Sure thing." He reluctantly followed the others into the house, wondering how his day could get any worse.

CHAPTER 18

MISSION ELAPSED TIME:
72 DAYS, 18 HOURS, 59 MINUTES, 51 SECONDS
86.9 MILES ABOVE EARTH

The "impactless" separation of the orbital module and instrument compartment from Clayton's crew module had nearly given him a heart attack. The violent vibrations he'd felt were the explosive bolts stripping the Soyuz into three parts. Only the crew module was intended to withstand the heat of reentry and land safely on the planet.

"I think I wet myself," he said breathlessly. "I really do. A little bit of piss leaked out. Not kidding. A grown-ass man just wet himself."

He mentally chided himself for having forgotten the separation. He'd known it was coming. He'd planned for it by lowering his visor and closing his helmet.

"I'm gonna smell like piss when I get home. Freaking great. At least I didn't eat asparagus."

He laughed, though he wasn't sure if it was because what he'd said was funny or if it was a nervous reflex. He had been convinced, while urinating on himself, the ship was falling apart on reentry.

He composed himself and checked the systems. This was when he learned if he lived or died. It was time to dip into the atmosphere.

"Please be right," Clayton begged. "Please be right. Please be right."

The first gentle tugs of gravity pushed him into his seat. He opened his eyes to a bright light from the circular window to the side of the capsule. Outside the window was a reddish glow.

It was the plasma burning against the exterior of the Soyuz as the ship surfed the atmosphere like a wave. The onboard computers automatically adjusted the craft positioning, spinning it to the right or left to keep it on target. Clayton was ninety seconds into his ride through the atmosphere when he saw the first alarm.

Fighting the increasing pull of gravity, he picked up his tablet to check the alarm codes. He scanned the display to confirm what he feared. The automatic controls were failing. He was about to lose his wave. The ship's trajectory was off.

Clayton quickly grabbed the control stick and spun the craft to increase its lift. He then rotated in the other direction to try to find the proper line. He couldn't do it. All of the indicators told him he was off. The alarms were sounding. There were too many for him to read, decipher, and attack. He made a command decision.

"All right," he said, "time to dive."

As the Soyuz shuddered and the increasing heat of the thickening atmosphere began creeping from the shields designed to protect it and the crew, Clayton employed a last-ditch maneuver. He manually initiated what was called a ballistic descent.

Unable to ride the planned trajectory through the atmosphere, Clayton opted for a slightly steeper descent. It was risky, but it was his only shot. With the ballistic descent, the capsule began to spin, but it didn't need the rotational controls to avoid tumbling out of its path.

There was a downside, however, and Clayton felt it bearing down on him the moment he made the call. Instead of reentering the atmosphere with four times the normal force of gravity pulling downward on his body, the ballistic descent created nine times that force.

Nine times.

His hands were pulled from the controls to his sides. The computer tablet on his chest felt like a lead plate underneath an elephant. His head curled at his neck. He had trouble breathing. His vision narrowed and he could sense he was on the verge of losing consciousness. He fought it, working to keep his ten-pound eyelids open. He took slow, even draws of breath as the capsule spun like an electric top and barreled toward Earth.

"Anti-g suits, my ass," he managed to mumble through the drool spilling from his lips. He carefully shifted his eyes to the window. The plasma was still there. It was red and burning.

Then, as quickly as it had started, it slowed. The atmosphere had done its job and the Soyuz was traveling at two hundred and forty meters per second. Clayton was through the worst of it.

He was still traveling at nearly three-quarters the speed of sound when another explosive shudder shook him in his seat. This time, Clayton was ready for it.

"Parachutes deployed," he said, checking the indicators. He was a little more than six and half miles up. Two small chutes were slowing his descent even more. The main chute popped and violently shook the craft with a sickening hiss. When it stopped, Clayton heard something he'd not experienced in more than seventy-two days: the wind.

Outside the falling brick of the Soyuz, the wind was screaming. The parachute ride, which Clayton had assumed would be quiet and almost peaceful, was anything but that.

The capsule was yanked side to side like a yo-yo on a bungee cord as the side-launching parachute righted itself. Combined with the gravity, the roller-coaster ride made Clayton want to vomit.

"I can't land with piss in my suit and puke on it," he said. "Not gonna happen."

He closed his eyes and rode the jerky, frightening drop, bracing himself for a hard landing. The Soyuz was designed with Soft Landing Engines. They fired in the seconds before landing to offer one last deceleration.

There was nothing soft about the landing.

Even with massive shock absorbers in the seats, which automatically cushioned the landing, Clayton's body was jarred when the Soyuz slammed to the ground. It sounded and felt as if he'd collided with an eighteen-wheeler. His jaw hurt, his body ached, and his head felt thick and heavy as if someone had filled it with wet sand. But he was alive.

He was alive and he was on Earth. Somehow he'd done it. He'd gotten himself and the bodies of his friends off the ISS, into the Soyuz, and back to solid ground.

The heavy, relentless pressure of gravity kept Clayton in his seat for longer than he expected. He tried to stand shortly after the cataclysmic landing but lost his balance and fell over onto Boris. He shifted his weight back into his seat, the weight of Earth's pull resisting every movement he made.

He laid his head back against the seat and shuddered at the sudden urge to vomit. He somehow managed to get his hands over his mouth and gagged. He swallowed and winced against the sharp burn as it sank back down to his stomach. He couldn't remember the last time he ate. The taste was unrecognizable the second time he swallowed it. His stomach was twisting, his head ached, his fingers felt thick, and his legs were like stumps.

During training, instructors told him that everyone adjusted to reentry at their own pace. Some people got sick; others didn't. The longer an astronaut lived in microgravity, however, the harder it was on the body when returning.

He'd also heard, anecdotally, that shorter astronauts recovered faster. He wasn't short. Chances were he'd even grown an inch, his spine having expanded while in orbit.

After three more failed attempts to stand, Clayton managed to hold his own weight. He pushed upward for a moment, the weight of breathing still difficult. His thighs burned from the gargantuan effort it took to bear his weight and maintain his balance in the cramped quarters of the Soyuz.

Once he was sure he wouldn't fall again, he opened the hatch. It took every bit of strength he could muster to operate the simplest of machines. He grunted as would an Olympic weightlifter until he'd opened the doorway.

The cold was the first thing that struck Clayton when he popped the hatch. It was arctic. The wind was blistering and carried with it ice and snow.

He couldn't tell if it was actually snowing or not. It was too dark to see anything, and there was no moon.

For a split second, he wondered if there *was* a moon, if he'd actually landed on Earth. The surroundings felt that alien to him. He popped on a flashlight, holding it tightly so as not to lose it to the howling winds, and shone it through what he assumed was a blizzard.

He couldn't see more than a few inches in front of his face. The ice and snow were driven horizontally into his eyes, nose, and mouth. The air was refreshing but bordered on caustically cold. He looked up, blinking past the flakes and pellets, and aimed the narrow white beam skyward into the milky darkness. It revealed nothing.

Where was he?

Normally he'd be able to get a vague read on where he'd landed. His compass was shot. It couldn't tell him north from sideways. His portable GPS was broken. He couldn't even see the stars to guesstimate where he might be.

He ducked back into the capsule and out of the wind. Wisps of snow drifted in through the open hatch.

He could be in any hemisphere. There was no way to rule out any of them. He wasn't in an ocean, as best he could tell. That was good. He'd beaten the odds.

It was highly unlikely he'd have landed at either pole. His entry, especially as steep as it was, would have made that less likely. He also wasn't in New Zealand or Australia. It was summer there.

Russia was a possibility. So was much of Asia north of the equator. The Cascades. The Himalayas, the Alps were possible too. Though, he'd breathed the air without much trouble. The oxygen was plentiful enough that if he were in either of those larger mountain ranges, his elevation was relatively low.

England was out of the question. Iceland or Greenland maybe. No, he couldn't hit that far north. Nothing above fifty-one-point-six degrees, give or take. Most of North America was on the list. Central and South America were off; it was summer for most of South America. The Andes wouldn't typically be like this in January. Snow maybe, perhaps cold, but not a blizzard.

Thinking it through, Clayton ruled out the southern hemisphere. Somewhere north of the equator was his best guess. It was a high altitude but not ridiculously high.

What frightened him wasn't that he couldn't pinpoint exactly where he was. That wasn't the immediate concern. He couldn't worry about whether or not he'd landed in a territory or nation hostile to the United States. There'd be time enough for that if it became an issue. What bothered him was that he had no idea how remote his location might be.

The chance that NASA, ESA, or Roscosmos had a clue where to find him was slim to none, and slim was caught somewhere in the magnetic mess left behind by the CME. He was on his own. His spirits were buoyed by the knowledge he had plenty of food, weapons, and shelter. He wouldn't have to worry about water. He could melt ice and snow. He was trained to survive in the wilderness. All astronauts were. That part of the training had held his attention, unlike the Russian language.

At a point, though, he'd run out of food. He'd get dangerously cold. He'd only be able to stray so far from the module without risking getting lost or freezing to death.

Clayton laughed at himself for worrying about getting lost. He *was* lost. He didn't know where he was. Nor did anyone else.

The radio!

If the portable HAM radio had worked in orbit, there was a chance he'd be able to reach someone, somewhere. Plus, the snow had to stop at some point. The blizzard couldn't last forever, could it?

Once it cleared and there was daylight, he'd have a much better idea of what he was dealing with.

"One day at a time. One hour. One minute," he said, shutting the hatch. "Don't get ahead of yourself."

He was exhausted. He needed sleep. He needed to get warm.

Clayton awkwardly maneuvered himself in the capsule until he found one of the white Nomex bags that contained the snowsuits. He struggled with the brown straps before he freed the bag and unraveled it. There was virtually no room inside the VW Beetle-sized space, but he managed to squeeze into one of the suits. He'd use the other two as blankets.

Once the snow stopped, his first job would be building a fire and a shelter. That was what the training had taught him. He was too exhausted to do either right now. Sleep would clear his head, rejuvenate him. Clayton climbed down into the commander's seat and sandwiched himself between the bodies of his crewmates. He drew the other two suits over his body and shifted in the seat until he was as comfortable as he could get. He extended the suits' edges over Ben and Boris. They were still his crewmates. The mission wasn't over yet.

It wasn't over until he was in Jackie's arms, until he could look his children in the eye, until he could eat a huge plate of lasagna at Frenchie's Italian Restaurant.

The mission wasn't over until he was truly home.

CHAPTER 19

SATURDAY, JANUARY 25, 2020, 9:45 PM CST
CLEAR LAKE, TEXAS

Jackie stepped onto the porch and quietly closed the front door behind her. She peeked through the sidelight next to the door and, confident she'd slipped out without notice, walked to the end of her driveway. She pulled her sleeves over her hands and tucked them under her arms. It was colder than the night before. An involuntary shiver coursed through her.

She looked up to the cloudless sky and was struck by the stars. They'd never shone so brightly. She'd never seen so many of them. They freckled the moonless expanse with varying degrees of light. It reminded her of her honeymoon in St. Lucia.

She and Clay had been on the second night of their weeklong getaway. He'd stood behind her, facing the Atlantic Ocean on the black sand beach that framed a cove between two jagged mountains. The resort was behind them, the faint strains of string-heavy jwé folk music echoing from the lawn above the din of insects and reptiles in the surrounding rainforests.

The stars that night seemed close enough to touch, as if someone had hung them in the sky. She'd purred at Clay's lips on her neck, his breath in her ear. Their future together was in those stars, she'd thought. It was an unmistakably magical moment. She'd forgotten so much of that trip and the others they'd taken as a couple, then as a family, over the years. That night, however, standing with their bare feet sinking deeper into the coarse grains of volcanic sand, the warm Caribbean tide washing in and out from Pitons Bay, was indelibly inked into her memory. It was as fresh as the moment they'd met, their first kiss, and the births of their children.

She stood in the driveway, lost in her thoughts, her eyes stinging from the bitter particulate that still hung in the air. She could feel Clay's arms around her waist, his hands strong and reassuring. Together they could conquer anything, including those stars.

Jackie searched the sky for something familiar, a constellation, a planet, anything that would connect her with Clay. There were too many stars for that and she gave up.

"Please come home to me," she whispered. "I need you. The kids need you. I can't lose you to the stars, Clayton."

She'd told Marie what little she'd learned from her conversation with Irma Molinares at NASA, then shared it with the rest of her boarders. All of them, Marie included, handled the news with a pragmatic stoicism.

"No news is good news," Marie had said. "Until we hear bad news, everything is good."

Even Chris refused to believe anything was wrong in orbit. He'd insisted if they could survive the religious cult, thieving father and son truckers, and malevolent store clerks, his dad could climb into a capsule and fall to Earth. Jackie had agreed with them, but privately it was a difficult position to hold. Those stars, as bright as they were, seemed so far away.

Jackie took stock of where she stood. Her son was home. He was safe, despite the threats he'd faced on the road. He seemed unfazed. That was something positive, but she'd have to keep an eye on him. She knew Chris could bury his emotions.

Her home was fine, unlike the ones across the street. Even though she didn't have a generator, the house was comfortable. Together they had plenty of food, water, and there was still hot water for showers.

She wasn't sure what to think of the woman named Nikki or the other camper named Mumphrey. They were polite enough, but she couldn't get a read on either of them.

Rick was Rick. She was grateful to him for getting Chris home so quickly, but she wasn't thrilled to have him in the house at the same time she was sheltering Karen. The tension was thicker than thick. It would thankfully be short-lived. Rick, Nikki, and Mumphrey would be gone in the morning.

Karen and Kenny were staying. Jackie had insisted. Chris would need a distraction, which Kenny could provide, and she didn't like the idea of Karen being home alone.

Reggie had gently and privately protested the idea of adding two more mouths to feed. He worried what that would do to their food and water supply.

"We're talking about adding a twenty-five percent burden to our resources," he'd reasoned. "From eight people — including Chris, who's now home — to ten. That's a sizable strain for an indefinite future."

"I understand you contributed to those resources," Jackie had said through her teeth. "But this is my house. What makes Karen and Kenny any more or less of a burden than you and Lana? Or Betty and Brian?"

Reggie's face had flushed. He'd stuttered a nonsensical answer before relenting. "You're right. You're absolutely right."

Betty seemed to have calmed from the initial shock of losing her home. However, Brian was agitated at the irregularity of his schedule. While Jackie was hopeful he'd adjust to a new routine, she wasn't optimistic.

Candace had proven to be a valuable asset in a short time. Despite her unspeakable loss only twenty-four hours earlier, she was levelheaded and smart.

Jackie was housing thirteen people including herself. Thirteen. Not a lucky number. She wasn't prone to superstition, but she didn't like it. She rationalized that there were twelve people staying with *her*. That was more reasonable. Her eyes scanned the sky and she took in a deep breath through her nostrils, blowing it out through puffed cheeks.

"One day at a time," she said to the stars. "One hour at a time. One minute at a time. We'll be okay, Clayton. But you have got to get home."

THE ADVENTURE CONTINUES EARLY 2017…

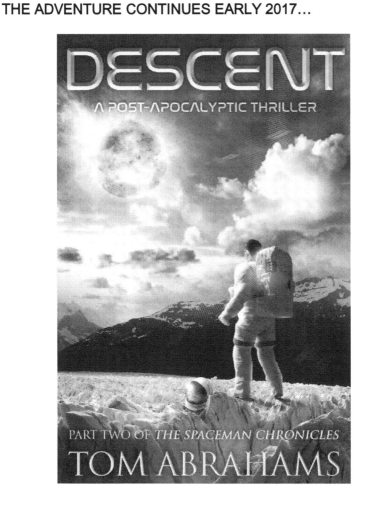

Join Tom's Preferred Readers Club. You'll be the first to know about new releases, promotions, and special opportunities reserved only for members. It's free to join.

CAN'T WAIT FOR THE NEXT INSTALLMENT OF
SPACEMAN?

CHECK OUT THE AMAZON INTERNATIONAL BEST
SELLING TRAVELER SERIES

ACKNOWLEDGMENTS

Thanks always begin with my crew: Courtney, Sam, and Luke. I could not burn the candle on one end or both without your guidance, love, and support.

A large, Jupiter-sized shout to my editor, Felicia A. Sullivan, who does incredible work and always finds a way to make my work better than it was before she got it.

Thanks also to Pauline Nolet for her expert eye and proofing talent and to Stef McDaid for giving the book a professional look I could not manage on my own.

A huge debt of gratitude goes to my friend from across the ocean, cover artist Hristo Kovatliev. He takes a very vague direction and turns it into a brilliant, stunning piece of art. Thank you.

I also must give thanks to the men and women who helped make sense of the science in this book. Astronaut Clayton Anderson answered endless questions, sent photographs, and spent his time explaining what it was like living on the ISS. Dr. Loren Acton, also a NASA astronaut and brilliant professor, read a very rough draft and gave expert instruction about what was missing and what was wrong. Ben Honey, NASA engineer, was also incredibly adept at answering questions, telling me what was and wasn't plausible. He was a great resource. Also, Gina Sunseri, producer at ABC News and resident space expert, was a Rolodex of information. Steve Kremer provided excellent help with the HAM radio sequences and was an outstanding sounding board. Tim Heller, a guy who knows a little bit about weather, was a critical early reader of the rough manuscript. And to Steven Konkoly, Russell Blake, Nicholas Sansbury Smith, Patricia Wilson, Sabrina Jean, Cathy Northup, and Lynn Blake -- the trusted beta readers who gave me their input, a sky-high thank you. Lastly, I thank my parents, Sanders and Jeanne, my siblings, Penny and Steven, and my mother-in-law, Linda Eaker, for their viral marketing efforts. And to my father-in-law, Don Eaker, I know you're reading this somewhere among the stars. You always believed in me.

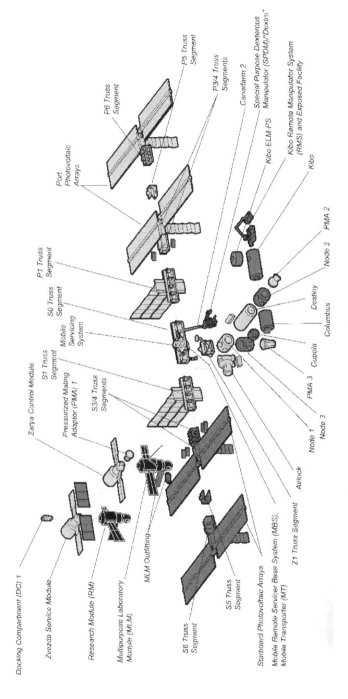

Diagram of the International Space Station from NASA.gov

Printed in Poland
by Amazon Fulfillment
Poland Sp. z o.o., Wrocław